TRAPPED

I ran to the window and looked out. The clouds seemed to be hovering just above the roof as the wind wailed around the window, scattering millions of snowflakes through the gray atmosphere. I turned back, desperately searching the room for some sort of weapon with which to defend myself.

There was nothing . . . *nothing!*

Soon he will break down the bedroom door, charge through, and kill me. There is no way he can let me go free. I know too much. Somehow I have to get out of the house.

The window is cold against my trembling hands; the latch is frozen. I heave with all my strength. It is stuck!

I *must* escape. Otherwise no one will ever know the truth.

Fear grips me, icing my blood. I shove hard on the latch, and this time it moves beneath my weight. I lean against the window, pushing with every ounce of strength. Suddenly it flies up, and I lunge forward.

Snowflakes fly on the wind; the arctic air sweeps over me. Leaning out the window, I am praying for someone—anyone—to appear on the deserted road. But there is no one—no one to help me. A scream for help would merely be a waste of breath.

I have dispatched my last ally, and he has sent back the enemy! Any second he will break through. I shall have to go out on the ledge—there is no other way!

GOTHICS A LA MOOR—FROM ZEBRA

ISLAND OF LOST RUBIES
by Patricia Werner (2603, $3.95)
Heartbroken by her father's death and the loss of her great love, Eileen returns to her island home to claim her inheritance. But eerie things begin happening the minute she steps off the boat, and it isn't long before Eileen realizes that there's no escape from *THE ISLAND OF LOST RUBIES.*

DARK CRIES OF GRAY OAKS
by Lee Karr (2736, $3.95)
When orphaned Brianna Anderson was offered a job as companion to the mentally ill seventeen-year-old girl, Cassie, she was grateful for the non-troublesome employment. Soon she began to wonder why the girl's family insisted that Cassie be given hydro-electrical therapy and increased doses of laudanum. What was the shocking secret that Cassie held in her dark tormented mind? And was she herself in danger?

CRYSTAL SHADOWS
by Michele Y. Thomas (2819, $3.95)
When Teresa Hawthorne accepted a post as tutor to the wealthy Curtis family, she didn't believe the scandal surrounding them would be any concern of hers. However, it soon began to seem as if someone was trying to ruin the Curtises and Theresa was becoming the unwitting target of a deadly conspiracy . . .

CASTLE OF CRUSHED SHAMROCKS
by Lee Karr (2843, $3.95)
Penniless and alone, eighteen-year-old Aileen O'Conner traveled to the coast of Ireland to be recognized as daughter and heir to Lord Edwin Lynhurst. Upon her arrival, she was horrified to find her long lost father had been murdered. And slowly, the extent of the danger dawned upon her: her father's killer was still at large. And her name was next on the list.

BRIDE OF HATFIELD CASTLE
by Beverly G. Warren (2517, $3.95)
Left a widow on her wedding night and the sole inheritor of Hatfield's fortune, Eden Lane was convinced that someone wanted her out of the castle, preferably dead. Her failing health, the whispering voices of death, and the phantoms who roamed the keep were driving her mad. And although she came to the castle as a bride, she needed to discover who was trying to kill her, or leave as a corpse!

Available wherever paperbacks are sold, or order direct from the Publisher. Send cover price plus 50¢ per copy for mailing and handling to Zebra Books, Dept. 3075, 475 Park Avenue South, New York, N.Y. 10016. Residents of New York, New Jersey and Pennsylvania must include sales tax. DO NOT SEND CASH.

THE WAILING WINDS OF JUNEAU ABBEY

PEGGY DARTY

ZEBRA BOOKS
KENSINGTON PUBLISHING CORP.

ZEBRA BOOKS

are published by

Kensington Publishing Corp.
475 Park Avenue South
New York, NY 10016

First printing: July, 1990

Printed in the United States of America

For my editor, Ann La Farge, who wisely suggested Alaska

Other Zebra Books by Peggy Darty

The Widowed Bride of Raven Oaks

Prologue

I must escape!

He is after me. Soon he will break down the bedroom door, charge through, and kill me. There is no way he can let me go free. I know too much. Somehow I have to get out of the house. The window is cold against my trembling hands; the latch seems permanently frozen. I heave with all my strength. It is stuck!

His footsteps are thundering up the stairs—*I must* escape. Otherwise, no one will ever know the truth.

Fear grips me, icing my blood. I press hard on the latch, and this time it moves. I lean against the window, pushing with every ounce of strength. Suddenly it flies up, and I lunge forward.

Snowflakes fly on the wind; the arctic air sweeps over me. Leaning out the window, I pray for someone—anyone—on the deserted road. But there is no one.

Heavy blows are crashing against the bedroom door; any second he will break through. I shall have to go out on the ledge—there is no other escape. I lift my skirts and yank off my crinoline, then I tighten the strap on my boots.

The wood of the door is splintering!

I must not stop to consider the consequences of the narrow ledge. I will simply go.

Bunching my skirt in my hands, I crawl through the window as the door behind me gives way with a crash.

Like a giant hand, the wind slaps me back against the

wall of the ledge. Thank God, I can cling to the rail! One thing I know, he will not follow me onto the ledge. Only a fool would step onto a narrow, ice-slickened ledge that promises a long fall. And yet, I prefer to die trying to escape rather than leaving my fate in his hands.

You will not die, a voice in my brain commands. *You will escape and stop this dangerous man from harming anyone else.*

I can hear him laughing as he stomps across the floor. He is certain I will fall, and this has made his task easy.

The hem of my skirt is whipping in the wind; the frigid air rushes up my bare legs. With tiny, cautious steps, I inch my way along the ledge, far enough to escape the hand that is flailing from the window, grabbing for my skirt. He is now dangerously near.

I want to scream as tears of rage and terror fill my eyes. I can't make it!

Yes, you can.

"You will freeze in three minutes," he calls threateningly. Then the window slams down, and I hear his cruel laugh, snatched on the wind to echo madly in the dying daylight.

Against the wind and falling snow, I can see the bell tower above me, an ominous shape in the gray light. The steps? Where are the steps?

The wind-driven snow is pelting my face like sharp needles; my eyes are blurring. He is right: if I do not act quickly, I will freeze to death.

He has extinguished the light in the bedroom; he is so smug and certain of my fate. For a moment, I consider trying to get back inside, but he is waiting there, ready to give a hard shove when I try to crawl back into the bedroom.

Anger, blessed anger, fills me, sharpening my determination not to be outsmarted by such a man. He has obviously forgotten the old steps, so long abandoned. Clinging to the rail, I inch my way around the ledge, squinting through blurred vision and whipping snow. *The stairs . . . where are the stairs?* Only a few more treacherous steps along the ledge and I will reach them. With my right foot, I test the wood, find it solid, then press down, moving my left foot in the same manner. The slickened ledge is a death trap; if I make one step that is not deliberate, that is not planned and negotiated with infinite skill, I am gone.

The stairs are only three feet away!

Carefully, I move my right foot again . . . but there is no wood! With my back flattened to the wall, and my hands on the rail, I look down . . .

A piece of the ledge is missing!

My heart is hammering; my teeth are chattering. I am beyond knowing how cold I am.

Go on. Go on!

Can I possibly reach the stairs if I jump? If the steps or the handrail are not secure, I will plunge to a certain death.

I am screaming. I cannot stop myself. If only someone would appear out of the storm to save me! Across the meadow, I can barely see the cemetery where Russian crosses rise like white fingers. Uncle Joshua is there . . . poor Uncle Joshua who died at the hands of the killer inside.

I must live to tell what he has done.

I blink away the moisture on my lashes and concentrate on the steps again. Either I jump or I freeze. Steeling myself, I lunge forward out of sheer desperation. The rough wood splinters my palm, a pain that brings a leap of joy. For miraculously my feet have landed on the steps, and the handrail is secure against my trembling grasp.

A numbness is creeping over me; a warning. Through the swirling snowflakes, I count the steps leading up to the tower. Six.

I bunch the hem of my skirt in my left hand and lift it above my boots, while I cling to the rail with my right hand. The Taku wind is wailing louder now, tossing my hair in my eyes, blinding me until I can brush the wind-tangled ends from my forehead.

The second step.

The third step.

Then the fourth.

The fifth step is breaking beneath my foot!

I do not hear the wood splintering, but I feel it give way. I am swinging in thin air! The weight of my body is pulling me down, down, down. My hands are frozen to the rail. *I am going to fall.*

Get your footing again, the voice that has guided me on is now the only sound I hear, though the wind rages and I feel the heave of sobs in my chest. Blood fills my mouth; I must be chewing my bottom lip, but I feel no pain.

One step, only one more step. Reach for it . . . reach for it now, or you're dead.

My body is still swinging, but my right foot lands on the lower step, gaining a weak foothold. My left foot follows. I am temporarily anchored.

The top step. I have to stretch for it.

With both feet now secure, I stretch as high as I can reach. The tips of my fingers brush the icy step. If I can touch it, I can reach it. I must!

Something is happening, something strange and wonderful. A strength I have never possessed flows through me, drawing my body upward. First my right hand is moving up the rail, then my left hand, moving my body with a determination born of desperation.

Finally, by lifting my knee, then my foot, I am on the last step.

I am looking into the tower window, dark, desolate, but promising the shelter that will save me. The window glass is broken, there are only a few remaining shards around the edge.

Lifting one arm over my face, I dive through the window, too numb to feel or care about splintered wood or broken glass. The wooden floor is a haven for me as tears of terror now turn to tears of joy.

The tower is narrow, dark, but beside the window a long shelf holds two blankets and an old mackinaw. The wind is shrieking through the open window, spitting snow and mist into the tower.

My body no longer seems human; my muscles are like

iron, unwilling to bend, as I reach for the blanket and with stiff fingers stuff it into the open window. The howl of the wind is muffled, the frigid air is shut off.

The board floor holds a faint warmth from the rising heat within the house. I tear the buttons from my wet dress and shinny out, wrapping my frozen body in the other woolen blanket. The mackinaw, stiff from cold and age, provides a tent for me. The fur of the hood is a caress to my frozen face. I crawl to the farthest corner, my body drawn tightly into a ball beneath the cover. I am safe for now.

Later, when the storm subsides, he will go outside, expecting to find my body frozen in the snow. When he does not find me, he may suspect that I am in the tower, but he cannot get to me, not for a while. And I shall hope, and desperately pray, that my one true friend will come looking for me.

For now, I must stay warm, keep calm. I will try to think pleasant thoughts to chase from my mind this day, the worst day of my entire life. Yes, I will think of something else . . . I will think of those first days in Juneau. I will think back to how it all began . . .

Chapter 1

Looking back now, I see that something small and rather insignificant can forever change a life. A letter read before the fire one rainy evening in San Francisco, a letter from my Uncle Joshua in Alaska.

Uncle Joshua was a poet, and his descriptions of snow castles and waterfalls, northern lights and a midnight sun had fired my imagination through a long, lonely winter. And so it was that when news of his death reached the family, I was the one who volunteered to go to Juneau, where he had finally settled after wandering throughout Alaska.

The long trip was rewarded at once when the steamer docked in Juneau and I stood gasping at the rugged beauty before me. Sculpted mountains disappeared into cotton clouds, forming a mystical backdrop for the cozy village nestled in the arm of Gastineau Channel. Stumps scarred the lower ridges of the coastal mountains, testifying to good lumber which had constructed the quaint shops and small cabins. The steep-pitched roofs held narrow smokestacks; a few were already puffing tiny wisps of smoke, although this was early October.

"Isn't Juneau the most beautiful little place you've ever seen?" The exuberant woman who had become my traveling companion nudged me.

"Yes," I smiled at her, "it is. How many times did you say you've been here?"

"This will be the third time. And you know the saying—third time's the charm!"

I glanced at the pert woman who had boarded the steamer in Portland, where my cousin Tom and his frail wife Edith had eagerly disembarked. Like a mother hen, Edna Vanderhoof had hovered over me for the remainder of the journey, but I hadn't minded. She was intelligent and witty and, unlike my mother, thought nothing of my traveling on without the relatives forced on me back in San Francisco.

I shook myself back to her comment. "Third time's the charm?" I repeated, trying to follow her train of thought, which was as elusive as the sea gulls winging noisily about the ship.

"A rich husband!" she whispered, poking me even harder in the rib cage. "Not that Harry would mind," she raced on, her blue eyes intent. "He said to me before he died, 'Edna,' he said . . ."

I forced a bland smile and returned my attention to the busy little town, focusing my thoughts on the purpose of this long journey, which was *not* to snag a husband. That final fracas with my ex-fiancé lay like a stone in my memory. I had no interest in a man at the present, other than Uncle Joshua, my mother's black-sheep uncle, who was my reason for coming. Or, more specifically, the death of Uncle Joshua.

Passengers and cargo were being unloaded at the wharf, and Edna bade me good-bye and flew off into the crowd. I hesitated, waiting for the crowd to disperse. I needed time to clear my head, make my plans, think what to do first. With that challenge, I sauntered around to a quiet spot and studied the blue waters of the channel while reflecting on the life of my mysterious uncle.

Joshua Martin, at thirty-five, had finally broken the confines of the family newspaper business to pursue a dream of roaming the Alaskan frontier. To soothe his absence at the editorial desk, he had promised stories of adventure from this distant, mystical place, and in the beginning, two or three wonderful stories had trickled back. But then, he had apparently chosen to live adventure, rather than to write about it. The last hastily written letters related his latest project—panning for gold.

I had defended his lifestyle to Mother and Tom, who considered him irresponsible, and even to my fiancé Thad, who having gained a prestigious foothold in the newspaper business after a long struggle, couldn't imagine deserting it. But I understood Uncle Joshua; I even admired him for being true to his dream. My own dream, thwarted by the family, had been to put to use the business sense that I had inherited from my father. Unfortunately, 1895 was not the proper time for women to inherit men's jobs, and I bitterly resented being unable to take over my father's desk upon his death. I had been a "quiet" reporter with Thad until he was chosen to assume my father's job; then nothing was ever the same between us. Perhaps I was jealous; certainly I was angry when, in a clumsy attempt at humor, he suggested I was more suited for apron strings than suspenders.

Mother, Thad, and Tom had united solidly against me, and while I did not break the engagement at first, my romantic notions toward Thad were slowly killed off by boredom. At that point, Uncle Joshua's letters began to provide the excitement I hungered for, and I pored over them long and hard. Upon settling at Juneau, he wrote of an abandoned Russian church that he had purchased and fashioned into a unique home. Leave it to Uncle Joshua to do something different!

Inflamed by the sense of adventure burning in my veins, I could not, to Thad's mounting frustration, agree to marry. I was not ready to stay home and tend the fires, make the tea, have the babies. Our breakup had come the day before we received the news of Uncle Joshua's death. A letter had come from his banker in Juneau, who had advised us of Uncle Joshua's outstanding accounts, which needed to be settled as soon as possible. It was obvious that someone had to go to Juneau to take care of matters. Since the immediate family had dwindled to Mother and me, I considered myself the logical choice. Unfortunately, a second cousin and his wife were sent along as chaperons. But then Tom and Edith's stomachs were no match for the high seas. I had countered their pleas to disembark with them in Portland by repeating the message from Gordon Walling, the Juneau banker.

"If a member of the Martin family doesn't appear in Juneau by the end of the month," I stated emphatically, "Uncle Joshua's house . . ."

"Church!" Tom had interrupted with a snort.

". . . will be sold to pay off his debts. And there are other matters to be investigated as well."

At that, we all fell silent. For none of us could imagine how Uncle Joshua had completely exhausted the considerable fortune he had inherited.

"Aren't you getting off, Miss Martin?" The voice of the ship captain startled me back to the present. I blinked and stared at his pleasant smile.

"Oh. Yes, of course." I glanced around the empty deck. "I was just waiting for some of the crowd to disperse."

"Particularly the talkative ones, I imagine." A humorous expression touched his features, and I knew he was thinking of Edna Vanderhoof.

"How long will you be staying?" he asked.

"Well . . . when will the boat return?"

"The steamer comes twice a month, but only one time with passengers. The second time is merely for mail and cargo. We'll be delivering and picking up passengers a month from today."

I nodded, smiling. "Then that's how long I'm staying."

"Incidentally, we'll be docked here for the afternoon. If you need to send any mail out, better get it taken care of today. This will be your last chance for two weeks."

"Two weeks?" I echoed, horrified. I could hardly imagine that sort of delay. "I'll need to let my mother know I arrived safely. Thank you for telling me this."

"It's been a pleasure having you aboard," he said, waving to me. "Take care in Juneau."

"Thank you," I smiled, lifting my skirts to pick my way along the well-traveled gangplank.

Take care. It was to be the best advice I had been given. For despite my thirst for adventure, I had no way of knowing, when I disembarked, that I was headed for the most dangerous experience of my life, one far more complex than my active imagination could have created.

As I reached the dock, the crowd was still milling. Someone carelessly bumped me, sending my hat spiraling through the tangle of people.

Dazed, I followed the direction of the hat, which landed in the outstretched hand of a grizzly-looking older man standing by a wagon loading cargo. His was the only form of transportation that I saw, and so I waved to him, indicating I wanted both the hat and a ride, once my trunk was fetched.

He was a big man with blunt features and a fur cap perched on a gleaming bald head. His greeting was merely a series of grunts as I climbed into the wagon unassisted. In the process, another passing wagon splashed fresh mud onto my traveling suit. By the time the surly driver had loaded my trunk, my patience was wearing thin. I took a deep breath and stared at the distant wooden buildings, erected on pilings as a safeguard against rising tides.

The driver lumbered to his seat, settling his heavy weight down slowly; still the wagon shook.

"I'd like to go to the local bank," I announced.

"Which one?" he asked abruptly.

I searched my memory for the name of the bank but remembered only the banker who had written. "Gordon Walling is the man I must see," I replied. "Do you know him?"

He nodded. "You want to go to his bank," he stated flatly, laying a frayed whip over the ponderous horses.

"His bank?" I had spoken the question aloud, thinking of the difference in one man and a bank, as compared to San Francisco's many banks and boards of directors.

"His bank," he repeated, staring dully into the distance.

I cleared my throat, glancing around, trying to absorb the many impressions of this bustling town where smells of salt, fish, and fresh-cut lumber floated on the air.

The steepness of streets reminded me of San Francisco, but only for a moment, for those same streets were potholed, crudely planked, and soggy with mud. It was a bustling new town with a sense of the wild west at every turn. We had passed a mercantile, a jeweler, a hotel, a saloon. A wagon with rubber buckets stood before the fire department. I smelled fresh baked bread and glimpsed a Chinese man standing in a doorway smoking a pipe as we turned a corner.

Suddenly a man darted across the street in front of us, and the driver swerved, uttering an oath about rude Americans. I noticed that his words were slurred with a strange accent; occasionally an English word gave way to something foreign. When I inquired, he told me he was Russian, that he had come to Alaska as a young man back in the sixties, before America had acquired Alaska.

When I asked if he had ever returned to his homeland, a look of sadness clouded his face. He shook his bald head and lapsed into a brooding silence.

Glancing back at the shops we were passing, I could see that the Russian influence still lingered here, on street signs with strange exotic names. As I followed one narrow street, I spotted an octagonal building with an onion-shaped dome. Immediately I thought of Uncle Joshua's church-house.

"Is that the only Russian church here?" I asked, peering into the distance.

"We started another one. A crazy American bought it." This was followed by a few surly words that I suspected were most uncomplimentary to Uncle Joshua.

"Was the church in use when he bought it?" I challenged, knowing it had been started, then abandoned.

Just when I had decided he was going to ignore my question, he growled a reply.

"Some of the people left . . . there was not enough labor

to complete it. Then this one was built." He nodded toward the small church in the distance.

"Well, if the other church was abandoned, I wouldn't call the American crazy," I said, too smugly.

He turned and looked at me with blue eyes as cold as glaciers. "He went crazy after he tried to make a house out of a dwelling meant to be sacred!"

Uncle Joshua was not crazy, I was about to reply, but his hard stare sent a chill down my spine; instead I turned my attention back to the streets, crowded with men in work clothes, saloon girls, and an occasional woman dressed in last year's fashions. I didn't know a soul here. I must curb my tongue until I made a friend or two. I began to wonder where I would find such a friend. Edna had been swallowed up in the crowd.

The wagon lurched to a halt before the bank, and for the second time within the hour, I lost my hat. It landed in the mud of the street, and this time I gave it up for good. My blonde hair must have been a rarity in Juneau, because I was immediately the object of several bold stares.

"Where to put your trunk?" he asked, his fur cap slightly askew on his shiny bald head.

I glanced toward the crowded boardwalk, where men in work clothes and knee-high boots stood talking.

"Bring the trunk inside the bank," I instructed, seeing no other alternative except a narrow space beside a popular spittoon.

The driver hoisted the heavy trunk to his shoulders, and I followed behind as we entered the bank. Just inside the door, he dumped the trunk beside a straight-backed chair where an elderly man sat dozing. When my trunk hit the floor beside him, the man bolted up and stared wide-eyed at me.

I plunged my hand into my reticule, quickly seeking the driver's fare, a sum which seemed exorbitant, considering the short ride and his rude behavior. Once I had dismissed him, I sauntered to the nearest clerk and inquired for Gordon Walling, the man who had written the letter.

I was ushered down a short corridor and into a small office where a man in his early thirties was seated behind a cluttered desk. He stood as I entered the room, and I saw that his dark waistcoat and striped trousers held the stamp of a good tailor. His light brown hair was neatly trimmed, as was his thin mustache. Behind small spectacles, his bright blue eyes were friendly, yet curious.

He came around the desk and offered me a chair. "Good morning," he said, removing his spectacles and placing them in his vest pocket. "How may I help you?"

I settled into the chair, smoothing down my hooped skirt, as I looked across the desk, where he had taken his seat again.

"My name is Abigail Martin," I answered. "I've come to settle my uncle's accounts."

He blinked and stared at me, obviously puzzled.

"You wrote concerning Joshua Martin's debts. I am his niece."

At the sound of my uncle's name, his polite smile vanished. He removed his spectacles from his vest pocket, hooked them over his ears, and studied me curiously. "You've come a long way, Miss Martin," he said, his eyes sweeping over me with interest, but then, as though remembering something, a frown rose between his brows. "You say you are Josh Martin's niece?" he seemed to be struggling with this bit of news.

"Yes, I am. Mr. Walling, how did my uncle die? Was it his heart?"

Another look of surprise crossed his round face. "You didn't get a note from Doctor Willis?"

I shook my head, confused.

The frown deepened as he dropped his eyes to his desk. "Mail from Alaska to the lower states is awfully slow. And Doc Willis has more than he can do." He looked back at me and sighed. "Miss Martin, your uncle shot himself late one night after a bout of drinking."

I gasped and stared.

"His friends at the saloon said Josh was depressed over

money matters, that his happy mood turned sour after too many drinks."

I sat back in the chair, trying to take in this bit of startling news. *Uncle Joshua committed suicide?* It was too dreadful to think about.

"He's buried in the cemetery near his house," he said quietly.

I swallowed, trying to force my mind back to the purpose of this visit. "I . . . had no idea," I stammered, then tried to collect my thoughts. "Well," I sighed, "My family is most anxious to have Uncle Joshua's accounts settled. And I would like to find a buyer for the house," I finished shakily.

He folded his hands over a stack of papers and looked at me gravely. "A buyer?"

"Yes. We don't want Uncle Joshua's home sold at a street auction, as you suggested."

He began to shake his head. "There may be a problem in selling that place, Miss Martin. You do know that the dwelling started out as a Russian church, don't you?"

"One that was never completed, I understand."

"Well, yes; that's true," he conceded. Clearly he had not expected me to be so determined to defend my uncle.

"The letters he wrote indicated his house was his pride and joy," I said. "I intend to see that his wishes are dealt with accordingly." I opened my reticule and withdrew the draft from our bank in San Francisco. Once he saw the amount, I expected his mood to change. My hopes sank, however, when he shook his head again as his eyes swept over the draft.

"This is a drop in the bucket, Miss Martin."

I stared at him, unable to believe what he was saying.

"I'm very sorry to be the one to deliver the bad news. Obviously you didn't realize the extent of your uncle's gambling."

"Gambling?"

I had never known Uncle Joshua to be a gambler, but of course I had not seen him in two years. When he lived in San Francisco, I recalled Mother's comments about the many evenings he spent at his clubs. Was he gambling then? This second shock pushed me deeper in the chair. The Uncle Joshua I remembered was a dapper young man with laughing eyes and a quick wit. A daredevil, Mother often said. It was quite conceivable that he was a gambler, given his nature. Was this how he had exhausted his money?

The man opposite me was considerate enough to allow a few minutes to pass without speaking. As my mind groped with this astounding news, he pushed his chair back and wandered over to stare out the window.

I took a deep breath, trying to summon the courage to face the horrible truth. If Uncle Joshua had run through his share of the family fortune, and the draft I had brought was insufficient, what should I do?

The banker was glancing back at me, and I cleared my throat, trying to think how to respond.

"Miss Martin, I liked your uncle," he said quietly. "We became friends soon after he arrived in Juneau. In fact, I grubstaked his first expedition into the mountains."

"Were you repaid?" I asked quickly.

He pursed his lips and studied his hands, the silence answering my question quite clearly.

"Did he ever find gold?" I asked suddenly.

"Not that I know of."

My sympathy for Uncle Joshua was rapidly turning to anger. How could he have become so irresponsible? I realized now that Uncle Joshua had not only lost money at the gambling tables, but that his elusive search for gold had probably cost him as well. I looked at Gordon Walling. "Exactly how much more money is needed?" I asked.

He opened the drawer and withdrew a stack of papers. "Around five thousand dollars." He handed the papers to me. "Please take a look at these."

As I leafed through the notes, I could see the figures were carefully detailed and agreed upon by my uncle in a signature that was clearly his. I sighed and returned the papers.

"He owed most of the stores here, and a few individuals, and," he dropped his eyes, "the saloons, of course, until they closed his credit. I made him one large loan to get the creditors off his back. He secured the loan with his house, but then he came back. . . ." His voice trailed off.

Silence fell, heavy with gloom. I sat twisting my gloved hands in my lap, trying to think what to do when Gordon Walling came around the desk and looked at me sympathetically.

"I imagine you must be feeling the effects of the long trip. We can talk about this later. After lunch. Will you join me?"

I shook my head, too stunned by what I had just learned to think of food. "No, thank you." I stood. "I'd like to take a few days to think this over."

He nodded understandingly. "Of course. The Occidental Hotel is comfortable and well managed. It is electrically lighted."

"I intend to stay at Uncle Joshua's place," I interrupted.

Gordon Walling's mouth fell open. I paused for a minute, allowing him time to regain his composure.

"It's a couple of miles up the inlet," he finally responded. "I don't think you'll be comfortable . . ."

"I would still like to try it. Oh," I remembered the draft, "and I would like to open an account here."

It was the first time he had looked pleased since he'd heard my name. "We'll be happy to have your business, Miss Martin," he smiled, leading me back down the hall to the reception area. "Incidentally, you're lucky to have arrived on a sunny day. In Juneau, we're as apt to have rain as sun. Here we are." He stopped at the desk of an older gentleman who peered at me curiously. "William, this is Miss Abigail Martin. She wants to open an account with us."

When I handed the little man the draft, I was relieved to see that at least he was impressed with the amount, even if Gordon Walling had not been.

"I need a paper and pen, please," I said to him. "I have to

send a letter out on the steamer."

"Of course. Please take a seat there," he said.

As I dashed off a letter to my mother, I tried, as gently as possible, to relate what I had just learned. I specified the amount of money needed, with a request that she advise me of her decision immediately. I also told her about Tom and Edith, but by now she already knew that I had gone on alone. She was probably wringing her hands this very minute.

I couched the above news with a cheerful ending, saying the people I had met here were being very helpful. I assured her that I was being taken care of, that she had no cause to worry.

Finally I addressed the letter and gave it to the man who was still watching me curiously.

"I'll see that your letter gets in our mail going out on the steamer," he said, turning the letter over in his hand, studying it thoughtfully.

"My buggy is waiting," Gordon said upon returning. "I'll drive you to Josh's place. Your trunk has already been loaded."

"Thank you!" I was relieved to have a more pleasant driver than the surly man who had brought me. When I saw the fancy buggy with brass-trimmed harness, hitched to shining bays, I felt even better. This time I would be riding in style.

As we entered the street, I noticed there were no other buggies, no hitching rails, and very few horses. When I commented on this, Gordon smiled.

"There aren't many horses in Juneau. The area is small, and of course it's difficult to bring them in, since the only way to get here is by boat. Also, no feed is grown locally. We have to import feed from Washington State. I expect all that will change in time."

As I took my seat in the buggy, and he tapped the reins on the sleek horses, I became aware of eyes following us as we rode through the town. Gordon tipped his hat to the men milling on the street corners, and I read a look of respect in their eyes. For the first time since my arrival in Juneau, I felt a sense of relief, despite the awful news about my uncle.

"How long have you been here?" I asked.

"Ten years. I came up from Seattle when Juneau was just a mining camp. Now we have the basics of any respectable town—schools, churches, newspapers, a variety of stores. A lot of money is being made here."

"And lost." The words tumbled out before I could stop them, and I instantly regretted such a bitter reply. After all, it was my uncle's own carelessness that had gotten him into trouble.

"Yes, a man has to be careful," Gordon said. "Ever since gold was discovered out in the channel, there's been a steady flow of tenderfeet. Most end up losing their grub-stakes."

I sighed, trying to push those unpleasant thoughts from my mind. "Did you get involved in the gold mining?" I asked.

"Only on a small scale. I've financed a few ventures, but my profits have been low. A mining company has been established here now, and they tunnel gold out of the hillside."

"Yes, I've read about that," I replied vaguely. "That's an interesting totem pole." I pointed to the tall, intricately carved cedar pole on the edge of town.

"You'll see those around. The Tlingit Indians had a settlement here."

The totem pole was very tall and brightly painted with intricately carved figures. At the top of the pole, I could see something that resembled the face of a bird with a sharp beak. Objects like this were highly valued in the shops in San Francisco.

We had left the town behind and were following the rough road that led north up the inlet. The boggy wetlands of the channel bordered the road on one side, while the mountains disappeared in fog on the other.

"I'm afraid you're seeing Juneau at a drab time," Gordon spoke up. "The cottonwood leaves are gone, and the snows haven't come to give color. You can't see the mountain peaks today, but we already have termination dust . . ."

"Termination dust?"

"Oh," he chuckled, "of course you don't know what that means. It's a term the miners used for the first light snows; it means the termination of their mining."

The landscape here was lonely and remote, with only an occasional log cabin paralleling the road.

"The Zarnoffs live over there," he pointed. "They'll be your closest neighbors."

As we approached, the door to the large log cabin opened, and a heavy-set woman eyed me cautiously beneath a fringe of gray hair.

"That's Mrs. Zarnoff," Gordon said, as he tipped his hat. "She's a bit eccentric, but she can be of help." Behind his spectacles, the blue eyes held an expression of concern. "Miss Martin, I must admit I don't think it's wise for you to stay out here alone. If after a night or two you wish to return to town . . ."

"I'm sure I'll be fine," I persisted stubbornly. I knew as I spoke that I was being rash. Somehow I felt compelled to prove to everyone that my uncle had not been crazy in choosing to live in a building intended to be a church.

And just as I thought of the church, it loomed into view.

It was a narrow, boxlike structure rising two stories to an enclosed tower that held a small glass window. An addition on the back of the house jutted out from the first level. On the second story, a thin rail encircled a narrow ledge, creating a circular appearance that was totally out of harmony with the rest of the building. Obviously my uncle had added that on his own.

A stained-glass front window provided the only color against the weathered gray boards. My first impression was that it was the bleakest, loneliest place that I had ever seen.

"Well, here we are." Gordon looked doubtfully at me.

I gave him a weak smile, then studied the landscape surrounding the house.

A meadow stretched to a lush green spruce-and-hemlock

forest. At the far end of the meadow, a picket fence enclosed several crosses. My heart sank.

"Is that where Uncle Joshua is buried?" I asked, swallowing.

"Yes, it is. The three-bar crosses are Russian graves. I believe your uncle's grave is marked by a one-bar cross."

Silence, like an ocean fog, wrapped around the setting—a soft, eerie silence broken intermittently by the distant lap of water out in the channel. As Gordon handed me down from the buggy and reached for my trunk, I felt as though I were standing on hallowed ground, that we were trespassers in a spiritual realm no longer intended for humans.

"There's a creek up that little road," Gordon pointed. "There used to be a mining camp back there. Some Russian immigrants had settled here and started the church back in the eighties. A squabble broke out among them about the same time the stream played out of gold. Most of the people left, and there wasn't enough labor to finish the church."

"But it seems such a waste," I said, shaking my head and staring at the lonely dwelling. "Their time and money . . ."

"Well, the lumber came from the woods, and they used their own tools. Another church has been built down in Juneau."

"Yes, I saw it."

"Well, shall we take a look inside?"

I merely smiled, unable to voice any sort of reply. I had the feeling I had made a terrible mistake, but for the sake of pride, I needed to make at least an attempt to stay here.

I stared at the front of the house as we approached. A small stoop supported by two poles overhung the front steps, providing protection against the elements for those entering and leaving.

"The keys were delivered to me after Josh died," Gordon was saying as he reached into his coat pocket and withdrew a brass ring holding two narrow keys. He experimented with first one key and then the other until the lock finally clicked. "I'll leave the keys with you now," he said, twisting the knob. The door would not budge.

It held stubbornly until Gordon heaved his weight against it; only then did it groan and drift open.

"I'll get your trunk," he said, leaving me to explore alone.

Unpainted boards enclosed a large room about 45 feet square, cluttered with heavy furniture. The first thing my eyes met was a hideous face! Then I saw that it was some sort of mask hanging on the wall. I walked into the room and looked around. A long couch was covered with thick white fur. Nearby, a coffee table held a brass lantern and an interesting carving of a bird. The room contained an assortment of Indian artifacts—pictures designed from beads, whalebone, and ivory. As I started across the room to examine a picture, my heel caught something, and I stared down into the glassy eyes of a grizzly.

I screamed.

"What's wrong?" Gordon shouted from the door.

I swallowed. "This bearskin rug took me by surprise."

"Unusual place, isn't it?" he asked, lugging my trunk inside.

"What is that thing on the wall?" I asked, pointing to the grotesque face.

He stared at it for a moment. "It looks like a Tlingit ceremonial mask that your uncle decided to hang as a picture."

With growing concern, I let my eyes roam back to the bearskin rug, then to the animal fur on the sofa. Either Uncle Joshua had become a hunter or else he had a friend who hunted. I didn't like keeping company with dead animals.

Gordon turned toward a passageway behind a partition. "Here are the stairs. This room had a cathedral ceiling before Joshua enclosed the upper area for a bedroom."

I followed Gordon up the tiny, close-set stairs, which made a resounding creak at every step. As I climbed upward, the air became close and musty.

By the time we reached the second story, I was gasping for breath. Gordon heaved the trunk to the floor with a thud and glanced back at me.

"I like it," I said, surveying the large, pleasant room. The east and west windows admitted patches of sunlight gilding the heavy sheen of dust that covered the floor. An armoire large enough to hold my clothes filled the opposite wall. The most striking feature in the room was the mahogany four-poster bed, a Mallard. When I saw it, I burst into laughter, startling Gordon.

"The Martins dote on this kind of bed," I explained, glancing at his puzzled face. "Would you believe Uncle Joshua had his bed frame shipped up here? In spite of his attempt to live the rugged life, I see he still held onto one special luxury."

I wandered over to examine the strange blanket that covered the bed. Heavy wool, dyed yellow and green, sported designs of abstract faces. The blanket was obviously well crafted and valuable, but I wondered how comfortably I would sleep beneath those strange, exotic faces.

"A Tlingit blanket," Gordon said over my shoulder.

When I saw that he was pressing a hand to the center of his back, I felt a stab of guilt. My trunk, crammed to bursting, had obviously done its damage to him.

"I appreciate your trouble," I said quickly, thinking what a bother I had been.

"Quite all right. Are you ready to explore the rest of the house?"

I nodded, and followed him back down the narrow stairway.

"We get far more than our share of rain," he said as we crossed the big room again. "I'm sure you'll need to leave the doors open, air the place out."

I opened and closed the doors of two tiny rooms at the end of the big room. These were merely closets, overflowing with boxes of books. A small, L-shaped kitchen huddled behind the big room. While I was no authority on kitchens, I could see at a glance that this one contained only the bare essentials, or perhaps not even that, I amended, seeing no sink. A wood stove was braced against the back wall. A rickety eating table and two chairs with broken rungs filled the remainder of the room. Open shelves held tin cups and plates. A battered kettle centered a questionable stove in the far corner. I frowned at the stove, painfully aware of my ignorance of stoves and fires.

Gordon ventured into the kitchen and lifted the lid of the stove. A rank smell flew at us. Gordon sneezed, and I retreated toward the doorway as he dropped the lid and removed a handkerchief from his pocket.

"You're sure you can manage here?" he asked, wiping dirt from his hands.

"Yes, for the short time that I'll be in Juneau."

Gordon's blue eyes darkened behind his spectacles. He was probably thinking that I possessed a bit of my uncle's crazy streak, and perhaps he was right.

"Well, you'll need some staples," he said, looking around. "In the meantime, I insist on returning for you in a couple of hours. That should give you time to unpack and look around. We'll have an early dinner in town, then tomorrow you can buy groceries."

I was staring at the stove, privately wondering if I could manage. I was accustomed to a comfortable life in the city, shamefully pampered by a maid and a cook. Wasn't I looking for a challenge when I drowned out my mother's dire warnings and stubbornly set out on this adventure? The idea had seemed so compelling back in my cozy living room in San Francisco but obviously I was in for a greater challenge than I had expected.

Squaring my shoulders, I tried to dredge up some of my old resolve.

"I'll purchase groceries tomorrow. For tonight, I accept your dinner invitation," I answered gratefully.

He nodded, obviously not surprised. "Do you have a timepiece?"

I reached into my coat pocket and withdrew my father's gold watch.

"Nice," he nodded approvingly. "I'll return around four. That should give you ample time to reconsider the hotel."

I kept my smile in place. "We'll see. Thanks for your help, Mr. Walling."

Below the blond mustache, a guarded smile touched his narrow lips. "Don't you think it's time we dispensed with the formalities? Please call me Gordon."

"Very well. And I'm Abigail."

With a reminder that he would return at four, Gordon picked a path back across the dust-layered floor. His retreating footsteps trailed a lonely echo through the big room as the front door closed with a bang, and I jumped in response.

I wandered to the center of the big room and looked it over again, from the glassy eyes of the bear at my feet to the distorted face of the ceremonial mask on the wall.

"Hello, Church-House," I called out. "We might as well try to become friends."

Such absurd conversation, and yet I felt I must make peace with whatever spirits might linger.

The rank smell of a house closed up for too long rushed over me again, and I hurried across to open the front door. Lifting my skirts, I descended the steps and stood surveying the meadow leading to the deep evergreen woods.

It was a few seconds before the sound penetrated my thoughts, but once aware of the steady chunking, I quickly located its source.

The tall, dark man was standing off to my right at the far edge of the woods, his ax poised above a fallen log. And he was staring straight into my eyes!

Chapter 2

Abruptly he turned, and with one mighty thrust sank the ax blade into the stump of the fallen tree. Before I could collect my senses and dash back inside, he leaned down, scooped up an armload of wood, and headed in my direction. I hesitated, watching curiously as he crossed the meadow, his knee-high black boots making long, purposeful steps. He wore a flannel shirt and jeans, and even from a distance, the eyes held me, eyes the color of jade. Broad cheeks, slim nose, and high forehead were partially shadowed by the fur cap slanted rakishly over dark brown hair.

"Hello," he called out.

"Hello . . ."

He was handsome in a rugged way, but there was something more appealing than his good looks. He had a casual manner, a friendly smile, and a hint of mystery in the green eyes that sparkled in the sunlight.

"You'll need some firewood, Miss Martin," he said to me. "October days grow cool in the afternoon, and even colder at night."

"How do you know who I am?" I blurted.

"Moccasin telegraph! News travels fast here, but news of a beautiful woman's arrival in Juneau is speedier than the Morse Code."

I stared at him, not knowing how to respond to a compliment from this stranger.

"Juneau is quite a change from San Francisco, but once

you adjust, you may come to like it. I'll just take the wood inside," he said, sidestepping me to bound up the steps and through the kitchen door.

A lifelong warning against strangers hovered in my mind, then disappeared. This was Alaska, where everyone was a stranger. In order to survive, I would have to trust some of these people.

When I entered the kitchen, he was arranging the wood inside the stove. "Know how to tend a fire?" he asked, glancing over his shoulder.

"Sort of." I had never in my life tended a fire, and I was determined to learn, but I was more interested in the man than in the stove. I stared at his thick hair, a very dark brown. It grew low on his neck and waved in deep ridges.

"What's your name?" I asked abruptly.

"Scott Morgan. I knew your uncle." He opened the door of a tiny cabinet behind the stove and withdrew a brown bottle, along with a stack of yellowed pages from newspapers.

It was obvious that he had been a frequent visitor here, since he seemed to know where everything was kept.

He began to tear the newspaper into strips, then he tucked the strips beneath and around the wood. "Coal oil," he said, uncorking the bottle and dribbling the contents over the newspaper and wood. I concentrated on the way he was doing everything, for I was certain with my sensitivity to cold that it would be necessary to keep a fire at night.

He had pulled a match from the pocket of his red flannel shirt and was now scraping the tip across the stove. When it sparked, he dropped it onto the kerosene-soaked paper. A fire blazed up, and he closed the stove door.

"That should take care of you. By bedtime it will have burned down to a low fire that will knock off the chill until tomorrow. Then I'll come back and . . ."

"You won't need to come back," I interrupted. "Now that I've watched you, I think I can manage." It wasn't that I disliked the idea of seeing him again; I just didn't want to be in the debt of this handsome stranger.

He looked me over carefully with those magnetic green eyes. Then, a caustic grin tilted the corners of his mouth as he reached forward and, to my surprise, lifted both my hands, turning them over in his calloused palms. I stared up at him, too stunned to react.

"Forgive me for saying so, but I would wager these hands have never built a fire. It would be a shame for that soft white skin to bear the ugly scars of a burn."

At last my sanity returned, and I yanked my hands free. "I'm perfectly capable," I retorted, "otherwise I would not be here."

"Why *do* you insist on staying in this strange house?" he asked, turning to saunter about the kitchen. "Josh would never believe it."

It occurred to me this might be the person to shed some light on my uncle's mysterious life.

"Mr. Morgan . . ."

"Scott . . ."

"How well did you know my uncle?" I pressed on.

He leaned against the open door, crossing his boots at the ankle. "We were friends," he repeated the statement he had made earlier. "Josh was the most interesting man I've ever known. He was a man's man; he could talk about explorations into the mountains, landing a giant salmon, the business world in California . . ." he paused, flashing that lethal grin, "or about gambling . . . or women. But more important," he was serious again, "we talked about the great writers of our century. Josh was a writer." His eyes dropped to his feet and he was silent.

I swallowed, absorbing what he had said. "Mr. Morgan . . ."

"Scott . . ."

"I came here to pay off my uncle's debts. I was astounded to discover the extent of those debts. We had no idea." I bit my lip, wondering how much I should reveal.

His pleasant expression became one of grave concern as he looked back at me.

"Apparently he spent a lot of time at the gambling table,"

I said, studying his face for a clue.

Again, his eyes dropped. "Yes."

I began to pace the floor, my hands clenched. "What a waste of time and money!"

"A matter of opinion."

I stopped pacing and stared at him. So! This man was the same kind of rogue my uncle had become. "Did you gamble with him?"

"Sometimes."

"Did you win or lose?" I knew I had exceeded the boundaries of polite conversation, but somehow I couldn't stop myself.

"I usually lose," he grinned, as though it were of no great consequence.

Automatically, my eyes flicked over his rough clothes, noting in the process a frayed thread here and there. Companions like this Scott Morgan had influenced Uncle Joshua to abandon the common sense of his upbringing and throw caution to the wind. My anger was building. I glanced back at the stove, which was already radiating heat into the small room.

"Thank you for building a fire," I said curtly. "I'll be fine now. You need not trouble yourself again."

I could hear the rude dismissal in my tone, but I didn't care. The anger I felt was to remain throughout most of my stay; unfortunately, Scott Morgan was now the prime target.

"What is your first name?" he asked, ignoring my stinging comment.

"Abigail."

"Good day, Abby." He left the house without a backward glance, thereby missing the shocked expression on my face. No true gentleman called a lady by her first name without asking permission. But this man was no gentleman.

Curiously, I cracked the door open and watched him walk briskly across the flats to the bay. A canoe was beached there, and he pushed it from the shore out into the water and hopped in. He lifted a paddle and the canoe sped into the bay.

As the boat moved north in the slate gray water, I suddenly realized how little Scott had told me about Uncle Joshua, when there was so much I wanted to know. He had told me even less about himself.

I closed the door and stood in the big room, trying to feel at home in this strange dwelling. I recalled the driver who had taken me to the bank, muttering a complaint against Americans in his native tongue. When I asked about his homeland, I could see the nostalgia in his eyes, and I wondered now about those people who had worked on this dwelling. Life must have been difficult for them. I could read a lifetime of hardship in the driver's face.

But perhaps they weren't all as unhappy as the driver, I thought as I climbed the stairs to the bedroom and stood before the window looking at the distant crosses in the small cemetery. I thought of Uncle Joshua and felt a deep sadness. I turned from the window and with a sigh began to open my trunk. As I shook out the new dresses I had purchased, I realized that more practical clothes should have been chosen. When I thought of home and friends, I knew that no one there could picture *me* living in an abandoned Russian church that overlooked a cemetery! Nor would they believe that a woman as independent as I had been had turned into a tongue-tied schoolgirl in the presence of Scott Morgan, the dark, mysterious stranger who was probably as wild as my uncle had been.

As I hung my clothes in the armoire, I saw it had been stripped of Uncle Joshua's clothes, although a pair of snowshoes still leaned against the inside wall. Where had his clothes gone? I glanced again at the large room that filled the upper second story. A rusty gold pan lay in a corner. An old fiddle rested on a table in the corner. Odd, I thought sadly, what my uncle had kept.

I wandered over to the Mallard bed and gently touched the mahogany post. Tears sprang to my eyes. I suddenly felt very homesick as I looked at this bed, the only link to the life my uncle had left behind.

I touched the coarse woolen blanket, staring at the green and yellow faces woven into the threads . . . the faces of tribal chiefs, I imagined. While this kind of covering was a drastic change from my white satin spread at home, I felt certain the wool would keep me warmer. Already the heat from the stove downstairs had begun to ease the sharp chill, while the resin smell of spruce branches had begun to chase away the mustiness.

I opened a chest of drawers and found a tablet. When I flipped it open, I discovered a collection of Uncle Joshua's poems. Sentimentally, I turned the dog-eared pages, appreciating the perfect rhyme and meter on which Uncle Joshua doted, and the sterling beauty of each passage.

As I read the poems, however, I noticed a subtle change in my uncle's moods. Tributes to Alaska's beauty gave way to morbid accounts of lost gold and lost love. The sadness was almost tangible. I could read no more. I closed the notebook and returned it to a corner of the drawer. Yes, it was conceivable to me now that he had taken his life.

Tears flooded my eyes as I thought of the witty, charming man who used to come to our house, bringing peppermint sticks and humorous poems. It seemed to me that Uncle Joshua had traded a happy-go-lucky outlook for one of sadness and gloom. As I put my clothes away, I tried to pull myself out of this sad mood and think sensibly. But I was hardly being sensible, living in a remote Russian church with a window overlooking the forlorn cemetery where my uncle was buried!

By the time I had freshened up and renetted my hair, I heard the thud of horses' hooves and buggy wheels on the narrow road. A peek through the window brought Gordon into view. I hurried back downstairs and eagerly met him at the front door.

"I'm ready," I called, tossing my cloak about my shoulders.

A knowing smile touched his mouth. "Perhaps you're also ready to reconsider the hotel?"

"Not yet." I stepped outside, locked the door, and

dropped the key into my skirt pocket.

"The days are growing shorter now," Gordon said, handing me into the buggy. "If you had arrived in the summer, you would still see people out working in their gardens until very late."

"I wouldn't mind the long days, but isn't it hard to adjust to short days in the dead of winter?"

"At first it was, but then I grew accustomed to it, like everyone else." He helped me into the buggy and glanced up the road. "How do you plan to get to and from town?"

"I enjoy walking."

"It's a long walk," he said with a wry smile. "I think it would be a good idea to hire your neighbor, Mr. Zarnoff. He makes his meager living hauling freight for merchants or providing transportation for visitors. Now that the summer season is over, there'll be less work for him. He'd probably be glad to take you to and from town. Would you like to stop by his place on the way into town? You can meet him and discuss transportation. He and his wife are older and not in very good health. He needs the money."

"I suppose that's best."

As we approached the Zarnoff's house, I spotted a large man puttering around his yard. Then, as we approached, he turned, and my heart sank. It was the driver who had met me at the ship and delivered me to the bank!

"Oh no," I gasped.

"What's wrong?"

"We've already met, and I think he's a very disagreeable man."

Gordon merely chuckled. "He's not so bad. He *is* dependable." He waved and called to the man. "Hello, Mr. Zarnoff."

He lumbered across to the buggy. He didn't bother to conceal the look of disapproval as our eyes met.

"Mr. Zarnoff, I'd like to introduce you to your new neighbor, Miss Abigail Martin. You remember Joshua Martin? She's his niece."

I caught my breath as the introduction was given and

Zarnoff's hard stare hit me. We were both remembering my inquiry about the church and his claim that my uncle had gone crazy while living there.

"Hello again," I called lightly, hoping to make a fresh start with the man.

He nodded curtly, his eyes returning to Gordon.

"Miss Martin will be requiring a driver from time to time," Gordon continued pleasantly, unaware of the heavy tension in the air. "I've told her you might be able to provide that service. She will pay you, of course."

The opportunity to make some money slightly altered Zarnoff's grim expression. "Yes," he said directly to Gordon.

"Then I'll be getting in touch with you," I said, expecting him to look at me again. He did not.

Gordon bade him good evening and we were off again.

"Pleasant man," I said bitterly.

Gordon merely chuckled.

Dinner at the hotel was far more enjoyable than I had imagined. Gordon explained that the proprietor had once owned a hotel in Denver and had used the same decor here. Wall sconces cast mellow light against the brocade walls and over tables covered with white linen.

As I settled into a cushioned chair and looked around, I felt the day's tension slipping away.

Fresh salmon and vegetables were cooked to perfection and served on silver trays and fine china. I ate heartily, despite the interruptions of those who stopped to speak with Gordon. As they did, their eyes strayed curiously to me. One old man in particular fixed bold eyes upon me and continued to stare.

"Pardon me," he finally apologized, "but it's such a pleasure to see a beautiful woman here. Your blonde hair and fair skin are very pretty."

Feeling embarrassed, I thanked him and looked nervously about the room. I suddenly met my reflection in a gold-framed mirror over a buffet. I was a natural blonde, thanks to my Swedish mother, whose clear blue eyes and fair skin I had also inherited. While she had always impressed upon me the sinfulness of vanity, I was practical enough to realize I had been blessed by my resemblance to her; and on a small frame, my hundred and five pounds were evenly distributed.

"I hope you aren't embarrassed," Gordon broke through my thoughts. When I glanced at him, his eyes were moving over the crowd, and there was a pleased expression on his face, as though he were enjoying the compliments more than I was.

While there was still an air of reserve about this man, I was beginning to feel more comfortable with him. Conversation was easy because he asked the right questions. I had managed to give him a complete history of the Martin family, the newspaper business, and my long engagement as well. On our return home, however, I found my pleasant mood fading.

"When did you last hear from your uncle?" Gordon had asked.

I thought back over the winter months. "Around Christmas. His last letter was very cheerful, and he never even hinted of his debts. Or . . . his depression." I dropped my eyes.

He sighed heavily as he lifted a hand to smooth his mustache. "No. He didn't want his family to know."

I had been deep in thought as we rode along, but as darkness descended like a black cloak about us, I turned in the seat and looked across at Gordon.

"How well did you know my uncle?" I asked.

The curve of his hat brim, his small nose, and his round chin were etched in silhouette as he silently considered my question. "Not as well as some of the other people here," he replied. "But I must admit that when he first came to Juneau, everyone liked him. I think Josh's problems began with the woman."

"The woman?"

"No one was quite sure who she was, or where she lived. There were rumors that Josh spoke of her when he was deep in his cups. To my knowledge, he never named her."

"I wonder who she was," I said, staring at the unusual totem pole as we passed.

Had a broken heart been the real cause of his suicide? In San Francisco Uncle Joshua was known as a confirmed bachelor, and never to my knowledge had any woman threatened his bachelorhood. My curiosity was whetted by the mention of this mysterious woman, and I knew before I left Juneau I must find out who she was.

We were approaching the Zarnoff cabin, and now the door was yanked open and the woman, silhouetted in the back light of a lantern, stared out at us until we had passed.

"I've heard of nosy neighbors," I said, "but I've never had one who fit that description like this one!"

Gordon chuckled. "The Zarnoffs are a bit eccentric, of course, but they won't bother you."

I had my doubts. My bad impression of the Zarnoffs was not improving.

We had reached my bizarre house, and I felt a sense of foreboding as my eyes traced the dark tower. Gordon leaned back in the buggy, drawing rein on the horses. As I glanced over the still and silent surroundings, I suddenly recalled the man who had been chopping wood over in the forest.

"Do you know Scott Morgan?" I asked, as Gordon handed me down from the buggy.

I could not see his face clearly, but I sensed my question had taken him by surprise, for suddenly his hand tightened on my arm. "Not very well," he replied after a moment. "He's just another sourdough, I suppose."

"Sourdough?"

"Someone labeled the miners 'sourdoughs' because they used a special sour dough for making their biscuits. Silly term, isn't it?"

I shrugged. "Mr. Morgan brought me some firewood."

We were approaching the broad front steps, and in the glow of the lantern from the window, I could see that Gordon was shaking his head. "I should have thought of firewood. You'll be needing a fire, of course."

"Mr. Morgan built a fire for me in the wood stove. He said I should let it burn low to have heat through the night."

As I removed the key from my skirt pocket and inserted it into the door, I glanced at Gordon and saw that he was leaning back, staring at the tower. "Josh enclosed the tower, but it can't be approached from within the house. It's an unusual home," he smiled grimly.

Home? I didn't see how anyone could think of it as a home. "I now understand why you feel it will be difficult to find a buyer," I said.

He shook his head and looked back at me. "I'm afraid it will be impossible."

I sighed. "I haven't decided exactly what to do."

"When will you be leaving?"

"I've booked passage on the steamer when it returns." I smiled. "Thank you for a lovely evening."

He took my gloved hand and lifted it to his lips. "My pleasure. And remember, Mr. Zarnoff can drive you wherever you need to go. I'm a town commissioner, and we have some meetings planned this week. Still, if you need anything . . ."

"I'll be fine," I assured him. As he tipped his hat and walked away, I felt an apprehension creeping over me, with the knowledge that I was now alone here. I watched as his buggy melted into the shadows of the road and the thud of horse hooves died away.

My eyes moved through the darkness to the distant island across the channel where lanterns in cabins glowed like fireflies in the night. With the exception of those lights, there was only darkness and the lapping of the water against the shore. I turned to go inside and was stopped dead in my tracks as a wild sound pierced the night. I froze, listening. It came again, bringing a layer of goosebumps to my skin. Then all was silent. I flew inside and bolted the door. What was that sound? I wondered, hugging my arms against my chest, as I strained my ears. It sounded . . . inhuman. Then the silence stretched on.

Across the room, red eyes glittered in the ceremonial mask. The open mouth revealed jagged teeth set in a grimace of pain. Wisps of black hair were convincingly real. Had they come from someone's scalp?

I quickly looked away, trying to think of something rational. The fire in the stove—yes, I must keep the fire going. Sidestepping the grizzly's open mouth, I crossed the big room and lit a candle, then headed for the kitchen, grateful for Scott Morgan's fire.

Obviously Gordon did not have a favorable impression of the man, which meant that I should keep my distance. An adventurer, he had said. A sourdough! Scott Morgan sounded very much like the man my uncle had become.

I entered the shadowed kitchen and checked the fire, still burning low. Then, with a sense of relief, I wandered back through the big room and finally extinguished the lantern. The cry I had heard must have been some sort of night animal. I must not dwell on it.

The lantern flickered out. The feeble light of the candle hardly penetrated the vast darkness. A moaning wind prowled around the house, rattling loose boards. Never had I felt so alone.

I hurried toward the stairway, toward the comfort of the big Mallard bed.

Once I had climbed the stairs and placed the candlestick on the bedside table, however, I was aware of how tense I remained. How could I possibly relax enough to sleep?

I thought of Uncle Joshua's tablet of poems and pulled it out of the drawer, determined to read until I fell asleep.

An Alaskan night, void of moonlight, inked the windows, and I quickly undressed, consoling myself that the high windows would discourage peepers.

I stretched out in the soft bed, pulling the thick blanket to my chin, while trying not to look at its eerie design. I read over the first pages of my uncle's poems, appreciating their beauty and sensing his fascination with Alaska. I sighed. This was the way I preferred to think of Uncle

Joshua, a man happy with his new life before bad luck had overtaken him.

When finally my eyes grew heavy, I placed the tablet on the table and extinguished the candle. The weariness of the long trip finally took its toll, and I drifted to sleep.

It could have been minutes, or hours, before the sounds from downstairs finally penetrated my deep slumber.

Chapter 3

I lay rigid, my ears straining. Something thudded below me, then there was silence. I had managed to persuade myself I had been dreaming when I heard another thud, then another. I sat bolt upright in bed and looked around the darkness. Foolishly, I had forgotten to bring up matches to light the candle. Another mysterious bump floated up from below.

I threw the covers back and sprang to the cold floor. One feeble ray of moonlight touched the window, while directly beneath me, slow, plodding steps crossed the living room. A cold sweat broke over my face, even though I stood shivering in my flannel gown. A robber? Instantly I thought of Zarnoff, the man with cold, hard eyes. He had not bothered to conceal his contempt for my uncle, who dared inhabit a sacred dwelling, nor for me, when he learned that I was staying here as well.

A heavy step sounded on the bottom stair.

Like icicles pricking my spine, fear shot through every nerve and fiber. He was coming up to my bedroom! Never in my life had I felt so helpless. I had nothing with which to defend myself; in the darkness, I couldn't locate any sort of weapon. I groped my way toward my trunk, hoping to push it against the door. At least this would block the intruder until I could think of something else.

My eyes had begun to adjust to the darkness, but before I focused on the footstool, my knee struck it, and I tripped and plunged headlong against the cold floor. For a moment I lay there stunned, my head pounding from the impact. The steps had ceased! I flounced about, trying to stand, even though my head was still spinning. With no other alternative, I began to crawl in the direction of the trunk, now vaguely silhouetted by the pale moonlight.

There was no sound from below.

When finally I reached the trunk, I held to it like an anchor as I slowly pulled myself upright. I leaned against the trunk, throwing my weight against it in an effort to push it across the room. It screeched across the boards, then banged as I shoved it hard against the door.

Footsteps were thundering over the floor downstairs. I listened, trying to follow their direction above the wild hammering of my heart. The slam of the back door gave me hope. I waited, but heard nothing more.

Flailing my arms about to locate objects in my path, I hobbled to the nearest window and peered out. The heavy clouds had drifted back to reveal a quarter moon. I pressed my face to the cold window, looking right to left.

Through the darkness there was nothing visible except the outlines of the three-bar crosses in the cemetery. I stared at the cemetery as ghost stories from childhood filled my mind. I crossed to the other window and peered out. Far across the flats, I could make out a shadow moving quickly along, then disappearing in the darkness. So! The midnight visitor was neither a ghost nor a figment of my imagination.

I stood at the window for several minutes, watching, listening. When I was certain there was no other sound from without or within, I made my way back across the bedroom and dislodged the trunk from the door. Then I seized the handrail and cautiously descended the stairs toward a puzzling tinge of light.

The light grew more distinct as I reached the bottom stair. My grip tightened on the rail; my heart beat faster. Oddly, that mysterious light gave me no comfort, it merely reinforced my fear; for it was visible proof that a mysterious presence had inhabited the house. As I cautiously stepped into the big room, I saw the lantern burning serenely on the table, the smell of sulfur from the match still drifting in the air.

I tried to swallow, but my throat was like sand. I stood motionless, my eyes flying over the room, inspecting every object, trying to see what, if anything, was missing. Everything appeared to be in order; still, that was little consolation when I realized that someone had entered the house, lit the lantern, and prowled around while upstairs I lay in a deep sleep. The idea that someone could do that brought another tremor of fear. *But he is gone,* I told myself. *There is nothing to fear now.*

I crept across, lifted the lantern, and headed for the kitchen. Tinned goods were spilled across the floor, and the doors to the small cabinet stood ajar. One of the wooden chairs had been overturned; this was probably the bang that had awakened me. I straightened the chair and felt the cold draft of air seeping through the back door . . . it was not quite closed.

The knowledge that I had failed to lock this door hit me like a bolt of thunder. I hurried over and gave it a hard slam, then turned the key in the lock, vowing never again to be so careless. A hungry prowler had come, that was all! Someone who did not know that I had taken up residence here. But if he came for food, why had he not taken the tinned goods? And why had he started up the stairs to my bedroom?

The next morning I awoke with stiff muscles. The long journey, the bad news of Uncle Joshua's indebtedness, and finally the midnight prowler lay heavily on my mind. I snuggled deeper under the warm blanket, dreading to get up and face the day.

But then I slowly became aware of a rhythmic sound somewhere in the distance. I sat up on my elbow, trying to identify the sound. It was a steady, even *chunk . . . chunk . . . chunk.*

Curiosity pulled me from beneath the warm covers, and

I hurried to the cold window to investigate.

The sunshine seemed unusually bright, to my sleepy eyes. I followed the chunking sound to the woods, and there, beneath a tall spruce, stood Scott Morgan chopping wood again.

I jumped back from the window and scrambled for my clothes. Had it been Scott Morgan who'd come into the kitchen the night before? He seemed to know where everything was kept; he would know where to find the lantern and the matches. Had he come to check on the fire? If so, there was no reason for him to come upstairs. . . .

Hurriedly I dressed, wondering if he intended to bring more firewood to me this morning. That was simply an excuse; what did he *really* want, I wondered. I had just finished netting my hair when I heard him pounding on the back door. Perhaps he had already tried the door and found it locked this time!

I turned and began to descend the stairs. A dull ache settled over my head, reminding me of last night's scramble in the darkness. And the intruder.

The knocking at the back door became more persistent. This time I was going to give the man a piece of my mind, let him know that I valued privacy more than his firewood. Perhaps he expected me to pay him for the firewood. Yes, that was it!

I opened the back door, ready to deliver a proper little speech and ask how much I owed him. When I looked into his green eyes, however, all rational thoughts vanished. For a moment we stood staring, and I couldn't seem to speak. Then I became aware of the brisk morning air, and I crossed my arms, shivering.

"Good morning," he finally spoke. "I left my ax in the woods yesterday. Since I had to come back for it, I thought I'd drop off some more wood."

"How much do I owe you?" I asked bluntly.

Ignoring the question, he let a frown settle between his dark brows. He entered the kitchen and stacked the wood beside the stove. "Fire's gone out," he observed upon lifting the stove lid. It was as though he spoke more to himself than to me.

Efficiently he repeated the process of the day before, building another fire. When he had finished, he slapped his hands on the sides of his jeans, then turned and looked at me with grave eyes.

"Don't insult me by offering money," he said coolly. "I—" He broke off as his eyes fell on the tinned goods, still tumbled about.

"I had a midnight visitor," I said, looking again at the disorder.

Puzzled, he silently knelt to pick up the tins.

"I foolishly neglected to lock the back door," I said, picking up a tin.

"Did you see him?" he asked.

"No. I only saw a shadow moving along the flats, then disappearing in the darkness."

"Was anything taken?" he asked, looking through the door to the big room.

"I'm not sure. He could have taken a few things from in here, but everything else seems to be in order."

He bounded past me into the living room, and I followed, watching him carefully. He stood in the center of the room, his hands on his hips, his eyes creeping over the room. Then he opened the adjoining doors and peered into the two closet-sized rooms. "Surely he didn't expect to find food in here!" he said, shoving his hands into his pants pockets.

Curiously, I wandered to his side to look into the closets.

"I imagine it was just a prowler who didn't realize anyone was staying here," I answered. "When he heard me stirring, he ran out the back door."

He turned and studied me thoughtfully. "Everyone in Juneau has heard that a beautiful woman has taken up residence in Josh's house," he finally answered. "It's hard to believe he didn't know that."

Beautiful indeed. His compliment threw me, momentarily. "Thank you for not referring to this place as a church, or church-house," I replied, "as everyone else has. They can't seem to accept the fact that my uncle converted it to a rather comfortable house."

He nodded as his eyes drifted over the room, lingering on the bearskin rug. "He loved this place."

"Why?" I blurted. "I mean, it was a rather bizarre thing to do, trying to make a house out of a church!"

He shrugged. "He probably saw it as a challenge."

I couldn't resist smiling. "Uncle Joshua loved a challenge. Incidentally, Mr. Morgan . . ."

"Please call me Scott, Abigail . . ."

"I didn't know until I arrived here that my uncle was so deeply in debt. And I didn't know about the mysterious woman in his life. Did you know who she was?" I asked, watching him carefully.

He shrugged. "We talked about books and the luck of the draw in poker, and Alaska. We rarely discussed women."

Why not, I wanted to ask.

"Don't pay much attention to the rumors. You're apt to hear some preposterous stories."

"Then you don't think there was a woman? Gordon said . . ."

The amusement in his eyes disappeared at the mention of Gordon's name. "Gordon Walling? He's no different from the rest when it comes to gossiping."

I searched his face, hearing the bitterness in his tone. I imagined he must have been the object of town gossip at some point, for him to be so sensitive.

"Mr. Walling has been very helpful," I said. "He notified the family of my uncle's death, and he's trying to give us some time to clear up his debts." *Debts that led to his suicide,* I thought bitterly. "About his death," I began, then paused, looking across at Scott. "Mother and I naturally assumed it was his heart, given the Martin history of heart seizures among the men of our family. It wasn't until I arrived here that I learned he had," I swallowed, hating the words, "taken his own life."

He turned and sauntered across the room to stare out the

window. "Do you believe that?" he asked.

I stared at his back, considering the question. "I don't know. What do you think?"

"I'm not sure," he finally replied.

"Did the authorities investigate?"

"The authority," he amended. "Hank Wilson, the Deputy Marshal, does his best between down-and-out miners. For so many years, the only law was the miner's law. That could be a rope, a gun, or merely tossing the criminal out in the wilds to the mercy of animals and mosquitoes."

I listened to the explanation, hardly appreciating the humor, because of my concern for my uncle.

"Did my uncle ever find gold?" I asked, as I thought again of his staggering debts.

He turned to face me. "If he did, he kept it a secret. Everyone believed Joshua was down on his luck, even though he sometimes boasted of finding gold. Still, he was practically penniless."

I shook my head. "We had no idea."

"Well, it isn't unusual for miners to lose everything."

Was he speaking of himself as well? I looked across at him, idly studying his thick brown hair, the dark stubble along his jawline, the firm mouth.

"You seem doubtful about my uncle's suicide," I said. "I would like to know why."

He had begun to pace the room, and now he lifted a hand to massage the muscles in his neck. "Mainly just because I don't want to accept the idea of suicide. It's such a waste."

"Mr. Zarnoff said he went crazy because he tried to make a house out of a sacred dwelling," I said bitterly.

He pursed his lips, making no comment.

I leaned forward, watching him carefully. "Do you suppose the person who came here last night was . . . ?" I didn't know what I intended to ask. Looking for something? Looking for *someone?*

"I suppose it was just a prowler. There are lots of men in these parts who are out of work, hungry, and disillusioned."

He frowned. "Take care to lock the doors from now on. I should be going," he said, although he lingered. "I have firewood to deliver."

"Is that your line of work?" I asked, then bit my lip, knowing it was a personal question.

"It's one of the things that I do. Well, good-bye," he said, with a small grin. Then he hurried out the door.

Whether he'd intended to or not, he had left me more troubled than ever so far as my uncle was concerned. I wandered through the house, looking around, but missing nothing of importance. I ended up at the foot of the stairs, staring at the narrow boards built into the close passageway. Someone had started up those creaking steps last night. If I had not made a noise, would the midnight prowler have come to my bedroom?

My thoughts flew back to the conversation with Scott and his obvious doubt about my uncle's suicide.

Had Uncle Joshua really taken his own life? I wondered. And if he did not take out his gun and put a bullet through his head . . . who did?

Chapter 4

I prowled through the house, my anxiety growing. Every step I took sent a loud echo rumbling, until finally I grabbed my shawl and headed outside.

Breathing the fresh air, cool and invigorating, I began to feel new strength surging back through me. I had prided myself on my father's business sense; this would be a good opportunity to put to use some clear thinking and reasonable logic.

I seemed to be falling deeper into a web of mystery, rather than settling Uncle Joshua's debts and laying the entire matter to rest. Now it seemed there were disturbing questions that must be answered for my own satisfaction, as well as for that of the Martin family. I knew upon my return to San Francisco, I would be questioned relentlessly.

And then as I stood in the yard staring vacantly across the short meadow, my eyes locked with the wooden crosses in the cemetery. I took a deep long breath. It was time to visit my uncle's grave.

Slowly I began to pick my way across the damp grass toward the cemetery. The sunshine I had glimpsed earlier had quickly faded, and now low clouds swelled, promising the rain that was so prevalent here in Juneau.

There were only seven graves enclosed within the picket fence. Upon pushing open the gate and entering, I discovered that the crosses were lettered with Russian names, except for the cross with the single bar.

A feeling of deep sadness washed over me as I walked over and read my uncle's name carved in wood on the bar of the cross. Tears blurred the dates of his birth and death as I stood paying silent tribute to the man who had been so filled with life when I knew him.

Home and family seemed far away now as I stood in the lonely little cemetery where the vast stillness was broken only by the sigh of the wind through the big spruces. As my vision cleared, my eyes fell to a small bouquet of dried wildflowers lying at the base of the cross. I knelt beside the grave, gingerly touching the flowers. Then, as my eyes moved over the mound and beyond it, a small patch of black caught my eye. Just beyond the grave something lay crumpled on the wet grass. I leaned over and picked up a small black glove. Mud on the glove had dried, then dampened again, leading me to believe it had been there for a while.

I turned the glove over in my hand, looking from it to my uncle's grave, then on to the bouquet of dried flowers. Yes, there *was* a woman in my uncle's life; or there had been. Curiosity burned within me as I turned and walked back to the house, the glove clutched tightly in my hand. Who was the woman? Why had he kept her identity a secret? And where was she now?

Glancing up at the clouds, I could see that rain was coming. The idea of spending a dreary day alone in the house held no appeal. My steps quickened as I hurried inside, dropped the glove on the table, fetched my reticule, and struck a path to the Zarnoff's house, seeking a ride to town.

While I had walked the distance to the Zarnoff's quite rapidly, I found as I approached that I was no longer in a hurry. Dread seized me. The yard was empty, the front door closed. I hesitated at the end of the walk, staring at the log house. As I hesitated, thinking what to say, the door was flung back and Mrs. Zarnoff stood glaring at me.

Her cotton dress had once been navy blue, but was now faded to gray. Shapeless sleeves held no cuffs; a frayed skirt was covered with a starched muslin apron. Her gray hair was whisked into a high chignon from which several wisps had escaped and bounced untidily about her neck.

"What do you want?" she asked in greeting.

I cleared my throat. "I want to hire a ride to town. Is your husband at home?"

Wordlessly she turned and shouted something in Russian into the depths of the cabin.

Presently Zarnoff appeared in the door, fixing a rude stare upon me, as though I had asked a favor of him.

I waited, trying to stare him down until he finally muttered something which I took to mean that he would get ready.

Such hospitable neighbors, I thought angrily, as I stood glaring down the road. I was beginning to wish that I had not been so independent, insisting upon staying here, rather than at the hotel. The hotel was much more convenient . . . and much *safer.*

Steps shuffled behind me and I whirled to face Mrs. Zarnoff who had returned to survey me curiously.

I stared back at her, ready to be as rude as she, but then she clasped her hands before her and spoke in a more civil manner.

"Will you be staying long in Juneau?" she asked.

"No, not long," I replied.

"You are not afraid down there?"

I lifted my chin. "No, I'm not afraid."

"The man will be coming by," she said quietly. "He always does."

The man?

"Do you mean Mr. Morgan?" I asked.

She frowned, obviously not familiar with that name.

"Scott Morgan," I explained. "He was my uncle's friend."

"No, that is not the name. A man named Bill."

Zarnoff cut off her words with an abrupt command spoken in Russian. In response, her face flushed and she yelled back, more Russian.

"Who is the man she speaks of?" I asked Zarnoff as I climbed up in his wagon.

He waved his hand dismissively. "The wife, she just rattles. She does not always know of what she speaks."

I stared pointedly at him, although his dark blue eyes evaded me. "I think she knew exactly what she was talking about, Mr. Zarnoff," I countered. "Who is this Bill? I have the right to know the name of a man who frequents the place where I live."

He laid a whip over the horses, and we lurched forward. His fur cap shot back on his bald head, and he quickly adjusted it, fixing his mouth in a thin line, as though determined to keep quiet. I continued to stare at him, refusing to be ignored.

"She is thinking of a man they call Lonesome Bill," he finally answered. "But I have not seen him in a while."

"Was he a friend of my uncle's?" I pressed.

His eyes drifted to me, as cold as ever. "He pretended friendship."

"Pretended? Does that mean he was *not* a friend? Could you please speak in a manner that I can understand?"

He muttered some Russian under his breath; I imagined it was unflattering to me. This time, however, I did not intend to be put off. The unpleasant memory of my midnight prowler still hovered threateningly in my mind, and I decided to be forthright with this incident.

"I don't care for uninvited visitors, particularly at midnight," I said emphatically. "Someone came in and pillaged around last night."

I could see that my remark had caught him off guard. Either he was a good actor, or he had no knowledge of the prowler. He turned in surprise.

"What happened?" he asked.

"He prowled about the kitchen, lit a lantern in the living room, then started up the steps. When I began to stir, he left."

Zarnoff's eyes lingered on me for a few more seconds before he tightened the reins in his hands and fell silent.

"Well, do you have any idea who might be coming to my house at midnight?" I persisted. "Or what the person was seeking?"

"Perhaps," he spoke in a gruff voice, "it was one of the spirits trying to reclaim a sacred dwelling."

"I don't believe that! And if anyone thinks I will be frightened off by such an idea, they are sadly mistaken."

That ended our conversation. The rest of the journey was passed in silence as we both stared at the road. If I had been in a more pleasant mood, perhaps I could have enjoyed the humor in my mode of transportation. Rattling down the road in a wagon driven by the surly Zarnoff was a far cry from the brass-trimmed Martin carriage and our courteous driver Jose, not to mention the sleek, well-cared-for bays, back in San Francisco.

But I was *not* feeling humorous, and so I stared gloomily at the passing scenery.

The small frame houses were huddled closely together with a supply of winter firewood already stacked on the plank porches. The steep-pitched roofs formed a row of tiny A's that stretched down the hillside to the channel, where fishing boats bobbed in the deep blue water.

The horse had slowed to a weary walk as we entered the business district and I glanced briefly around me. I could see the town was larger than I had first thought. I had already spotted a church, a school, another hotel, and a large mercantile.

"You can drop me at the general store," I said stridently.

"When to come back for you?" he asked gruffly.

I would have walked the distance if not for the packages and the threat of rain.

"Two hours should be sufficient." I climbed down from the wagon and hurried up the boardwalk, seeking some of the rubber boots I had seen everyone wearing.

I stepped inside the grocery and glanced around. The front of the building held tinned goods and an assortment of shoes and clothing. I purchased the rubber boots I needed, then sauntered to the rear of the building, fascinated by the butcher shop there.

A grotesque leg of something was hanging from a hook.

Venison, the butcher proudly announced while he trimmed a rib of roast. When I remembered I was no chef, I quickly returned to the grocery area and purchased some tinned goods. A stalk of imported bananas hung on a rope from the ceiling. I purchased a pound of bananas, then selected several apples from a wooden crate. After I paid for my purchases, I asked if I could leave them while I shopped.

The man was friendly and helpful. As I turned to go, I decided to venture a question or two.

"Did you know Joshua Martin?" I asked.

"Yes," he smiled sadly. "He was your uncle, wasn't he?"

I stared at him, aware that he had known all along who I was. I remembered Scott Morgan telling me that everyone in town knew of my arrival.

"Joshua was a good man," he answered slowly, his eyes dropping. "We were sorry that . . ." his words trailed off as though difficult to complete. "That he had a run of bad luck," he finally added.

I imagined he meant money, but I decided to play innocent, hoping he would reveal something new.

"Bad luck?"

His eyes held a puzzled expression. "Well, his . . . illness, you know."

I leaned across the counter and looked him straight in the eye. "Tell me what you know about his illness. He had not written us for a while."

Surprise flickered over his face; obviously he thought I knew as much about my uncle as everyone else, when in truth my uncle had become a stranger to me.

"Well, I meant his . . . drinking," he said, with a sorrowful look. "It seemed to get the best of him."

"Oh," I said, dropping my eyes. I thought about Uncle Joshua's life—the gambling, the disappointment over the big strike he never found, the mysterious woman. Yet I began to suspect that he had brought a great deal of the bad luck upon himself. "Did you know his friend Bill?" I asked curiously.

"Lonesome Bill?" His sad face relaxed in a pleasant

smile. "Sure. Everyone knows Lonesome Bill. He and Josh were close friends," he nodded reflectively.

An idea came to me. If this Lonesome Bill was such a great friend of Uncle Joshua's, maybe he could answer some of the questions that haunted me.

"Could you tell me where I could find him?" I inquired. He hesitated, looking embarrassed. "Well . . . I imagine he would be down at the Lucky Dollar. The saloon at the end of the street."

I thanked him and headed down to the saloon, where piano music drifted through batwing doors as a background for raised voices and raucous laughter. Gathering my courage, I pushed back the swinging doors and was instantly introduced to an environment which was foreign to me.

A haze of cigar smoke hung over the jammed room, and as I stepped inside, my feet immediately sank into the sawdust. No one seemed to notice my presence, for all attention was drawn to the scene at the bar on the opposite side of the room.

There, two burly men faced each other with enough distance between them to rest their right elbows on the bar. I stared, wondering just what was taking place. Each had the other's right hand gripped, with fingers locked, as both strained to lower the opponent's hand. Beads of sweat broke over one man's forehead, while the veins in the other fellow's neck bulged to bursting. Then suddenly the smaller man proved greater strength as he forced the other's hand to the bar with a resounding thud.

Everyone whooped and roared. Another round of drinks was exuberantly demanded.

I worked my way toward the nearest saloon girl. She was deeply rouged, and wearing a black satin dress and feathers. The young woman's eyes were glazed. She was either drunk or drugged.

"Excuse me," I said. "I'm looking for Lonesome Bill. Is he here?"

The glazed eyes swept the tailored lines of my short coat, then dropped to my skirt. I sensed there was nothing I could say or do to soften her resentment as I waited for her to answer. As I glanced around, I couldn't decide which man had been my uncle's best friend. They all looked wild and rowdy.

"The tall skinny one at the end of the bar," she finally replied. "The one about to lose his hat. That's Lonesome Bill."

"Oh," I said, finding him at last. "Thank you." My forced smile was a wasted effort, for she had already turned back to the table of men who had now discovered me and were openly staring. I could feel their eyes following as I approached the man she had indicated.

His long back held the bony hump of shoulder blades jutting against a worn flannel shirt. He wore dusty jeans and mud-encrusted rubber boots. A battered felt hat hiked up at the crown, revealing dark hair that overlapped his collar.

He had just reached for a tall drink as I approached.

Perhaps the whiskey and the excitement of the crowd had loosened his tongue, I thought hopefully.

Eyes followed me now; voices dropped as I approached the far end of the bar. Again I had neglected a hat, and my blonde hair set me apart from most of the other women in the saloon. I quickened my steps.

"Excuse me," I said, tapping his shoulder.

He whirled like a man on edge and fixed upon me the biggest eyes I had ever seen. They were like globes, gray-blue, slightly protruding. He had a long face with a lantern jaw and a nose that was crooked at the end, as though he might have once been on the losing end of a barroom brawl. The wide mouth fell open when he looked at me, revealing large yellow teeth. He was a pitifully unattractive man, and yet I sensed about him a kind of gentleness.

"Are you Lonesome Bill?" I asked.

"Yes'm." He made a swipe for his old hat, and his thin hair tumbled in all directions. "Are you . . ." he paused, as his eyes flew over me. "Joshua's niece!"

"Yes, I am."

His wide mouth reached halfway to his ears in a welcoming smile. "Ma'am, it's a real pleasure to make your acquaintance!"

"I'm glad to meet you, too," I replied. As I spoke, I realized something around me had changed. I could hear my own voice, clear and distinct, in the sudden hush of the room.

I drew a deep breath, determined not to say anything more when we obviously had an audience. "I was about to have a late lunch," I said, lowering my voice. "Would you care to join me?"

Coarse whispers were followed by snorts of laughter until Lonesome Bill's big eyes sent a silent warning over the crowd.

He nodded gravely, replacing his hat. "I'd be honored, ma'am."

As he turned to pay the bill, I kept my eyes pinned stubbornly to his back, ignoring the staring crowd. Then, with his hand on my elbow, he escorted me from the smoky room out into the fresh air of the sidewalk, and I heaved a sigh of relief.

"That's a wild bunch in there," he said humbly. "Hope you didn't take offense. They don't mean no harm."

"No, it's all right."

"Where do you want to eat?" he asked. "The best place would probably be Marie's. She's a nice lady from my home state of Texas who runs a decent little place. She knows how to make the salmon in these waters real tasty."

"That sounds fine," I agreed as he pointed toward a small, quaint restaurant with red gingham curtains at the window.

"Well," he said with another wide grin, "I hear you're living out at Josh's place. That takes some nerve!"

"Nerve?"

"Sure! Folks around here thought Josh was loco to . . ."

"Yes, I know," I broke in, unable to endure another diatribe about turning a sacred Russian church into a house. "But Uncle Joshua always had a mind of his own, and very few people changed it once it was made up."

"That's the truth," he chuckled as we crossed the muddy street, sidestepping a pothole that had been filled with brush and topped with gravel. "That was something I always admired in Josh!"

I stole a glance at the tall, gangly stranger walking beside me. He was obviously a plain country man possessing the kind of horse sense my father had respected, and which Uncle Joshua had sadly lacked.

"Well, here we are," he said, opening the door for me. We took a table near the door, and when I looked around, I was relieved to see that only a few people were having lunch, mostly couples who showed no interest in us. Marie was a stout, agreeable woman whose bright green eyes sparked with jealousy when she looked from me to Bill, who kept grinning in her direction.

As soon as he had placed an order for our baked salmon, I came right to the point.

"I'm very concerned about some things I've learned since arriving here," I began matter-of-factly. "I understand you were a close friend of Uncle Joshua's. I would greatly appreciate your answering a few questions that have been bothering me."

"Yes'm. If I can."

"The family had no idea of the extent of my uncle's debts," I confessed. "When I arrived in Juneau and went to see Gordon Walling at the bank, I learned it would take a large sum to settle Uncle Joshua's account. The bank was planning to auction off the house, even though Mr. Walling admits there probably won't be a buyer."

I paused as our meal was delivered. The fish had been baked to a golden brown and topped with spices, and while we both glanced admiringly at the food, I had lost my appetite. Lonesome Bill's expression had turned grave as well. I could see that he had cared for my uncle; I had the feeling he would help me.

"I hear that Uncle Joshua had become a heavy drinker," I began haltingly. "Mr. Zarnoff, my, er, neighbor, even said he was crazy!"

For the first time Lonesome Bill's big eyes slid away from mine. I hesitated, bothered by that gesture. "Well," I pressed, "do you think he was crazy?"

He swallowed noticeably, setting his large adam's apple in motion. "Well . . ."

"Just say what you're thinking, *please.*"

He looked me in the eye again. "It's true your uncle spent a lot of time at the saloon," he conceded, "but most men do. When the days get shorter, it rains a lot, then it snows. Saloons in Alaska are the gathering place. Only Josh . . ." he paused, studying his mug of coffee, "well, Josh drank more than the rest of us." I released my pent-up breath. Crazy meant *drunk,* I dared hope. It was easier to accept.

"I see." Now was the appropriate time to ask the other question, the one I dreaded most. I pushed the plate aside and looked at Lonesome Bill. "Please tell me what you know about his death."

The low murmur of voices, utensils touching dishes, a door slamming . . . all were sounds framing the silence as I awaited his answer.

He took a deep breath as his big eyes swept over the room, then slowly, reluctantly, returned to me.

"We had been at the Lucky Dollar that night . . ." he began in a tight voice.

"You were with him?"

"Yes'm. After we'd had a few drinks, he started dreaming about the lost rocker again."

"The *lost rocker?*"

He grinned. "This kind of rocker is a little wooden gadget that's used to filter gold nuggets from the water. An American by the name of Culver and a couple of his buddies hit a hot spot somewhere in southeast Alaska. They built themselves a rocker and went to work, but then the Indians attacked. Culver's buddies were killed, and he was wounded, but he managed to get back to his canoe with a sack of gold. He drifted in the ocean for a while—nobody knows how long. By the time he was found, he was in bad shape. Afterward, he couldn't remember exactly where the hot spot was."

"Josh took a real shine to that story. He kept dreaming of finding that lost rocker and the gold. Whenever he had too much to drink, he'd start to talk about the lost rocker. And after that would come the woman . . ."

"What woman?" I leaned forward in the chair, my eyes fixed intently on his face.

"There were a few things in Josh's life that he kept private. The woman was one of them. Anyway, we'd stayed at the Lucky Dollar until late . . ."

I listened, imagining my uncle in the rowdy bar where I had just found Lonesome Bill.

"Josh had been in good spirits the first part of the evening, but as the night wore on, he got depressed. He was sitting at the kitchen table, drinking, when I left him."

"When you left him?"

He nodded. "I rode up the valley with him that night just to be sure he got home all right . . ." his voice trailed off as he stared into space.

I sat, breath baited, expecting him to say more, but he didn't.

Finally I summoned my courage. "How did he die?" Each word was like a stone in my throat.

The gray-blue eyes were moist now. "The next morning when I came here for breakfast, Marie told me everybody in town was talking about Josh, that he had shot himself. I felt terrible," he finished, his voice thick.

Somehow I had always assumed that Uncle Joshua had taken his life outside a rowdy bar; or perhaps I had merely closed my mind to the possibility that he had taken his life in his own house. A chill ran over me as I searched Bill's long face, waiting for more details than I had been given.

"It's hard for me to believe he would take his own life," I said, my voice quivering now. "How do they know it was my uncle who . . . used the gun?" I finished miserably.

Bill's face was flushed, his big eyes holding tears. I felt as miserable as he, but at the moment I was beyond tears.

"His gun, his bullet, and the note," he replied.

"The note?"

"He left a note. I reckon you could talk to Deputy Wilson. He kept the note." He removed a handkerchief from his pocket and wiped his eyes.

A note. Then it was true!

Surely too much liquor had made him melancholy, overly dramatic. His disappointments seemed exaggerated.

"Ma'am, why don't you put it out of your mind, if you can," he said on a long sigh. "It was a terrible thing, but there's nothing we can do for Josh now."

I swallowed, still trying to absorb what he had said. "Yes," I replied, after a minute. "There is something *I* can do. I can see that his debts are cleared, and that some decent arrangements are made concerning the house he loved." I looked at Lonesome Bill and sighed. "Thank you for answering my questions." I reached into my reticule, glancing at Marie, who had been covertly observing us from behind the dessert counter.

"Allow me, Miss Martin," Lonesome Bill said, as Marie strolled forward, sensing that we were about to leave.

I opened my mouth to refuse, but then I sensed he might be offended, so instead I thanked him for the meal.

"Come back again, Miss Martin," Marie said with a tight smile, as her eyes lingered on my skirt.

Lonesome Bill was remaining, and so I bade him good day. "Thank you for being my uncle's friend," I said quietly.

I left the little restaurant feeling a mixture of sadness and relief. While I had found out what I wanted to know, I hadn't liked the answers. As I stepped back onto the board-walk, my eyes met Zarnoff's cold gaze. He was seated in his wagon outside the restaurant, waiting. I stared at him, un-nerved by the fact that he always seemed to know where I was.

"I need to pick up my packages at the trading post," I told him, "then I'll be ready to go."

I collected my purchases, and we rode home in silence. I

was too miserable to think about trying to have a conversation with Zarnoff. Lonesome Bill had finally convinced me that my uncle's death was a suicide. I hadn't even felt compelled to go to the deputy and ask to see the note.

Distractedly, I paid the fare and climbed down from the wagon when we arrived back at the house. The heavy front door groaned an ominous welcome as I entered and sauntered back to the kitchen to put away the groceries. The sound of my footsteps on the wooden floor was magnified throughout the house as the lonely silence wrapped around me.

As I put my staples in the cabinet, I touched a tin that had been left on the kitchen floor, and I thought again of the prowler and felt a stirring of unease. Today had seemed like a week, rather than a single day; I wondered, with a sense of doom, if every day would be this long.

I turned, worriedly surveying the stove, as I shivered in my damp clothes. In spite of my independence with Scott Morgan, I dreaded trying to build a fire.

Then suddenly my eyes fell on the scarred wood of the kitchen table and I froze.

Directly in front of me was a small dark stain. Blood. Uncle Joshua's blood? I gasped and sprang back. He had sat here, in this chair, drowning in drink and misery, and . . . taken his life!

The beat of the rain on the roof accelerated with my anxiety, and for a moment, I could almost feel Uncle Joshua's loneliness and despair.

What had gone through his mind that night? Why had his life suddenly seemed so unbearable? Hadn't he known his family would welcome him back to San Francisco? If he was lonely, despondent, why didn't he come home?

Money . . . or lack of it. And pride. He was penniless, and yet he had been too proud to wire home for money.

My eyes moved over the tiny kitchen, lingering on the plain cupboard and shelves, such a contrast to the mansion he had left behind. A deep sadness washed over me as I thought of Uncle Joshua's wasted life. He had been a talented writer. If only he had tried to market his work with an important publisher after growing discontented with newspaper work. He had been a good journalist, and his poems were excellent.

I could not look at the bloodstain again, and so I left the kitchen and stood before the closed doors of the small closets. Uncle Joshua had filled these rooms with boxes of books which I would prowl through when I summoned the energy.

I wandered into the living room and looked caustically at the bearskin rug, then at the glittering eyes of the ceremonial masks. I was thinking of what to do with those objects when the distant yelp of a dog reached through the softly falling rain. I peered out the window. Through the gray screen of rain stretching across to the channel, I made out two forms approaching, a man and a dog. The rain beat down upon the man's dark slicker as he ran along, accompanied by the large gray husky, whose head was tilted back as he looked at his master and barked again.

They were turning up the path to my house, and now I could see the face within the rain slicker. It was Scott Morgan.

He had already spotted me before I could back away from the window, and now he lifted a hand in greeting.

I walked over and opened the door, wondering about his visit.

"Hello," he called out, his voice muffled in the rain.

"Hello. What are you doing out in this weather?"

"This is *fine* weather," he defended, a grin forming on his damp face. "Any chance I could get a cup of tea?"

As he reached the stoop, his green eyes gleamed like polished stones in his bronze face. A strand of dark hair held the moisture of raindrops. He smelled of spicy spruce, salt, and wind, and suddenly my heart was beating faster. "Come in," I said, stepping aside.

"Wait here, Bering." He turned to the big dog, who immediately dropped to the bottom step.

"Bring him in," I said, looking at the dog's wet fur and

feeling sorry for him.

"Sure you don't mind? Josh always let him come inside, but . . ."

"Bring in . . . *Bering,* did you say?"

He nodded, easing out of his slicker. "Named him after Vitus Bering, the Danish navigator who led the Russians here."

"I remember Uncle Josh mentioning him," I said. "Actually, I think it was when he wrote an article on the fur trade in Alaska for our newspaper that he made a decision to come here."

"Is that right?" he grinned. "Tell me about the article."

I hung his slicker on the coat rack, trying to remember. My uncle had come for dinner and he had talked on and on about Peter the Great becoming obsessed with learning about the land east of Russia.

"Let's see. It told the story of the Siberian cossack explorers who took back furs and wild tales and," I smiled, "Uncle Joshua played up Czarina Catherine's fascination for the furs. But then, what woman wouldn't want a beautiful fur coat from those sleek sea otter pelts?"

He laughed. "Josh knew how to write stories."

I looked back at the dog, not wanting to feel sad about my uncle. "And so you named your dog after Vitus Bering as a tribute to the first explorers?"

"Actually, it was George Stellar who first set foot on the islands," he said, reaching down to ruffle the dog's thick fur.

"Stellar was a botanist who came along on the voyage. He had a passion for plants and refused to turn back until he had explored the islands. He spotted a large bird with blue plumage similar to that of the American bluejay. That led him to believe they had reached America."

He looked down at the dog, who was now wagging his tail and gazing adoringly at his master.

"My friend here didn't take to the name *Stellar,* so we settled for *Bering.*"

I smiled, thinking of what an amusing man Scott Morgan was. A far cry from my ex-fiancé whose interests were limited to printing presses and circulation figures.

"I'll put the kettle on," I said, remembering his request for tea. I came to an abrupt halt in the kitchen, however, when I realized that the stove was cold.

"I just got back from town," I explained to Scott, who had followed me and now stood framed in the doorway.

"Allow me." He walked to the stove and repeated the fire-building ritual while I turned to the counter to open the tea I had purchased. Belatedly, I began a search for the kettle.

"It's in the bottom cabinet, there on the left," he said.

"Thanks."

"Josh kept water in a container on the right side," he called over his shoulder.

I found the kettle, then the container—containing not one drop of water.

"Empty," I sighed.

"He got his water from that little creek coming down through the woods."

I was trying to work up the enthusiasm to go trudging out in the rain when I heard his weary sigh. "I'll do it."

He grabbed the container and dashed through the living room to reclaim his slicker. The dog had wandered in and dropped down beside the stove, as though he had often been a guest. To cover my embarrassment at being so helpless here, I knelt beside him, stroking his damp fur. I had always loved animals, but I had never been allowed to keep a pet at home.

I regretted having Scott go back out in the rain for drinking water, but I was desperate for tea, and I imagined he was as well. I would need a supply of water if I intended to stay on here, a challenge that increased with each passing day.

Bering laid his head on his paws and quickly fell into a contented sleep. I wandered over and cracked the back door, wondering about that creek. Through the drizzling rain, I could see Scott across the meadow, just in the edge of the woods.

I sighed, closing the door. The matter of obtaining water

was simpler than building a fire. From now on, I could get the water myself. I set out the cups and tea then wiped the inside of the kettle with a clean cloth. Then I paced the kitchen, feeling tense and uncomfortable. By the time Scott returned with the water, the fire in the stove was already radiating over the kitchen. He filled the kettle with water, placed it on the stove, then dropped in a chair.

"I like your dog," I said, hoping to get our minds off the empty container and the cold stove.

He looked at the sleeping dog for a minute. "He's actually a descendant of the timber wolves," he replied. "Bering and I became friends a couple of years ago, when I found him abandoned at the wharf. Someone told me he belonged to a fisherman who went out to sea and never returned."

"Oh."

More silence.

"Where do you come from?" I asked, taking a seat at the table.

"Portland. Like your uncle, I was intrigued by stories of Alaska. I had to come see for myself."

He didn't bother to elaborate, and I tried not to pry.

I folded my hands on the table in front of me, forgetting about the bloodstain that soap and water had failed to remove. Now, staring at it again, I yanked my hands from the table.

"Have you found any gold around here?" I asked nervously.

A grim smile touched his face as he ran a hand distractedly down the front of his flannel shirt. "I found a couple of nuggets out in the channel when I first arrived, but that was it."

"Lonesome Bill was telling me about the Lost Rocker," I remembered. "That's quite an interesting story."

"Yeah," he said, staring thoughtfully at his empty mug. "Miners believed if they could find the rocker, they could find a cache of gold."

"Do you have any idea where it is?"

"Nope. Somewhere in southeast Alaska, and that's a

broad range. Josh wanted to believe it was up the valley near the big glacier, but the rocker, I imagine, has long since been buried under an iceberg or washed out to sea." He paused and sighed. "The only wealth I've discovered here is in the stories I collect. I've sold a couple of articles to *The New York Times*, so I suppose the year hasn't been a total loss."

"You're a writer?" I asked. I remembered now that he had acknowledged Uncle Joshua's work and commented on their conversations regarding other writers. I leaned back in the chair and studied him with new interest.

"Writing is the only job that pleases me," he answered with a careless grin. "I odd-job around while I'm writing."

"Are you working on something now?" I asked as the kettle began to sing.

"Yes." His eyes were fixed on the plume of steam rising from the kettle. His silence indicated he did not care to elaborate on his work, so I got up and made tea.

"How long are you staying?" he asked.

"Just until the money arrives." The answer had tumbled out, and now I bit my lip and belatedly reminded myself that I could take a lesson from him about silence at the appropriate time.

His green eyes darkened, for of course he sensed my apprehension after blurting out an answer.

I forced myself to look him straight in the eye. "Uncle Joshua's debts must be paid before I leave Juneau."

He didn't know I had already brought a sizable draft, a matter which I hoped Gordon Walling had not raised. No, Gordon would not do that; I trusted him. I only wished that I could trust this handsome stranger sitting here in Uncle Joshua's kitchen.

"Where do you live?" I asked casually, trying to change the subject.

"Couple of miles up the inlet. I took over a miner's abandoned cabin, fixed it up a bit. It's very peaceful up there." He reached down to stroke his dog's head. "Bering and I appreciate peace and quiet."

In spite of my attempts to be wary of him, the man was far more fascinating than anyone I'd ever met.

"More tea?" I asked, when he caught me staring.

"No, thank you. I must go," he said, coming to his feet. "If you should need an errand boy, the Zarnoffs' grandson has come to visit. I think he's about fourteen years old. He hung around my cabin some last summer. You'll see him running up and down the road out there. He could be a messenger for you if you needed one."

"Thanks."

Bering jumped up and began to switch his tail, eager for another run. Scott reached for his coat and I followed him back to the front door. "It's still raining," I said, cracking the door and looking into the thick gray mist.

"Around here a light drizzle means nothing." He turned back for a moment as his eyes moved over my face and figure. "Sure you're not afraid to stay here alone?"

What good would it do to admit that I was? "I'll be fine," I said, forcing a smile.

Still he hesitated. "Maybe you'd like to see the big glacier up the valley sometime."

I thought it over and decided I would. When I returned to San Francisco, I wouldn't want to feel I had missed anything. But as I caught myself staring at the man before me, I had a strong suspicion that I was more interested in being with him than in seeing the glacier.

"Well, why not?" I said lightly.

A slow smile touched his lips. "I'm working on a story this week. By Saturday I should be ready to put it in the drawer and have some fun. I'll come back for you then." His eyes strayed toward the kitchen, and suddenly he frowned.

"I can keep the fire going," I said.

"Are you sure?"

"I'm positive!" It was becoming a matter of pride to survive here, and pride was possibly my worst flaw.

"I'll see you on Saturday, then." With Bering at his heels, he bounded across the yard in the drizzling rain. I closed the door and went back to the kitchen to finish my tea. For a few minutes I sat glaring at the stove, trying to devise a plan to keep the fire going. I would just keep adding a stick of firewood, I decided, studying the generous supply he had left behind the stove.

Presently a loud banging on the front door brought me out of the kitchen and across the living room to the front door. I was wondering what Scott had forgotten as I quickly opened the door; then I froze. Mrs. Zarnoff stood on the stoop, staring at me.

She was huddled into a rain slicker with a deep hood that half obscured her face.

"Come in," I said, as she nodded a greeting.

From the depths of her pocket, she produced a small jar and extended it to me. "Some of my berry jam," she said.

For a moment I was stunned by her friendly gesture. "Thank you," I finally responded as her eyes wandered over the big room and she fell silent, lost in thought.

A peasant scarf covered most of her gray hair, framing her large, wrinkled face. Piercing dark eyes were close set above a flaring nose, narrow upper lip, and heavy chin. Beneath her slicker she wore the same faded dress.

Suddenly her eyes darted back to me, and I shifted uncomfortably. I had no idea how to carry on a conversation with her, when an air of hostility seemed to radiate from her like heat from the stove.

"Let me take your slicker . . ."

"I cannot stay," she said abruptly, turning back to me.

"Let me at least give you a cup of tea," I insisted. "It will strengthen you for your walk back."

Slowly she began to shrug out of her slicker; then she turned and dropped it on the hook by the door. "I would prefer to drink it in here," she called as I started toward the kitchen.

Puzzled, I glanced back. "All right. I'll just be a minute."

The kettle still simmered on the stove. I put away the jam, rummaged for another clean mug, and poured tea.

She was sitting on the edge of a chair, watching me curiously. "How long will you be here?" she blurted.

Trying to adjust to her abrupt manner, I handed her the tea and took a seat. "Just until the steamer returns."

Her eyes were roaming the walls again as she sipped the tea.

I took a deep breath, trying to think of something we could discuss.

"What part of Russia do you come from?" I asked, trying to think of a subject that was far removed from this church-house and Uncle Joshua. A light sparked in the depths of her narrow-set eyes. "A small village in the south," she replied, her tone softening. Her eyes dropped to her cup. "In winter the roses and mimosa bloom," she said softly.

"Oh? It sounds like a very pretty place."

"Our home was not cold; everyone believes we froze," her voice became harsh again. "It was not cold, our village. And it did not rain . . . day after day . . . after day." The words thudded from her tongue, in the cold, flat tone that characterized her.

"Do you think of going back?"

She glared at me. "There is no going back! There is never any going back." Each word was coated with bitterness. How I wished I had never brought up the subject.

"I wanted to go back," she said softly. "We had been in Sitka for only two years when your country bought Alaska." She shook her head slowly. "It was very sad. I will never forget that afternoon in October, such a clear and beautiful day, but only a few of our people gathered around the harbor for the ceremonies. There were a hundred of our troops, and twice as many American soldiers."

She paused, drawing a deep breath, remembering. "They marched up Barinoff Hill and lined up there before the governor's house. Our flag was blowing lightly in the breeze. There were the pretty speeches, the boom of the guns and then they lowered the flag. I will never forget," she said, swallowing, "how our beautiful Princess Maksutova wept when a sailor lowered our flag."

I cleared my throat. "It must have been a very difficult

time."

She heaved a deep sigh, and her broad shoulders began to sag beneath the faded dress. "I must go," she mumbled, pulling to her feet with effort.

"What are you going to do with this place?" she asked, staring at me.

"I . . . am not sure. What do you suggest?"

"It should not be a home!" She had crossed the room to place her empty cup on the coffee table. "It should be—" she broke off suddenly, staring at the small black glove I had found at the cemetery.

I glanced down at the glove. "I found that at my uncle's grave. Would you happen to know to whom it might belong?"

"No!" she snapped, still staring at it. Then she put down her cup and whirled for the door. "I must go."

Puzzled, I watched as she seized her slicker and hurriedly pulled it on. Suddenly I remembered what Scott had told me about her grandson.

"By the way, I understand your grandson is coming to visit."

The grim expression on her face softened. "Yes, they live in Sitka. They are coming today."

I nodded. "I was wondering if your grandson might be willing to run errands for me, since I am without transportation. Except for your husband." When she hesitated, I added, "I would pay him, of course."

She pursed her lips, considering the thought. "Yes, he would do that," she finally conceded.

As she trudged out the door, I remembered the jam and thanked her.

She hesitated, looking at me curiously. "Thank you for the tea," she said quietly. Then she turned and marched across the yard in the rain.

I closed the door and heaved a sigh of relief. I should have been grateful that she was kind enough to walk a half mile in the misting rain to deliver her homemade jam. What, I wondered, had prompted her to do such a thing?

News travels fast here, Scott had said. What had he humorously termed the local delivery of news? *Moccasin telegraph.*

Suspicion darted through my thoughts as I recalled his invitation to sightsee, and now her visit with the jam. Was it possible that the news of my bank deposit was flying over Juneau by means of moccasin telegraph? And had the contents of the letter to my mother been relayed by the curious clerk at the bank, who had covertly read the message?

No, of course not. I did not want to think like that—but I did. I found myself pushing chairs against the doors, double-checking the locks, lighting all the lanterns and candlesticks. When I sat down for a late snack, a wild, eerie cry brought me out of the chair. I waited with baited breath. Again that wild, terrible sound split the silence. I ran into the living room and peered through the window. A pale moon sifted its silver rays over the yard, the deserted road, the distant channel. I squinted, searching for the outline of a canoe, but there was nothing. The opposite island seemed a million miles away in the silent darkness. I waited, tensed, listening.

Only silence.

I checked the locks on the doors again and pushed the heavy chairs even closer.

Tomorrow I would ask about that strange, eerie sound. And when I went to bed tonight, I would stay away from the window. I would not look at the cemetery, not even a glance.

Chapter 5

I slept surprisingly well that night, despite the fact that I had eaten too much bread and jam. For the first hour I had tossed and turned, listening for sounds downstairs, or outside. When there was nothing but the soft drizzling rain to break the night silence, I finally relaxed and drifted to sleep . . .

. . . and awoke with nausea bolting through me. I stood, fought a wave of dizziness, then sank onto the bed again, trying to swallow against a parched, sore throat. My head began to throb as I stared bleary-eyed at the ceiling, trying to analyze what was wrong with me. A cold? An allergy? Something I had eaten?

Mrs. Zarnoff's jam?

Panic threatened, but I tried to remain calm.

No, it was not the jam, I told myself. The jam would not give me a sore throat! While Mrs. Zarnoff might dislike me, surely she would not poison me.

Obviously I had taken a cold. Or perhaps one of my allergies was acting up again, an allergy to jam, perhaps.

I locked an arm around the bedpost to steady my balance until my vision cleared. Then I staggered to the window and met a dismal gray day.

More rain. But what difference did it make, anyway? I would not be venturing from the house, perhaps not even from the bed.

Tea. I would have tea; that would help. Moving at a snail's pace, I tugged on my housecoat, then thrust my feet into slippers. Gripping the rail unsteadily, I trudged down the stairs.

I looked the living room over carefully, relieved to see that everything was exactly as I had left it. I plodded on to the kitchen, stoked up the fire, and unlocked the back door. As I cracked the door, I could see a heavy fog curling over the yard and woods. It gave me a feeling of being cut off from the rest of the world. Gordon had said the mountains were too steep to cross. Since Juneau nestled against the channel, people traveled by boat. And now, as I stood enveloped in the fog, the awareness of that isolation sharpened even more. The steamer would not return for two weeks. I could not escape if I wanted to!

Escape! Why had I even thought of that word? There was no reason to feel I must escape. I stared into the fog, and for a moment the gray wisps gave the impression of something moving . . . *someone* moving!

I slammed the door. It was this nausea that had worked on my nerves, set me on edge. And yet I could not deny there was a certain claustrophobia that settled about one here; perhaps it had bothered Uncle Joshua. Perhaps that was why . . .

I glared at the kettle, impatiently awaiting the hot water for my tea. My stomach still felt queasy, but the jolt of crisp air had cleared my head.

Shivering, I strolled into the living room and looked around.

"What are you going to do with this place?" Mrs. Zarnoff had asked. There was nothing I could do unless Uncle Joshua's bills were paid. The bank obviously owned the house, but it was unfair to expect them to sell it. Gordon had admitted that no one would want it.

I crossed my arms and looked about the room. There was a distinctive mood here, like a character too strong to be molded or changed to suit anyone else. My eyes fell on the glove lying on the coffee table, and I wandered over and picked it up.

Small, delicate, black.

As I turned it over in my hand, I recalled the look on Mrs. Zarnoff's face. It was almost as if, for an instant, she had recognized the glove. But of course it was too small for her large hands. More than likely, she was simply admiring something of quality which she had never been privileged to own.

I dropped the glove on the table, more curious than ever about the mystery woman, but now the kettle was singing, and I was desperate for tea.

I spent the day in bed, listening to the beat of the rain on the roof and sleeping quite comfortably as the nausea subsided. I was never quite sure what had made me ill, but I did not touch Mrs. Zarnoff's jam again.

The fog had rolled away by the next morning. With renewed courage, I dressed in a cheerful woolen suit of pale blue, with matching feathered hat, and set off down the road. In the beginning, I had planned to walk to town, but by the time I had reached the Zarnoff's house, I was more inclined to seek a ride.

As I approached, the smell of fish wafted through the air, and I saw that a wooden frame had been set up in the side yard. A tall, dark-haired man was laying chunks of pink fish over the frame. As I approached he turned to face me, and I saw a younger version of Zarnoff. His features were large and blunt, like his father's, only he had thick dark hair. Unlike Zarnoff, he knew how to smile.

"Good day," he nodded.

"Good day," I replied, spotting Mr. Zarnoff and his grandson puttering about in the back of the yard.

When Zarnoff saw me he hurried forward, introducing first his son, then his grandson, Jamie.

"Nanna said you want me to run errands," Jamie said with a friendly smile. He was tall and muscular for his age, and wore corduroy trousers and a flannel shirt.

I had forgotten all about the errand business, but now his friendly smile reached out to me.

"Yes, I may need you to run an errand now and then," I said. "I will pay whatever you or your parents feel is fair."

"Yes'm. I pick up groceries for my mother and for Nanna. I could do that for you."

"Good!" My eyes wandered to the window. I was thinking of Mrs. Zarnoff and the mysterious jam. A curtain fluttered, and I saw a dark-haired woman with an oval face framed in the window. A rather pretty woman, I thought, before the curtain dropped and Zarnoff asked if I wanted a ride to town. When I replied that I did, he motioned me to the wagon, where the horses were already hitched.

In the backyard, I could see a tiny cabin mounted on log stilts. The smell of smoke was fresh around the cabin, and I imagined this must be where the Zarnoffs stored their fish and food.

"We can go now," he said.

I waved to the smiling boy and his father as I climbed into the wagon, and we set off for town. As the wagon jostled along, the heavy, familiar silence stretched between us, as usual.

"You have a fine-looking grandson," I said, glancing at Zarnoff, whose face was grim beneath his fur cap. At the mention of his grandson, however, his features softened.

"Thank you," he said, his voice less gruff. "He is a hard worker."

As he spoke, I realized this was the greatest compliment he could give, for Zarnoff was obviously a man who had known a lifetime of hard work. Perhaps that was the basis of his resentment toward my uncle, who seemed to have wasted time and money at the gaming tables. The fact that Uncle Joshua had used family money to acquire a church the poorer Russian families had built through hard work and sacrifice was like salt poured into a festering wound.

For the first time, I began to see Zarnoff's point of view; I could even respect him for it.

"How long has your son lived in Sitka?" I asked. I could see that my question, innocently friendly, had put him back on the defensive again, as though I were invading the family privacy.

"A few weeks," he answered gruffly. "He is a fisherman." He looked at me sharply. "The run of Kings and Reds was better there than here this fall."

Kings. Reds. He was speaking of salmon. That led me to think of animals, and the eerie cry I had heard.

"Mr. Zarnoff, is there some kind of animal that makes a strange sound?"

He whirled and stared at me.

I bit my lip. Why had I asked him that? He was sure to blame a strange sound on a spirit reclaiming their sacred dwelling!

"What do you mean?" he barked.

I shrugged, glancing away from his piercing eyes. "I heard a strange sound last night. I think it was some kind of animal."

When he did not reply, I regretted having asked him. My second question would have been about the glove and the mysterious woman, but I was certain he would be even less responsive. And there was also my odd illness, and Mrs. Zarnoff's jam.

I leaned back in the seat and dispensed with conversation. It was not likely that I would learn anything from Zarnoff. We were approaching the outskirts of Juneau, and I was glad to think of something more pleasant . . . like shopping.

"How long you will be in town?" he asked.

"I'm not sure. An hour, perhaps two."

"I will wait at the livery."

"Fine. You can drop me at the bank."

As he drew up at the street corner, I climbed down, smoothed my skirts, and headed into the bank to see Gordon.

"Mr. Walling is meeting with the town commissioners," the clerk at the desk announced as he studied me in his usual curious manner. "I hesitate to interrupt him."

"Oh no, that isn't necessary. I just wanted to say hello."

I left the bank, thinking about the letter I had written to

my mother and hoping the money would be forthcoming on the steamer. I was so deep in thought as I stepped onto the sidewalk again that I collided with Lonesome Bill.

His big eyes fell on me and widened in surprise as he tipped his battered felt hat and nodded a greeting.

"Morning, Miss Martin."

"Good morning."

"Are you enjoying your stay in Juneau?" he asked politely.

"I'm afraid I've been too concerned over my uncle's affairs to enjoy myself," I admitted frankly. Suddenly I thought of the mystery woman again. I didn't think I could leave Juneau without trying to find her. "Bill," I lowered my voice, "I'd like to ask a favor of you."

"Well," he nodded, "I'd be obliged to help if I can."

We had begun to attract glances from those passing on the boardwalk. "Maybe we should speak in a more private place," I said, as a saloon girl dawdled, obviously listening.

"We can go to Marie's if you want to."

"That's a good idea. And this time, I insist on buying your lunch! It's the very least I can do."

A lopsided grin cut across his craggy cheek. "All right, if that's what you want to do."

It was past the lunch hour, but we found Marie painstakingly slicing a huge chocolate cake. Again she attempted to be friendly, although her eyes were guarded and suspicious when I spoke to her. After we ordered, I took a deep breath and plunged into the subject foremost on my mind.

"Bill, I intend to pay off my uncle's debts and do something about the house. When I leave here, I'd like to have something settled in my mind."

He nodded, grimly. "You're still wondering why he killed himself."

I hesitated. It wasn't what I had intended to ask, but I decided to let him talk.

"Did you ask the marshal to see the note?"

The note? I had decided not to punish myself further, but perhaps seeing the note was the most sensible thing to do.

"No, I haven't, but I will." While we were on the morbid subject, I decided to ask one more thing. "On that last night you were with him, did he seem so depressed that he would actually," I swallowed, "put a gun to his head and . . ."

Marie delivered another variation of salmon, and we glanced distractedly at her. When she had disappeared, Bill looked across at me and sighed. "He didn't seem that bad at the saloon. He was ordering drinks, bragging like always about his secret gold."

"His gold?" It was the first I had heard of this.

"I told you about the Lost Rocker." The lopsided grin was sad, his big eyes reflective. "Well, whenever he got too much to drink, he sort of, well, let his imagination get the best of him. He used to dream about discovering that Lost Rocker. And we'd talk about how it would be if he did."

I speared into the fish, listening intently. "How it would be?" I repeated.

"Well," a shy grin crossed his lips. "How we'd spend our money, where we'd go."

"Did Uncle Joshua want to come back to San Francisco?"

"Well," he hedged, biting into his fish, "sometimes he got homesick, but mostly he talked about going up north again, seeing more of Alaska. He took a real fancy to this country, you know. I reckon Josh felt like the rest of us," Lonesome Bill continued, with a tone of sadness. "He was sick of city life, he used to say. He wanted to live in a place where he could draw a deep breath of clear, pure air." His big mouth lifted in a lopsided grin. "Josh was a trailblazer at heart, I reckon, wanting to explore the unknown, carve out new paths."

I nodded. "I know that sense of adventure was always burning in his veins. I'm amazed he spent so many years living the conventional life in San Francisco."

But then, as I thought back, I realized that my uncle had asserted his independence and adventure in other ways—controversial editorials, stories of fires, sports events, and always the political scene in which he attempted to keep both sides sparring.

"But you don't believe he ever found any gold."

Bill sucked his bottom lip between his tobacco-stained teeth and looked at me for a thoughtful moment. As he did, I could feel the heat of Marie's stare. Before he could answer, she appeared with the teapot, a curious expression on her plump face.

"No, thank you." I refused the tea, watching Bill, awaiting an answer. After she left, he shook his head. "To tell you the truth, Miss Martin, I was pretty drunk myself. It was one of those long, rowdy nights. We'd had a good time at the saloon." He shook his head, pushing his food aside. "I remember we argued about who'd get the richest someday. Just a lot of nonsense. When I left him," he continued somberly, "he was sitting there at the kitchen table with a bottle and a glass. I never thought . . ." His words trailed off as he stared into space.

He never thought he would take his own life. "I see," I answered finally, when the sad memory had overtaken him completely and he seemed unable to go on.

Well, it was as much as I would ever know, I supposed. I would let the matter rest.

We finished the meal in morbid silence, and I realized it would do no good to keep digging away at the sad truth. Uncle Joshua had taken his life that night.

"What was it you wanted me to do for you?" Bill asked, suddenly remembering my request.

I touched the napkin to my lips and looked across at him. "I want you to discreetly ask around to see if anyone knows the identity of the woman my uncle was seeing."

"But nobody knows," he spoke up, too quickly.

"How can you be sure? She has to be here in Juneau. Someone knows her. Juneau isn't that big." My mind ran on as I tried to analyze the situation. "Could it have been one of the saloon girls?"

"No, ma'am. Wouldn't be no reason to keep her a secret. To tell you the truth, I always figured she was married;

that's the only reason Josh would have wanted to keep quiet about her. But then . . ."

"*What?*" I pressed. "What were you going to say?"

"Well," he leaned forward and lowered his voice, "everybody knew Josh had a real fierce imagination. It got to the point we almost expected tall tales from him. The gold mine . . . then the woman." He shook his head and looked sadly at me. "It was like, well, he told things the way he wanted them to be, instead of the way they really were."

I considered that possibility for a moment. I might have doubted the existence of such a woman if not for the flowers and the glove.

"Bill," I lowered my voice, "a woman came to his grave and left some wildflowers."

"She did?"

"And she dropped a small black glove. There *was* a woman," I said firmly.

He looked startled. "Well, maybe there was," he said, lifting a hand to stroke his chin. "I'll ask around. Farrel, the dealer at the blackjack table, knew Josh pretty well. And he's got an eagle eye. He don't miss a thing that goes on in the saloon, or in town. I'll ask him," he said, nodding thoughtfully, as though for the first time he believed there actually was a woman.

"I would appreciate it," I said, paying the bill. "You know where I live."

"Yes'm. I'll look into it," he said. He glanced warily around the room, as though he were already in pursuit of the information I was seeking.

As I waved to Marie and stepped out into the brisk afternoon, I wondered, again, if it were not best to let the matter rest, but I just couldn't do that. I think I believed that by finding the woman, I would discover there had been some happiness in his life before the end.

I started toward the livery to meet Zarnoff, but upon remembering the note, I found myself turning toward Deputy Wilson's office. It was small and inconspicuous. Tentatively, I pushed open the door to find a man dozing in his chair, his feet propped on a desk cluttered with papers and cigars. I coughed loudly as I closed the door. His head flew back, unbalancing a gray felt hat.

"Morning," he said, swinging his feet from the desk and eyeing me with suspicion. He was a big man, of about fifty, with a bulbous nose and keen blue eyes beneath wiry brows.

"Good morning. I'm Abigail Martin . . ."

"Josh's niece?" He came to his feet, looking me over curiously. It was obvious he had already heard I was in town.

"Yes, that's right."

"I'm Hank Wilson," he said. "We were all sorry about your uncle's death." He removed his hat and placed it over his heart for a second, a gesture which I considered odd.

"Thank you." I glanced at his face. "I understand my uncle left a suicide note."

He shoved his hat back and looked at me. "Yes'm. He did." He turned to a small safe in the corner, then knelt, turning the knob in a full circle, then back a half circle. The door swung open, and my heart beat faster as he reached into the safe and picked up a piece of paper that had been folded into a small square. I stared at the paper, recognizing it as a ruled page from my uncle's tablet.

He looked down at the note for a second, turning it over in his large, callused palm. "You can have it," he said, handing it to me.

I reached for the note, quickly dropping it into my handbag. I would wait until later to read it. I could not bring myself to share my uncle's last message.

"Thank you," I said in a tight voice. A question rose in my mind, and I groped for a tactful way to ask it. I didn't want to imply that he had not done his job properly. I tried to sound casual as I looked up into his keen blue eyes. "When you . . . found my uncle, were you satisfied that his death was . . ."

"A suicide? Yes'm. When Mr. Zarnoff came for me, I went right up there and investigated."

Mr. Zarnoff.

His eyes never wavered from mine as he finished the explanation. "The bullet came from his own gun. The angle of the shot, and the note in his own handwriting . . ." He paused, shrugging his heavy shoulders. "There was no reason to suspect anything else."

I listened carefully, turning his explanation over in my mind. One important fact stood out above all else, however.

"Mr. Zarnoff came for you?" I repeated.

He nodded as a deep frown began to work its way across his broad forehead. "As soon as they found him, Mr. Zarnoff came to get me."

I swallowed. "They?"

"Mr. and Mrs. Zarnoff." He spoke slowly, analyzing my reaction to his words. "I reckon I thought since Mr. Zarnoff has been driving you around, you already knew. But then," his tone softened, "I understand you probably would rather not talk about this."

My pulse was racing as I stood at the door, my hand tightly gripping the wooden handle.

"Well, it *has* been difficult to think about. It seems so out of character for Uncle Joshua." Why was I saying this when I had almost accepted the suicide? Almost . . . and yet, fresh doubt kept cropping up in my mind.

"I understand how you must feel, but it's true. Josh did take his life. Mrs. Zarnoff found him that morning when she went over to clean house for him."

Clean house for him. The words marched ominously through my mind. I stared into the face of the big man who was trying to be as gentle, yet as forthright, as possible. *When she went over to clean house for him . . .*

"I guess I didn't realize the Zarnoffs were so . . . close to my uncle," I finally responded.

"Miss Martin, the Zarnoffs ain't close to anybody! They just live to themselves, mind their own business, do their work. But it's my understanding that when Mrs. Zarnoff went for the routine cleaning, like she did once a week, she found him there at the kitchen table." He shook his head. "I'm real sorry."

"Thank you." I smiled sadly. "You've been most kind. Good day." I left his office in a trance. Perhaps it wasn't necessary for Mrs. Zarnoff to tell me that she had come weekly to clean his house and that she was the one who had found him dead. But it seemed strange that she had not. It seemed even stranger that Zarnoff, in our long rides to and from town, had said nothing.

The wagon was waiting just down the street. Suddenly my eyes met Zarnoff's cold stare, which now held a different expression . . . one of curiosity.

For a moment, I could not stop staring at him, and as I did, something began to tremble deep within me. He trotted the horses forward to where I stood, but this time I could not bring myself to climb into the wagon. My eyes dropped to his huge, gnarled hands, tightly gripping the reins. I swallowed, trying to think of a reason not to get in the wagon.

Just then, Gordon Walling called my name and waved to me from across the street. I waved back eagerly as he crossed the street and reached my side.

"Miss Martin, I'm sorry I missed you when you came by the bank," he said, nodding a greeting as he glanced at Zarnoff. "Where are you headed?"

My eyes flicked from his pleasant smile to Zarnoff's sullen face. "I was headed home, but if you're free . . ."

"For the rest of the afternoon," he said, removing his gold watch from his vest pocket, and checking the time. "Will you have dinner with me?"

"I would love to!" I burst out, startling him with my eagerness.

Gordon's blue eyes gleamed behind his spectacles as he looked from me to Zarnoff. "I'll see her home," he said.

I yanked open my handbag, for money to pay Zarnoff. In the process the suicide note flew out and landed on the sidewalk. My eyes fell to the note and I froze.

Chapter 6

Gordon leaned down and retrieved the note for me, showing little concern for its contents. Zarnoff, on the other hand, stared intently. I saw the glimmer of recognition in his sharp eyes, and his face was pale and drawn as I paid him the fare.

Zarnoff then laid a whip over the horses' heads, and the wagon bolted from town at a suspiciously high speed.

Gordon recounted the day's events, and I pretended to listen as we strolled to the hotel for dinner. All the while, however, my thoughts remained on the note and Zarnoff's reaction to seeing it.

By the time we were seated in the dining room and Gordon had ordered our meal, I could no longer hold back my frustration.

I blurted out the news about my uncle being found by the Zarnoffs, and their subsequent strange behavior.

"Let me give you some advice," Gordon said after listening to my story. "I don't believe they harmed your uncle, but still I wouldn't say anything to them about his death. They're sensitive people who would probably take a simple question as an accusation of some sort."

I shifted uncomfortably in the velvet-cushioned chair and dropped my eyes. "I didn't mean to insinuate that they had harmed him. I just . . ."

"Wondered why they hadn't mentioned more about your uncle's death?" He nodded understandingly. "Maybe it's because they're eccentric and superstitious. I don't know Mrs.

Zarnoff that well because she keeps to herself. When she comes to town, I never see her talking with anyone." He shrugged, took a sip of coffee, then looked back at me. "It's just their way."

I had hoped that Gordon would be more reassuring, but he had in fact confirmed what I'd suspected all along.

"Do you know their son and his family?" I asked.

"Vaguely. James is a fisherman. They recently moved to Sitka."

"I suppose I should be discussing with you the important matter of Uncle Joshua's debts, rather than dwelling on my suspicions about the Zarnoffs," I told him. "I've written Mother for money, and I trust that a bank draft will arrive on the next steamer."

Gordon studied his silver fork, turning it over. "That's very unselfish of you," he said at last, "being so compassionate about your uncle. Most families would have wanted to put their money to use in their home state, rather than way up here."

"Well, my uncle still has some stock. I assume the reason he didn't sell that stock was because he kept hoping for a run of luck with his gold panning."

"I see." He nodded thoughtfully. "I appreciate your integrity concerning his debts, Abigail. I can assure you, not many people would be as responsible."

"The Martins have never owed money. We don't intend to ignore Uncle Joshua's indebtedness. I've written my mother; I expect she will liquidate his stock and send the money. So you see," I finished quietly, "it's his own money I'm using. Incidentally," I frowned at him, "did he ever say anything to you about some gold he had discovered?"

He adjusted his spectacles and peered at me sharply. "No, he never did. Why? Did you find something at the house that made you think he had discovered a hot spot?"

"No, but I spoke with Lonesome Bill, and he mentioned that my uncle was bragging about gold that last night, after too many drinks at the saloon. I think that legend of the Lost Rocker must have affected his thinking."

Gordon looked disappointed, but then he began to nod, comprehending the situation. "Yes, everybody talks about that Lost Rocker. As for Josh, he was always hoping to make a big strike. What does Bill think?"

"That it was just a brag," I sighed. "He said he sometimes confused reality with his dreams when he drank too much. Surely if he really did find a hot spot, as they call it, he would have confided in someone."

"Yes, and I'd like to think it would have been *me,* considering the size of his debt to us," he said sharply. "Forgive me for referring to it, but still . . ."

"Well, you're right, of course. It would have been the honorable thing to do." I realized that Uncle Joshua, despite his drinking and gambling, was still basically an honest person; I was certain of that. If he had found gold, he would immediately have gone to his creditors and told them.

The waitress had appeared with our bill, and now Gordon counted out the money and thanked her. As we left the dining room, I was still deep in thought about Uncle Joshua; however, I turned a corner and was immediately jarred back to reality as I came face to face with Scott Morgan and a beautiful woman.

He looked more handsome than ever in a tweed jacket and corduroy pants. The woman beside him was a tall, stately brunette dressed in a burgundy velvet gown. I had the fleeting impression that she might be older than Scott as he quickly whisked her past. I suddenly realized that his kindness to me had stemmed from his affection for my uncle, nothing more. I had not realized until this moment that I had hoped otherwise.

Once we settled into Gordon's buggy and the horses set off at a brisk pace, I couldn't resist asking Gordon about the woman with Scott. There must have been something in my tone of voice that revealed more than a passing interest, for Gordon gave me a curious look. Belatedly, I remembered Gordon's condescending attitude toward Scott when I mentioned his name that first day. A sourdough, he had said. *A gambler,* I could have added, *like my uncle.*

"I'm not sure who the woman is," Gordon replied with a frown. "She may be someone he met in another town who has followed him here. I'm afraid he has that reputation."

I turned on the leather seat and studied him through the growing darkness. "What do you mean by *that* reputation?"

"I believe, down in the States, the term used is 'ladies man.' " He gave a short laugh. "I haven't used that silly term in years. But," he sighed, "I'm afraid it applies to Scott Morgan."

"And probably to Uncle Joshua!" It was a blow to my pride to learn that the man who had intrigued me was known as a ladies' man. I hated that description.

"Your uncle?"

"Uncle Joshua was a ladies' man in San Francisco," I said grimly. "It's logical to assume that he did not change his habits when he arrived in Juneau. Incidentally, was there a woman my uncle fancied here?"

"Not that I know of," Gordon replied, "but then, my association with your uncle was purely business."

I sighed and stared into the shadowed road. "I should be asking that question of the men who frequent the saloons." Bitterness dripped from my voice, and I realized belatedly how badly I was behaving. I had completely lost my composure, and now I was being openly sarcastic about my late uncle. In truth, I was greatly disappointed in Uncle Joshua for becoming so lazy and irresponsible.

"Don't be too hard on him, Abigail," Gordon said, as though reading my thoughts. "This is a wild and rugged country; it brings out the best in some, the worst in others."

"I agree," I said, then lapsed into silence as we sped past the Zarnoff cabin. A lantern was burning in the window, and I could see the figure of someone moving about the living room.

Recalling my news about the Zarnoffs, I felt a rush of gratitude toward Gordon, who had saved me from another long ride home with a man I no longer trusted.

I stole a glance at Gordon's business suit and serious demeanor, appreciating the fact that such a respectable man had become my friend. He had gone out of his way to help me, which was more than I could say for anyone else.

"Gordon, I want you to know," I said in the kindest tone I had used all evening, "that I appreciate your thoughtfulness more than I can tell you. I would have been at quite a loss without your help."

"Not at all," he replied modestly, drawing rein as we reached the house. He hopped down from the buggy, then came around to assist me.

In silence, we walked up to the front door. I had opened my mouth to invite him in for tea, when my eyes fell on the cracked door. I stared at it in amazement.

"I could have sworn I locked that door," I said as we reached the stoop, then hesitated at the threshold. My ears strained for sounds from within, but there were none.

"Wait here," Gordon whispered, then turned and hurried back to the buggy. I stared after him, my heart pounding as I suppressed a childish urge to tag along. I glanced from Gordon to the cracked door, then back again. He was reaching under the seat of the buggy, and now I saw the rifle. My heart raced, for if Gordon was frightened enough to go back for a weapon, he must believe, as I did, that someone was waiting for us inside.

I pressed a hand to my breast, hoping to still my jumping heart. Gordon hurried back, lifting a finger to his lips to silence me as he pointed the rifle straight ahead.

"Allow me," he said, stepping in front of me and slowly pushing the door open.

The far corners of the big room were inked in shadows. Gordon looked right to left as dying daylight seeped into the cavern of darkness.

"There's a lantern there on the table near the door," I said in a whisper.

He walked to the table, fumbled about for the matches, then lit the lantern.

"I'll have a look around," he said, the rifle positioned in the crook of his arm. I lit a candle and lifted the candlestick high.

"I'm coming with you," I offered in a false show of courage.

We crossed the big room, and I was besieged again by that hideous mask with the jeering eyes and gaping mouth. As I crept along, my heel caught on the bear's open mouth and anger surged through me. Why hadn't I torn the mask from the wall and tossed the bearskin rug out the back door?

"Nothing seems out of place." Gordon spoke softly as I opened first one closet door, then another.

I glanced back over the room, looking for anything out of order. I was almost convinced that everything was just as I had left it until I spotted the desk drawer. It had been left ajar. I hurried forward and yanked it open. The papers were tumbled, the pens scrambled.

"Is something wrong?" Gordon asked over my shoulder.

"I'm not sure." With Gordon beside me, I stole a peek into the kitchen, the candlestick hoisted. The room was untouched.

"I'll go have a look upstairs," Gordon said in a low voice.

I hesitated, not quite brave enough to tag along. I recalled the horrible first night here, when I had been imprisoned in darkness as I lay rigid, counting each footstep on the creaking stairs.

I sank onto the sofa, my hands clenched in my lap, as Gordon lit another lantern and climbed up the steps. I shivered again, as his footsteps whispered over the floor overhead. Something bumped. I screamed for him.

"It's all right, Abigail," he yelled from the top step. "Come on up. There's no one here."

I jumped from the sofa and hurried up the stairs. When I reached the second floor, I looked cautiously about as he held the lantern high. When my eyes moved to the Mallard bed, a wrinkle in the blanket added an extra crease to the woven face and I almost gasped before my eyes adjusted and I looked around. "What was that bump I heard?"

"A chair had been overturned," Gordon replied. "You

probably did that as you were leaving."

I didn't think so.

"Abigail, why don't you close up this house and stay at the hotel?" Gordon asked, rather crossly.

I considered the suggestion, frankly wondering why I had exceeded stubbornness and insisted on punishment. I looked the room over carefully, then turned back to Gordon. "I don't like the idea of allowing someone to scare me off. And it's possible that I didn't close the door hard enough for the latch to catch. The wind could have blown it open."

"Abigail, your uncle had some rather unsavory friends," Gordon said, worried, "and he did owe a lot of money." He was looking cautiously around the room again as he wandered over to peer out the east window.

"Would someone expect to find money here when it was common knowledge that Uncle Joshua was flat broke?" I argued.

He shrugged. "Who knows?" He turned from the window and crossed the room. "Still, I don't think it's a good idea for you to stay up here all alone."

I wandered about the room, seeing nothing out of place. I would not have been surprised to find my pearls missing, but they were tucked safely in the blue velvet case. No, it was not a thief who had come to prowl; otherwise, the jewelry would have been taken. So . . . the desk drawer and front door . . . surely I had been careless, that was all.

I was conscious of Gordon's eyes upon me, and I knew he was waiting for my answer.

"Let's go downstairs and have a cup of tea," I suggested, sweeping past him and hurrying down the narrow stairs.

There were still a few meager ashes in the kitchen stove, enough to be poked into a low fire.

"Let me do that," Gordon insisted, taking the poker from my hand. "Thanks for offering tea," he said as he replaced the poker behind the stove and dusted his hands, "but I really don't care for anything."

"Then perhaps we can just sit and enjoy the fire." It was

an absurd suggestion, when I imagined us sitting in the tiny kitchen trying to make polite conversation; but the truth was, I was trying to delay Gordon from leaving. He, on the contrary, seemed anxious to go.

He reached for the rifle, which he had placed on a table. "I have a derringer out in the buggy which I insist upon leaving with you."

"I don't know . . ."

"Abigail, be sensible. If you're going to stay up here, you need a gun! Let me get it."

I nodded. I followed him to the front door, wondering if I could possibly shoot someone. When it came to defending my life, I decided that I could.

The darkness was complete now, so that I could barely make out his form as he trudged to and from the buggy. He returned with a small derringer which he carefully placed in my hand.

"It's loaded, so be careful. Just keep it by your bed. You'll feel safer."

I studied the gun, small yet heavy in my palm, and discovered that he was right. Already I did feel safer, knowing I had a weapon. I turned and placed it on the table.

"Thank you, Gordon." I smiled at him as he hesitated in the doorway.

"Be careful," he said, lifting my hand to his mouth, and pressing a kiss to my fingers.

"Thanks for everything," I said, as he descended the stoop and crossed the yard to his buggy, no longer distinguishable in the darkness. For a moment I wavered. But with the gun, and the certainty that no one was in my house, I felt secure.

I closed and locked the door, then pushed a chair against it. I crossed the room and opened the desk drawer again, inspecting the contents one more time. Perhaps I had upset the pens when I had looked for writing paper to make a grocery list. I remembered opening the drawer and seeing several pens neatly stacked beside the old photograph of . . .

I lifted the stationery, looked under it, around it. Where was the old photograph of Uncle Joshua? He had been dressed in overalls and a flannel shirt, sporting a healthy beard, and hoisting a gold pan. I looked in the other drawer, on top of the desk, my fingers moving in a frantic search.

The photograph was gone!

For a moment I stood staring into space. Then I wandered to the front door, opened it, stared across the meadow to the distant cemetery. Ghostly fingers of moonlight stabbed the darkness.

I grabbed a lantern and resolutely made my way across the yard, reminding myself of the gun in my pocket when the deep shadows swallowed me up. The lantern light bobbed and flared with my hurried movements, but at least it lit the path for me. I was too intent on my mission to be afraid.

When I reached the picket fence enclosing the cemetery, the wild cry of a coyote sent a volley of chills over my skin. My trembling hand found the latch to the gate and opened it, and I pressed on until I stood before Uncle Joshua's grave.

The small arrangement of dried flowers was gone. In their place was a small bouquet of greenery from the woods, arranged in a simple bundle and tied with a white satin ribbon.

I stepped back from the grave and heaved a deep sigh as a knot of tenderness clutched at my heart. The missing photograph . . . the fresh greenery. I turned and trudged to the house, the lantern more steady in my hand now. When finally I entered the front door and closed it soundly, I looked pointedly at the coffee table, to the empty spot where the glove had been.

Now I knew who had come and gone. I was sorry that I had missed her.

Chapter 7

The news of Mrs. Zarnoff finding Uncle Joshua, then the pressing need to avoid riding home with her husband, had detained me from reading the suicide note in town. I had not mentioned the note to Gordon at dinner, for it represented one last precious link with my uncle among a town full of strangers. I would not share it—not yet.

Our return home had launched my thoughts into another puzzle: the mysterious caller. Now, with a cup of tea to calm me, I sat beside the lantern in the big room with only a moaning wind for company and held the suicide note in my hand, as though it were insidiously evil. Maybe it was, for the message had come from a man on the brink, a man I scarcely knew anymore.

My fingers trembled as I unfolded the note, aware that this was my last tangible link with Uncle Joshua's mind. I took a deep breath, remembering the man who had bounced me on his knee as a child, brought me gifts on birthdays and at Christmas, and finally, upon leaving San Francisco, urged me to follow my dreams.

Tears sprang to my eyes. I couldn't bear the thought of the man I had idolized becoming so desperate, so disenchanted with the life he loved that he had ended it all here, one long, miserable night.

The paper crinkled in my hand as I smoothed it out and held the tablet sheet directly under the lantern. It was a simple sentence of seven words . . .

I do not wish to go on

At the bottom of the page, my uncle had signed his name. Not "Joshua," but "Joshua L. Martin."

My eyes moved back and forth from the sentence to the signature. I had seen his handwriting often enough to know this was genuine. And yet, as I looked at the sentence, carefully, painstakingly written, and then the signature, with the wide, familiar flourish at the end of each letter, I felt . . . cheated. Was I expecting a poem? No, but at least some sort of explanation . . . an explanation that would never come.

Carefully I laid the note on the table, swung my feet into the chair, and sat staring for over an hour. How can I explain just what it was that nagged me? I couldn't analyze the doubt that hovered in my mind, but my intuition screamed at me. Something was amiss here.

If my uncle had drunk himself into a deep depression, why had he condensed all his agony into seven simple words that seemed to be a mere prelude to something more—a story left untold?

Weariness crept over me, claiming first my body, then my mind. With a sigh of resignation, I folded the note and hobbled across to place it in the desk. Perhaps I would look at it tomorrow, or perhaps I would not look at it again. I checked the locks on the doors, reinforcing each door with a chair; then, with the lantern light casting gaunt dancers against the board walls, I climbed the stairs.

Carefully, I placed the gun beside the bed, feeling truly secure for the first time, silently blessing Gordon. I don't know how that led my mind to Scott Morgan, but somehow it did.

The next day was Saturday, the day he had asked me to go sightseeing with him. No doubt he was down in Juneau now with the woman. He had hardly spoken to me in the hotel; there was no reason to expect that the date was still on.

I undressed and turned back the Tlingit blanket, ignoring its weird face as I crawled into the soft bed. The wind was moaning through the woods now, and I shivered beneath the covers as a host of lonely thoughts whipped through my mind: Uncle Joshua buried in the cemetery across the meadow . . . the woman who had somehow gotten inside the house, reclaimed her glove, and taken one last memento of Uncle Joshua before visiting his grave again. Through the night, the distant howl of a wolf, trapped in loneliness as well, reverberated through the wind, and I snuggled deeper in bed.

As my eyes grew heavy, I realized I had forgotten to ask Gordon about the strange, eerie cry I had heard. But I had not heard it again; I would not worry.

What are you doing here in the wilds, alone in an abandoned Russian abbey? a voice in my head whispered. There was no answer for it. And then, with the flash of perception that sometimes comes when least expected, I knew exactly what I was doing. I was not trying to prove my strength or my courage to the Juneau people; I was trying to prove something to myself!

I might be gaining courage by staying here alone, but I was losing ground with Scott Morgan, not that it mattered. The beautiful woman at his side loomed in my memory, and I sighed. A ladies' man, Gordon had said. Well, I had been duly warned about the man. Now I must stay away from him.

But why was forbidden fruit always more tempting, I wondered, as I drifted off to sleep.

The forbidden fruit appeared at an astonishingly early hour the next morning, considering the circumstances of the previous evening. I was seated at the kitchen table, sipping tea, thumbing through the tablet of poems, when I heard the dog.

I hurried through the house to crack the front door. It was a gloriously beautiful morning, with no clouds to mask a pure blue sky. The air was crystal clear. It was the kind of morning that made one appreciate Alaska.

I blinked into the bright sunlight and focused on Scott Morgan and Bering, loping up the path to my house. As I watched the man approaching, my mind flew back to the previous evening, to the beautiful woman at his side. In spite of that agonizing memory, Scott was even more attractive than ever. A green tweed cap dipped jauntily over his forehead. He wore a white shirt and dark pants tucked in knee-high black boots.

"Good morning," he called as he approached.

"Good morning . . ."

"Did you enjoy your dinner at the hotel?"

"Yes, did you?"

He grinned. "We didn't eat."

I cleared my throat. "Would you like a cup of tea?"

"Let's not waste time inside on this beautiful day." His eyes fell to my housedress. "Did you forget?"

I ran my hand through my hair. "Actually, I overslept. What exactly did you have planned?"

"A ride up the channel and a picnic lunch near the big glacier."

I looked over his head to the sunshine and decided it was exactly the kind of outing that I needed. "I'll just be a minute."

"Be sure to wear boots," he called after me, "and dress comfortably."

With lightning speed I flew up the stairs and changed into a riding habit with matching hat, which seemed as appropriate as anything else.

When I returned, Scott was playfully tossing a stick out in the yard and watching with amusement as Bering retrieved it. I locked the door and waited as he finished the game of fetch.

He never seems to hurry, I thought, shifting from one foot to the other. But then, I supposed one need not hurry if there was no specific job waiting. I did not like to think of this attractive man in terms of hack writer, woodcutter . . . gambler! Involuntarily I sighed, and he quickly glanced over his shoulder, interpreting my sigh as one of impatience.

"Ready to go?" he asked.

I nodded. "It's a wonderful day, isn't it?" I commented as we crossed the tidal flats to his boat.

"It's glorious!" he exclaimed, reaching down to pick up a pebble and skip it toward the channel. I watched, amused by the boyish gesture. I couldn't imagine my ex-fiancé, or even Gordon Walling, doing this, but then part of this man's charm was his way of doing exactly as he pleased without trying to impress anyone.

He glanced back at me. "Watch your step," he warned as we crossed the wet sand to the boat. A small boulder near the water's edge held mussel and clam shells, left by a seagull who had feasted on the contents and now took flight as we approached.

Bering loped ahead of us, lunging into the stern and flopping down with a weary sigh. Scott held my hand as I stepped carefully into the little boat, taking a seat on a narrow wooden slat. The boat began to rock beneath our weight, and while Scott loosened the anchor, I glanced anxiously around the channel and on to the opposite island. This was a new experience, but I felt safer here than in the vast bay of San Francisco. This was not my first boat ride, but still I was a bit nervous. To ease my nerves and divert my mind, I plunged into conversation.

"Tell me about the story you've been writing," I said as we shoved off.

He dipped the oars into the water and began to row. "It's a piece about the Tlingit Indians. They migrated here a long time ago, and were a unique people who knew how to survive on the land while conserving it as well. They had different kwans . . ."

"Kwans?" I interrupted curiously.

"Territories. The various tribes moved about, hunting and fishing. They gathered berries, bird eggs, and clams. They had a rather unique society, divided into two groups. The eagle, or wolf, and the raven. They were forbidden to marry into the same group, interestingly enough. A child belonged to its mother's group.

"Well, that's different from the clannish ways of many tribes, and of even our own society," I said, laughing, thinking how snooty Tom and Edith, my cousins, and even Thad, my fiancé, had been.

"They were a fun-loving tribe. They tried to outdo one another with their feasts; guests were always showered with gifts."

"They were very artistic weren't they?"

"Very. Each clan has its own emblem, and it used that emblem in its arts and crafts."

"I'll bet your story is interesting," I said, my attention momentarily diverted by a bald eagle soaring overhead.

"Well, I hope the editor of the Portland newspaper thinks so." He followed my gaze to the sky. "Just keep watching that eagle. He's looking for food."

In a few seconds he dived to the water and emerged with a small fish clutched in his talons.

"Look at that!" I cried.

He laughed. "They're fascinating." His eyes slipped over me interestedly. "I'll bet a city lady like you doesn't often study the animals of the wild," he teased. "But then, San Francisco is probably more exciting. I've never been there, but Josh was always telling me stories. He said there were enough colorful characters there to fill a library with books about them."

I looked out into the gray water. "Yes, it's an interesting place."

"I remember he used to mention some character named Lillie something-or-other," he said, removing his cap and tossing it onto the seat as a light breeze ruffled his dark hair.

"Lillie Hitchcock Coit! She would make a wonderful story for you."

"Tell me about her."

I bit my lip and thought for a minute. How could I give a description that would do justice to Lillie, I wondered, smiling as I thought of the delightful woman who entertained everyone with her antics.

"Well, she's one of the firemen, so to speak. She has a passion for fire engines, or fires, or maybe just the firemen, I'm not sure. Every time there's a fire, Lillie goes dashing off to help them. And she comes to their banquets wearing firemen's boots and a dress short enough to delight the men and shock the women!"

Scott laughed, enjoying the story. Yes, I thought to myself, he is so very much like my uncle!

"She loves to play pranks," I continued, feeling more frivolous as I thought of the remarkable Lillie. "I've heard it said that sometimes young men passing her house on their way to the medical school get a view of a bare leg poked through her upstairs window as Lillie belts out, "Doctor, doctor, come saw off my leg!"

We were both laughing now; in fact, I couldn't seem to stop laughing. I suppose it was a relief, or a release, to think about something humorous and far removed from the tensions of my present home.

"We're almost home," he said.

"Home?"

"That's where I live." He inclined his head toward a quaint little cabin perched at the edge of the woods. Far in the background, I could see a huge white glacier with a pale blue tint.

"It looks like a painting with all the colors exaggerated in the clear sunlight," I exclaimed. The sky was like a blue velvet canvas on which everything had been carefully painted . . . sprawling aqua glacier in the background, the deep green woods, the square log cabin, weathered to brown-gray, even the smooth, pearlike rocks along the bar.

"It's nice to be with a woman who appreciates nature," he said with a smile. Even his teeth, straight and white, are nice, I thought, trying not to stare into the green eyes that set my heart to pounding. "Well," I said, looking at the cabin, "you're a real Thoreau, aren't you?"

"Yep. I hope you're hungry," he said as he hopped out of the boat and tugged at the rope to anchor it.

"I'm ravenous!" I took his hand and stepped onto the muddy bar. One cup of tea had been the extent of my nourishment.

"Good! I have a special lunch planned."

I glanced at him as we climbed up the plank steps built into the slight knoll, and I thought how full of surprises he was. There was never any predicting what he would do next. It was one of the reasons I was so intrigued by him.

Fresh cut cedar and the pungency of evergreens drifted through the air as we topped the steps into a world that was uniquely his own. A path, outlined with various sizes and shapes of driftwood, led past an open lean-to containing a dogsled, an assortment of fishing poles and buckets, a pair of snowshoes, and some gold pans. A few steps beyond, a wooden bucket filled with water obviously belonged to Bering, who had leapt out of the boat and raced ahead of us to lap greedily from it.

The front step of Scott's cabin was a halved log, where a pair of boots with silver spurs perched. Beside the cabin door, a wide stump provided a resting place, and I dropped down to catch my breath.

As he opened the door, I could feel his eyes sweeping over me, and I turned my attention to Bering, who had flopped wearily at my feet, curiously sniffing my boots.

"I'll just grab the picnic lunch," he called over his shoulder, stepping inside.

My eyes moved cautiously toward the open door. I could see a long, unpartitioned room with sleeping quarters and a tiny kitchen. The eating table was piled with books.

He stepped back through the door with a wicker basket and a blanket tucked under his arm. "We'll hike through the woods so you can get a view of the glacier. It's really something."

We followed a well-traveled path through a dense growth of towering hemlock and spruce. I could see that the so-called wood was really a lush forest where the trees reached for the sky and sphagnum moss was abundant. The air was cool and crystal clear, and I felt as though my lungs were being purified.

Soon, the forest broke open and we stepped into a meadow that ran beside a lake of indigo blue. In the distance, the glacier rose up before us, and I gasped and stared in awe.

I was looking at a mountain of sparkling aqua ice. It was the most breathtakingly beautiful sight I had ever seen.

"I wish you could see it in summer," he said. "All sorts of wild flowers grow in abundance around here. It's so beautiful it looks as though the setting has come from a portrait; it's almost too pretty to be real. Fireweed, lupine, forget-me-nots were all in bloom before you came. Too bad you couldn't see it then."

"I can imagine . . ."

"And the ice you're looking at once fell as snow, a very long time ago. The glacier is receding into the sea."

"Like Juneau."

He glanced at me quizzically.

"When I first arrived and looked at the town nestled in the arm of the channel, it seemed to me that the mountains were pushing the town back out to sea."

He laughed. "It's a unique place. There's nothing to equal this kind of beauty anywhere in the world. At least I don't think so."

"No," I shook my head. "I've never seen anything like it."

He took my hand, squeezing it lightly. "Let's eat lunch."

As he spread the blanket and opened the basket, I peered curiously inside.

"Rainbow trout," he proudly announced, withdrawing a tin bucket filled with bite-sized pieces of fish. "I caught the trout, filleted it, and smoked it over a low fire . . . just for you."

I stared, aware that he was in the act of charming me, and just as aware that it was working.

"I appreciate your trouble," I said as he pulled out a golden loaf of bread. "And you baked that, too, I suppose?"

"Nope, the credit goes to China Joe at the bakery. I *did* prepare the tea," he grinned, carefully lifting out a warm pot. Tin cups and plates followed, like gifts from Pandora's box, and we ate heartily.

I had never in my life tasted anything so wonderful. I knew that part of the enjoyment came from the beauty around us, and the fact that I was enjoying—far more than I should—the company of Scott Morgan.

As we sat enjoying the scenery, something moved on the rock just behind us, and I saw that Scott was watching with amusement.

"What is it?" I asked, glancing over my shoulder.

"It's a ptarmigan," he said softly. "That one's a female. They have three plumages." He glanced back at me. "She's a fashionable little bird, you might say, with her different garbs. One for spring and summer, one for autumn, and one for winter!"

I watched the small bird darting down from the rock. It was a gray-white, and as it sprang down and began to hurry across the meadow, I laughed at its odd, rolling gait.

"In the winter, they burrow into the snow. You hardly even notice them except for the dark eyes."

I smiled as the little bird turned back and made a different sort of call. "What an odd sound," I said looking back at Scott. "It almost sounds like a clock being wound."

"Yes, they're unusual. But then, I've found everything in Alaska to be special."

I finished the lunch, then sat back on the blanket and gazed in rapture at the glacier.

"It's beautiful," I sighed.

"Like you," he said as he leaned forward and brushed his lips over mine in a tender kiss.

I told myself it was the awesome setting and the wonderful day that lifted me into a special euphoria, but when I looked into his eyes again, I felt a kind of magic I had never known.

Then suddenly a voice in my memory spoiled that exquisite feeling.

A ladies' man, Gordon had said. And the memory of the tall, stately brunette joined the voice to topple me from the clouds back to earth with a jolt.

I dropped my eyes to the empty plates and fell silent as he watched me. I could not lose my head over this man. Not yet anyway.

"I think it's time to go," I said as I put the plates back in the wicker basket and drained my mug of tea.

"What's the hurry?"

"I have things to do at home." It was a silly lie, but I didn't know what else to say.

"How is your investigation coming along?" he asked in a slightly different tone.

"I beg your pardon?"

"I know you're discreetly looking into your uncle's last days," he said. "Have you discovered anything?"

"There was a woman in my uncle's life," I said.

"There was?"

I nodded. "First, I found some dried flowers on my uncle's grave, and a black glove only a few steps away. Now the dried flowers are gone, and there's an arrangement of greenery tied with a white satin ribbon."

"And . . . ?" he pressed, watching my face intently.

I decided to tell him.

"The black glove disappeared from the house along with a small picture of Uncle Joshua that I'd seen in the desk drawer."

He frowned. "You mean this occurred just in the last day or two?"

"Yes. When I returned from town, the door was cracked, even though I was certain that I'd locked it. At first I thought perhaps the lock hadn't caught when I closed it, that later the wind blew the door open." I stared at the blue glacier, remembering. "Once I walked inside and looked around, everything appeared in order at first, exactly as I had left it, but then . . ." I took a deep breath and shook my head. "If Gordon hadn't left a gun with me, I might have tossed and turned through another night."

"Gordon Walling?" he repeated. "He gave you a gun?"

I glanced at him sharply. "Why, yes. What's wrong with

that?"

"Nothing, if you don't end up shooting yourself."

The sarcasm in his tone, and the implication that I was too dim-witted to be trusted with a gun, sent a flash of anger through me.

"I'm perfectly capable of handling a gun," I added pointedly, "and taking care of myself."

"With Gordon Walling's help."

I came to my feet, brushing the crumbs from my skirt. "Yes, Gordon Walling has been a great help to me. And he's been more than understanding about Uncle Joshua's debts. He is a very good businessman, unlike . . ." I broke off before I said too much.

"Unlike Josh and me," he drawled. "Isn't that what you were thinking?"

I looked away, embarrassed, humiliated, angrier than ever, because he was so adept at reading my thoughts. I had never met anyone who was as perceptive as he, and it unnerved me completely.

"Shall we go back?" he asked, not looking at me again as he picked up the basket.

We returned through the forest to the boat in miserable silence. I tried to think of a way to undo the damage, but none came to my mind. I decided that Scott Morgan was overly sensitive. Even if I had spoken carelessly, I did not think he should have been so quick to take offense.

We got in the boat, and he rowed us back home. It was an awkward situation, with each of us pretending an interest in the passing scenery. At length, he looked across at me and sighed.

"I seem to have said the wrong thing," he said.

"And I'm a bit tense," I conceded. "Since I arrived in Juneau, it's been hard for me to relax."

"You may be right about the woman," he said, looking at the shoreline where the house loomed, strange and out of place in the peaceful surroundings.

As I looked from Scott to the house, I felt reluctant for the day to end. I couldn't stay angry with him. He was by far the most interesting man I'd ever met, even though he was a bit sensitive. None of the dapper bachelors in San Francisco, with all their charm, had ever impressed me the way this man did. He was obviously happy with himself and his life; what difference did it make if that life was rather unorthodox? I thought with a sigh.

"Tired or bored?" he asked, watching me again.

"I'm not bored," I replied, turning my eyes up to his face. "It's been a wonderful day."

We had reached the path leading up to the house, and I tried to think how to choose my words. If I invited him inside, I did not trust my emotions or his. This friendship was likely to blossom into a romance once the candles were lit and we were alone in the soft darkness of an Alaskan night.

I forced myself to think of our discussion concerning the woman and Uncle Joshua. Suddenly I stopped walking and looked at him.

"I hadn't known Mrs. Zarnoff was the woman who found my uncle."

"You didn't?"

"No. She never mentioned it, nor did Mr. Zarnoff. Doesn't that seem odd to you?"

He shoved his hands in his pockets and lifted his eyes to the house, tracing its angle against the growing darkness. "Not particularly odd, no. Why would the Zarnoffs want to talk about that? Or why would they think you would want to recall such a gruesome thing?"

I shook my head, walking on. "I don't know. It just seems . . . unusual."

He hurried ahead of me, turning the knob of the door, which was still tightly locked.

"Well, it doesn't appear there have been any visitors while we were away," he said, glancing over his shoulder. "I'll see you safely inside."

I handed him the key and he quickly unlocked the door, then stepped inside and looked around.

I lagged behind, trying to see if everything seemed in

order.

He opened the doors and peered into the closets, then went into the kitchen. The stove lid clattered, then I heard chunks of wood being dropped in.

I did not follow him into the kitchen or offer him tea. I needed to be alone, to sort through my erratic thoughts.

"Everything looks fine," he said, as he returned to the living room. I stood at the coffee table, lighting the lantern against the gray dusk seeping through the windows.

"Thank you for a lovely day," I said, trying to be pleasant, as though there had not been a tense scene between us.

"It was my pleasure," he replied. He opened his mouth, then closed it, not speaking his mind. We both felt inclined to say more, but an invisible barrier had descended between us an hour before.

We were standing near the door. Suddenly he turned, lowered his face to mine, and kissed me. It was a brief, tentative kiss, yet my heart began to race again.

"You are a beautiful woman," he said quietly. Then he opened the door and hurried down the steps.

I stood there staring after him until I caught myself. Then I quickly slammed the door and leaned against it, my head spinning. How had I let myself become so infatuated with this man? It was easy to be fascinated with him, I rationalized. He was handsome, intelligent, and witty; but I suspected it was that aura of mystery and intrigue that had drawn me like a moth to a flame.

Later, as I lay in the big Mallard bed, I decided to study Uncle Joshua's poems in an effort to divert my mind from Scott Morgan. I flipped through the tablet, enjoying his early poems, the ones that paid a glowing tribute to Alaska's beauty. Finally I skimmed over the later ones, which reflected a mood of gloom. I paused on the final poem . . . one that made little sense. Then, suddenly the last line jumped at me, and I reread it again.

"Beware of mosquitoes and silver spurs."

Silver spurs.

Abruptly I closed the tablet and lay staring at the small

taper beside my bed.

In my mind's eye I could see Scott's boots on the porch step. Rather ordinary boots . . . except for the silver spurs!

I tried to push that image from my mind, not wanting to pursue that thought. And yet my mind raced on . . . did Uncle Joshua's last sentence hold a secret message?

A warning?

My heart began to beat faster. Though there were no strange sounds in the house that night and no threats from a prowler, sleep did not come for a long, long time.

Chapter 8

By morning I had decided I must have a talk with Mrs. Zarnoff.

Since she was the one who had found my uncle, along with the gun and the note, I felt justified in asking her a few questions.

It was a dreary gray morning. Low-hanging clouds banked the sky, threatening more rain. Deciding to dress according to my mood, I chose the most somber navy woolen in the armoire and tugged it on over my thick petticoats.

Downstairs, my slippers sent small thudding sounds across the big living room, a sound magnified by the awesome silence which always served to remind me of how alone I was, how isolated. Avoiding the face on the wall, I stepped quickly into the kitchen, where a dwindling fire offset the chill of the house. I knew I must feed the stove. Carefully, I added two sticks of wood, then prodded the poker determinedly, until a blaze flared. Then I made tea and dropped down in the chair, thinking again of Scott. Why couldn't he be more stable, more practical? I liked everything about him except his irresponsibility, a major flaw. And what about my uncle's warning of silver spurs?

I recalled the woman I had seen with him at the hotel. Perhaps she was the type of woman he preferred. Sophisticated. Experienced.

My eyes fell to the table and I recoiled in my chair upon sight of the bloodstain. I crossed my arms, shivering.

Mrs. Zarnoff, I thought again; I *must* speak with her.

I hurried back through the big room to fetch my cloak and boots. As I shoved my cold feet into boots, then tied the strings of the cloak, I thought about what I would say to Mrs. Zarnoff concerning that terrible morning when she had discovered Uncle Joshua at the kitchen table.

As I opened the door, the dismal day greeted me, doing nothing to lift my sagging spirits. Reaching for my parasol, I locked the door and pocketed the keys. Quite likely, there would be a steady downpour before I returned.

My boots squished over the damp ground as I lengthened my steps and lowered my head against the light rain. Far in the distance, I could see a small canoe approaching from the south. Automatically, my heart beat faster. I didn't think it was Scott, and yet I peered cautiously, hoping. No, it was not Scott.

I had to end this annoying fascination with him. The sooner I settled Uncle Joshua's debts, the better. Surely the bank draft would be forthcoming in a matter of days.

While I was beginning to enjoy Alaska, I feared that I, like Uncle Joshua, was being drawn toward situations which were not in my best interests.

The Zarnoff house was only sixty yards away now, and absently I glanced back toward the channel. The small canoe was closer now, and I could clearly see the man in the canoe. It wasn't Scott, so why was I staring? The canoe glided along, the paddles moving, slowly, silently. It struck me, for the first time, how quietly one could approach. I thought of the midnight prowler, and my steps quickened.

The Zarnoff house looked desolate, deserted. No one milled about the two small outbuildings. The fish were gone from the racks, and I did not see the wagon. I pressed on, thinking it might be to my advantage to catch Mrs. Zarnoff home alone.

The yard was neat, well tended. Smooth, round rocks outlined the graveled path to the wide log steps and circled a flower bed. Of course, nothing was blooming now, but I could see thick greenery that offered a promise of color in the growing season. I had been too apprehensive to notice anything on my other visits, but now I could see that this was no ordinary cabin. It had been built with great care and pride. Large spruce logs, smoothly trimmed and dovetailed to fit snugly in the corners, framed the house. Small pieces of driftwood, chosen for their unique size and shape, were spaced decoratively about the narrow plank porch.

The sound of my knuckles rapping on the wooden door reverberated into silence. I gripped my parasol, glancing right to left, wondering where everyone was.

Presently, the door opened, and I was looking into the face of an attractive Indian woman whose dark hair was plaited in a thick braid that reached halfway down her back. She was small and slim, dressed in a colorful cotton housedress. As she moved her hand, silver bracelets jangled from her narrow wrist.

"Good morning," she said as her eyes flicked over me curiously.

"Good morning. Is Mrs. Zarnoff home?"

"No. They've all gone to town." Huge dark eyes lit a rather plain face, and yet there was about her a sense of style and grace that made her attractive.

"Would you like to come inside and warm yourselves?" she asked.

At my hesitation, she smiled. "I'm sorry that I did not introduce myself. I'm Nona, wife of James. We are visiting."

"Hello," I smiled. "I met your son Jamie. He's a fine young man."

I was grateful that I could honestly say that about one member of the Zarnoff family, although I could see that his pleasant disposition had come from his mother.

"My name is Abigail Martin," I hastily explained. "I'm Joshua Martin's niece."

She nodded, dropping her eyes.

"Here, let me take your cloak."

"Thank you." As I stepped inside and untied the strings of my cloak, my eyes wandered over the small living room, dwarfed even more by excessive clutter and heavy wooden furniture. Whipsawed planks were covered with rag rugs.

Nona hung my cloak on a wall peg, then glanced back. "Have a seat, please. Would you like a cup of tea?"

"Yes, I would. Thank you."

When she went into the kitchen, I studied the cabin. While it had appeared small from the outside, there seemed to be at least four rooms within, judging from the curtained partitions on each side of the living room, and the kitchen in the rear. My eyes returned to the fire dancing pleasantly in the hearth. An old iron bell sat on the hearth, and I wondered if that bell had been meant for the church that had now become my temporary home. On the opposite side, a small canoe, made for a child, held rubber boots.

Intricately woven baskets overflowed with discarded newspapers and a short-handled hoe.

The woman returned with a small tray and placed it on the table before us. The tray held a white crockery teapot, matching cups and saucers of a red design, and two pewter spoons.

"How do you take your tea?" she asked.

"Just plain, thank you."

She handed me a cup, then took her seat across from me. I felt her covert glances as I sipped the strong, hot tea.

"You live in Sitka now?" I asked.

"Yes," she said, stirring her tea carefully. "The fishing is better there."

I leaned back on the pillows, noticing the soft, sleek fur.

"From the sea otter," Nona explained, watching me. "It is the strongest fur, yet the softest. Mr. Zarnoff used to hunt the sea otter years ago."

"It's lovely," I said, trailing my fingers over it.

"Jamie told me he may run errands for you while we are here," she said.

"That's right. He could be a great help on days like today when I prefer to stay in, but then . . ." I broke off, not wanting to convey my apprehension to this woman who seemed to possess a kind of calm inner strength. I imagined it must take a great deal of that to be a Zarnoff.

"You must be lonely down there," she said.

I hesitated, hating to admit just how lonely I was. "It's quite a change from the hectic pace of San Francisco," I finally answered. "Are you a native of this area?" I asked.

She placed her cup on the table and leaned back in the chair, her hands folded in her lap. The bracelets jangled softly, and I looked at the handiwork, which was a design of birds.

"My people were Tlingit. We lived here in the valley." Her dark eyes rose above my head as she stared into space, remembering. "The men built log canoes, hunted the sea otter, gathered fish in nets. The women made clothing, dressed the fish. In winter we gathered in clan houses and made baskets from spruce roots."

My eyes strayed to the intricate baskets spaced about the living room.

"Yes, I made those," she said modestly. "We lived close to the land and in harmony with nature. It is very different now." Her eyes dropped again.

I nodded. I could imagine circumstances might be *very* difficult for her, considering the attitude of the Zarnoffs.

"Well," I came to my feet, "I must get back."

"Did you want to leave a message for Mrs. Zarnoff?" For the first time, I saw an expression of anxiety steal over her face. There was no point in discussing with her the matter that had brought me here.

"I'll see her another time," I answered. "How long will you be visiting?"

"I'm not sure. My son gets homesick for Juneau." The nostalgia in her tone indicated that she did, as well.

"Stop in for tea with me some day," I said.

She appeared startled by the invitation. For the first time, the friendly expression faded, replaced by a cool reserve.

"I will be busy here," she answered.

I was puzzled by her change of attitude, until I remembered that I was living in their sacred abbey, and they all resented that. I placed the empty teacup on the table and stood.

"Well, good day," I called, pulling on my cloak and grabbing the parasol.

"Good day," she said, quickly closing the door after me.

As I entered the road again, I cast a longing glance south. If not for the certainty of more rain, I would strike out for Juneau. A two- or three-mile walk might do wonders for my nerves, but I reined in such impulsive thoughts and forced myself to march home in the drizzling rain.

In an amazingly short time, Mrs. Zarnoff appeared at my door.

"You wanted to see me?" she asked.

I blinked and drew myself up to my full five foot three inches. "Yes, come in."

She stepped just inside the door and waited. Beneath her hooded cloak, her dark eyes held an expression of suspicion.

"Won't you have your cloak off?" I asked.

"I haven't time!"

"Then I'll come right to the point. I understand you're the one who found my uncle here the morning after he committed suicide." I was watching her closely as I asked the question, and suddenly she seemed to grow taller before my eyes, or perhaps it was the way her spine stiffened and she squared her shoulders, as though ready for battle.

"Come," she said, marching ahead of me.

I followed her to the kitchen.

She stood before the table, staring entranced at the bloodstain. For a moment, neither of us spoke.

"He was right there in that chair," she said, lifting a plump hand to touch the back of the chair, where I often sat.

"He was slumped over the table, his head on his arms."

"How?" I pressed, looking for some flaw to the story.

She glanced back at me; a flame of anger sparked in the depths of her eyes before she yanked the chair back and heaved her large frame into it. She spread one arm across the table, turned her face sideways, and pressed her cheek against the bloodstain. The other hand lay near her forehead.

"Like this," she said. Her voice was muffled with her mouth pressed against the table. "The gun was here in his right hand;

the bullet hole was here." She pointed to her right temple. "His tablet and pen were over there."

I closed my eyes for a moment. Why was I doing this? It was too horrible for both of us.

When I opened my eyes and looked at her, she was sitting upright in the chair, staring at me vacantly, as though lost in thought.

"The bottle was still half full," she pointed to the center of the table, "right there. And his glass was here, empty. His tablet lay over there. He had pushed the tablet away from him so as not to . . ." her voice trailed.

"Yes, I understand," I said hastily.

"He had written a note. His pen lay over the page. I gave the note to the deputy in town."

I would not tell her that I had the note. If anything had been concealed from me, I wanted to find it. She looked me straight in the eye and said in her firmest tone yet, "I am telling you the truth."

As I looked into the heavily lined face, drooping mouth, and sad, dark eyes, I realized that I believed her.

"Thank you, Mrs. Zarnoff," I replied after a thoughtful pause. "No one has explained anything to me. I couldn't help wondering."

She nodded, dropping her eyes. "I understand. I should have told you, but my husband . . ."

I looked at her. "Yes?"

"I came to clean the house," she sighed heavily. "He usually left the back door open. He was here," she pointed to the table. She paused, swallowing heavily. "I turned and ran through the back door. I ran all the way home." She lifted a hand to her sagging breasts. I could see that she was breathing heavily. "It was dangerous for my heart," she said, "but I ran. My husband hitched the wagon, and we went straight to town. I never came back here." She shook her head slowly, her dark eyes intense. "It was meant to be a sacred dwelling," she said, under her breath.

"What's that?" I pressed.

Her head jerked up, and she looked at me through hooded

eyes. "I should have cleaned the stain. I will do that now."

"No, that isn't necessary, and it's probably been too long. Please don't bother."

"I will try to do that now," she repeated firmly. I turned and walked from the kitchen into the big room and stood staring at the stained glass window. I recalled the first day she had come here, how she had wanted to take her tea here in the big room, rather than in the kitchen. I now understood why.

I could hear the cabinet door open and close, and something else banged. I sank onto the sofa and stared into space, sick at heart.

Why had I dredged up a memory that was such a terrible scene? I could hear a scraping sound from the kitchen, and I tried to summon the energy to go in and help. But I sensed she would not want my help. The back door slammed, and I wondered if she had left, but suddenly she appeared in the doorway and looked across the room at me.

She turned and marched across the room to the door.

"Thank you, Mrs. Zarnoff," I said, following her.

She bobbed her head. "Good day." Her heavy frame moved on down the steps and up the path to the road.

I closed the door and sauntered back to the kitchen. Her offer to clean the bloodstain from the kitchen table had been a gesture of kindness. No one had asked her to do that.

I stood in the kitchen glancing at the table. The blood stain was gone, but it had not been removed with soap and water.

Astonished, I stepped to the table, then gasped in surprise.

Mrs. Zarnoff had taken a knife and carved out the piece of wood where the bloodstain had been. At first I thought this was a terribly destructive act. The more I thought about it, however, the more sense it made: now I could look at the table without feeling sick at heart.

It seemed I had lived through three long days, rather than one, but finally, after an early supper, I lit the candlestick and climbed the stairs to the bedroom.

I slept more peacefully since I had developed a ritual of locking doors, double-checking the locks, then reinforcing the door with chairs. The wind sang a lonely song through the spruce trees as I entered the large bedroom and glanced toward the shadowed corners.

I listened to the wind. In Juneau someone had referred to it as the Taku wind. It seemed different than any I had heard down in the states. This kind of wind was stronger, lonelier.

I wandered over and peered out the window. Faint traces of moonlight drifted over the meadow and cemetery. If I had not been thinking of Uncle Joshua, and peering through the darkness in search of his tombstone, I would never have seen the black-cloaked figure. I blinked, pressed my face against the window.

The outline of the crosses rose like bony fingers. To find Uncle Joshua's grave, I merely had to look for a space where there was only a one-bar cross. As I stood there squinting into the darkness, something moved before my eyes. Had I imagined it? No, there it was again. A dark form began to emerge.

Chapter 9

I stood motionless, waiting, watching. Was it merely a shadow from the moving branches of the tree as the sweeping wind created human shadows? No! Now I could make out a hooded cloak . . . a person. The figure moved slowly across the meadow, then turned from the road.

With the candlestick trembling in my hand, I hurried back down the stairs and crossed the room to the window that faced south. The hooded figure was gone.

I stood watching, searching the distant beach. The channel was a dark, impenetrable mass, with only a few flecks of moonlight to silver the water. There was no canoe in sight.

Who had been to the cemetery, and why?

I paced the living room floor, afraid to remain upstairs alone. Uncle Joshua was not the only person buried here, I reminded myself. It was logical to assume that someone might visit another grave—but who would want to visit at such a late hour?

Was it the woman? I sat down, shivering. The house was cold despite the low fire, but it was something else that had brought goosebumps to my skin. I felt as though someone were watching me. For a moment, I could not move. Then slowly I turned my head and looked toward the windows, almost expecting to see a face. There was no one. *The visitor to the cemetery is gone,* I told myself firmly.

And then I knew where the eyes were. I whirled and looked at the hideous mask on the wall. The glaring eyes! I screamed out, then jumped up and ran over to yank the mask down from the wall. I hesitated before the door to the dark closet. Somehow I could not bring myself to open that door. Instead, I dropped the mask to the floor, face down.

I crept back to the window and looked out. There was no movement along the road, no canoe out in the channel. Scolding myself for being so childish, I trudged back upstairs to the bedroom.

I awoke the next morning feeling stiff and out of sorts, but I dressed in warm clothing and hurried downstairs. The living room was cold. When I checked the stove, the last ember had died. With an angry sigh, I slammed the lid. I was in no mood to build a fire.

I thought of the hooded figure in the cemetery and hurried toward the front door, changing from my slippers to my rubber boots.

Grabbing my cloak, I unlocked the door and flew out into the cold morning. A sharp sting in the air assured me that winter was on its way.

Hurriedly, I crossed the wet grass to the cemetery and stood before Uncle Joshua's grave. Beside the small bundle of greenery, now soaked from the recent rain, a small silver object gleamed.

I knelt, picked it up curiously, and turned the cold metal over in my palm. It was an oval piece of silver, hammered into an odd design. I frowned, puzzled. What meaning did this have? Was it a gift from an Indian? I whirled, glancing around me. None of the other graves held anything new. My eyes moved upward to the gray skies, as my mind flew back to the night before. So! The hooded figure I had seen here last night had come to Uncle Joshua's grave after all!

I laid the object back on the grave and searched the grounds again. The grass was pressed down in a small area near the grave as though someone had sat there for a while. *Who?*

I turned and plodded back to the house, glancing out toward the channel. I could hear someone whistling, and presently I saw the Zarnoff boy running down the road. He was wearing a mackinaw, and he was looking intently into the channel. Suddenly he stopped and leaned down to inspect something at the water's edge.

"Jamie!" I called to him, eager for company.

He stood and turned, a puzzled expression on his angular face before his dark eyes found me.

"Hello!" he called, bounding across the path to meet me.

"Good morning!" I smiled. "You're out early."

"I'm going up to fish with Scott Morgan," he replied pleasantly.

"Oh." I looked out across the channel, wondering about Scott again.

"Is he coming to pick you up?" I asked.

"No ma'am, but he only lives a mile or two up the bay. And I can walk it in a hurry."

"Do you like to fish?" I asked.

"Yes ma'am. But Mr. Morgan isn't a very good fisherman," he said, with a charming little grin. "Not as good as my father, anyway. But he makes fishing fun."

"He does?" I looked into the grinning face and wondered if his father wasn't similar to his gruesome grandparents after all. "But you say Mr. Morgan isn't a good fisherman," I repeated, amused.

"He won't use the right kind of bait!"

"Well, it's a good thing he has you to help him," I replied. I realized what I needed more than anything was a pleasant friend. I found myself trying to think of things to say to detain him. I liked Jamie Zarnoff.

"Do *you* know the right kind of bait to use?" I asked.

"Sometimes. Then sometimes I don't. Fish can be real tricky."

"By the way," I smiled at him, "when are you going back to Sitka?"

He frowned and studied the mud on his rubber boots. "I don't know. You got any errands you want me to run?"

"Well . . . not today. But why don't you check with me tomorrow?"

"Yes'm." He glanced anxiously toward the road. "Well, I gotta go."

"I hope you catch a big rainbow, Jamie," I called, staring after him as he dashed off. His rubber boots squished loudly through the lonely silence. I headed back up the path to the house, feeling the loneliness more than ever. As I walked through the front door, my eyes fell on the mask lying on the floor across the room. I hurried over and picked it up, opened the closet door, and laid it face down on one of the boxes. Then I slammed the door.

Determined to forget the mask, the hooded nocturnal grave visitor, and his strange offering, I tried to make some plans. I must sort through the boxes and do something about Uncle Joshua's possessions!

I wandered into the kitchen and stared at the cold stove, trying to summon the energy to build a fire, when I heard a tapping at the front door.

I hurried back and opened the door to face Lonesome Bill, who stood awkwardly on my doorstep, his battered felt hat clutched between his big hands.

"Mornin'," he said with a big grin. "Thought I'd better come up and check on you, see if you needed anything."

"Thank you; I certainly do! My stove has gone out and I'm not very good at building fires."

"Oh, yes'm. I'll do that for you."

I stepped aside, and he bounded through the door and into the kitchen. He had picked the perfect time to visit.

"I'm glad you stopped by," I said, as I reached the kitchen and looked at his long back, bent over the stove.

"You got anything to start a fire with?" he asked over his shoulder.

"It so happens I do." I plundered through the cabinet and found the old newspapers and brown jug. Bill didn't seem to be as familiar with the kitchen as Scott Morgan, who obviously had been a more frequent visitor. Yet this man was supposed to have been my uncle's friend!

"Sorry I can't offer you tea or coffee," I said.

"Don't need any, ma'am. Thanks."

As I sat down at the table, my eyes were drawn to the fresh scarred wood, and my thoughts flew back to Uncle Joshua. "Have you found out anything about the woman?" I asked.

"No, ma'am," he called over his shoulder. "That's what I came by to tell you. I've been thinking it might have been someone from Douglas Island, or as far away as Sitka."

He stood watching the flame ignite, then closed the lid and slapped his hands against his jeans. "That should do it," he said, turning back to me. His eyes strayed to the chair and the table, and for a moment he seemed lost in thought.

"Bill, I want to ask you something, while we're on the subject of my uncle. Did he ever say anything specific about the Lost Rocker?" I lifted my hand in a helpless gesture. "I know I seem to be dwelling on all of this, but I just can't put it out of my mind."

He nodded. "I understand. Let me see. Just the usual," he looked back at me. "That he'd found the Lost Rocker and was going back up to his secret stream when the ice broke up."

"He didn't mention the location of this stream?"

He shook his head. "If he had told me that night, I probably wouldn't remember. Like I said, I was near about as bad off as he was! We both had a good-sized dose of cabin fever after so much bad weather."

"But he died in April . . ."

"Yes'm. The first week of April. We'd had enough pretty weather to be getting out then, doing things; but then another snowstorm came in. The night you're asking about was right after that storm."

I bit my lip, staring at him, thinking about what he had told me. "Do you think Uncle Joshua might have gone up to that stream during that short time the weather was good?"

"He didn't say so," he replied.

I stared into his huge, protruding eyes. He didn't *say* so. Why did that simple reply arouse my suspicions?

"Even if he didn't say so, do you believe he did?" I pressed.

He removed his hat and scratched his head. "I don't know, ma'am. I hadn't seen him in over a week. Then we met up at the saloon and . . . you know the rest." He dropped his eyes.

I nodded. Obviously, this was all the information I was going to get from Lonesome Bill.

"Well, I reckon I'll be going if there ain't nothing else I can do for you."

I stood, glancing at the stove. Already I could feel its heat radiating across the room. "Thank you so much for building the fire."

"Glad to. How long are you staying?"

"Until the steamer returns."

He nodded. "Then I reckon I'll see you again." He was halfway out the door when I thought of the incident the night before.

"Oh, Bill," I called after him, catching up in the doorway, "someone came to my uncle's grave and left some sort of trinket last night."

"Trinket?"

"Well, I don't know what to call it. It looks like Indian handiwork."

He nodded quickly. "Yes'm. Probably something one of the Tlingits made. Sometimes they leave things on graves of their friends."

And yet—I didn't think it was an Indian I had seen last night in a dark cloak and hood.

"Well, I'd better hit the road!" he said. "Just wanted to come by and see if you needed anything. The weather's changing. Old-timers are predicting snow within the week."

"Snow?"

"Yes'm. From all nature's signs, we're in for a bad winter. That's one reason I wanted to check on you. Anytime now a blizzard could roll in overnight."

"Well, Jamie Zarnoff has offered to help me out if I need anything."

He nodded. "He's old enough to build a fire, I reckon."

I hadn't thought of asking Jamie to do that, but I would, if necessary. I felt more comfortable when I could pay for favors. Perhaps that was because I had been raised with household help, a situation which was a detriment to me here.

"Thanks for stopping in," I said as he turned to go.

He touched his hat again. "If you need me, you can send Zarnoff's kid to town. He knows where I live."

"Thank you, Bill. That's reassuring to know."

With a loose-jointed stride he bounded toward the deserted road. I closed the door against the sharp cold, feeling better about my circumstances as I wandered back to make tea. But then I discovered the water jug, almost empty. While the kettle heated, I decided to find the creek and get water.

I threw my cloak around my shoulders and hurried out the back door and across the yard. My boots made squishing sounds on the soft, wet ground as I searched for the area where I had seen Scott kneeling.

I found the creek easily enough, but when I knelt and lowered the jug, footprints in the mud caught my eye. Curiously I looked around. The footprints were everywhere. They appeared to be the same size—large, bold steps, all belonging to the same person.

Were these Scott's footprints? Surely not. There had been a day of rain, which should have washed the old footprints away. I traced them into the tall grass, but then it seemed as though the person had disappeared into thin air.

I turned back to the jug, trying to forget the footprints that had trespassed. I had begun to act like an amateur sleuth, watching, listening, dissecting everything anyone told me, and I vowed to stop being so suspicious.

The jug was heavy with water as I trudged back to the house. The singing kettle greeted me when I stepped inside, and the warmth of the kitchen settled over my cold face. I made tea and sampled some of the rolls from the bakery. Then I began to think of how to spend another long day. I decided I must get away from the house!

I had always found pleasure in shopping, so I would go into town and look for souvenirs to take back to San Francisco.

I dressed quickly, locked up the house, and set off in the gloomy morning for town. By the time I reached Zarnoff's cabin, however, I saw him hitching the horses to the wagon in front of the house. Why should I sacrifice my weary legs if a ride could be obtained?

Just as he was climbing into the wagon, I caught up and asked for a ride.

He nodded curtly, in his usual abrupt manner, and I climbed in. I glanced back toward the house, wondering about the rest of the family. I did not ask, however, as he seemed in no mood for conversation. We rode in silence, and I thought ahead to the souvenirs I would purchase.

As we approached town, the blare of the steamship horn drifted through the foggy morning. Zarnoff's head whipped toward the channel. "The steamer! It has come a day early! I have to go to the dock to haul freight. An hour. Maybe two hours!"

"I'm in no hurry," I replied. "I'll need to stay in town until the mail is dispensed."

We had reached the main street, and he slowed the wagon before the mercantile. "I'll find you," he said firmly.

As I climbed down from the wagon, I knew that was true. No matter where I went in the crowded little town, I often turned and found him watching me from a distance.

In anticipation of the letter, my steps quickened as I turned into the mercantile. "We just got these in," the saleslady was explaining to an elderly woman. I glanced curiously toward the item they were discussing and saw they were inspecting some all-woolen underwear for ladies. I pressed my glove to my mouth to conceal a smile. With luck, I would be gone before the cold weather set in.

I browsed around, finally purchasing some Indian bracelets for friends and a small bird carved from whalebone for Mother. As I stepped onto the sidewalk, I spotted a wagon and driver pulling up before the bank to unload cargo. I headed in that direction.

The curious clerk had spotted me as I took a seat beside the door, and now he hurried forward, peering at me in his usual obtrusive manner. "Good morning, Miss Martin. Can I help you?"

"Perhaps. I'm expecting a letter in today's mail. I gave this address," I explained.

"Oh," he glanced over his shoulder, "our freight is just arriving, and I see the mail sack. I'll check on your letter."

"Is Gordon in?" I called after him.

His eyes widened even more at the familiar way in which I spoke of his employer.

"No, he's gone over to Douglas Island. Could someone else be of service?"

"I was just going to say hello," I replied with a testy little smile.

His eyes flicked over me briefly before he left to check on the mail. Presently he returned bearing a thick envelope.

"You're in luck, Miss Martin. Your mail arrived."

"Oh, thank you!" I said, practically yanking the thick envelope from his hand. As I tore into it, another envelope fell into my lap. I recognized Uncle Joshua's neat script, but I ignored it for the moment, eagerly reading my mother's words.

> Dear Abigail,
>
> I was distressed to learn that you did not disembark with Tom and Edith. I do not think Joshua's debts necessitated you going on alone. I am disappointed that you did so, but as always, you have a mind of your own, and one that is not easily changed.
>
> I am relieved to read that you have made friends there, and I can only pray that those friends are honest and trustworthy and will take care of you until Tom arrives on the next steamship.
>
> (Tom!)
>
> I am sending another bank draft to cover the remainder of Joshua's debts. Then, you will be free to return with Tom.
>
> The day after you left, the enclosed letter arrived from Joshua. Apparently it had been placed on the wrong steamer. It seems to have traveled halfway around the country before finally reaching us. At any rate, it did arrive, and I was heartbroken anew to see his familiar handwriting and know it was his last communication with us. On the other hand, his message is cheerful, as you will see. There are some things within the

letter which might be helpful to you in winding up his business; therefore, I am enclosing it.

I will be in constant prayer and concern until you return. Please leave at once . . ."

I folded the letter, suddenly aware of the clerk's burning eyes. He was not looking at me, however, but rather at the other letter in my lap—the letter from Uncle Joshua.

Slowly, deliberately, I lifted the envelope and folded it carefully, watching him all the while. Then I placed it in my handbag. I would read my uncle's letter in privacy, without the prying eyes of the bank clerk, who was immensely disappointed not to get a peek at its contents.

When our eyes met, he blushed and faked a sudden interest in his neat desk.

"I would like to deposit this draft in my account," I said.

"Certainly!" His eyes popped upon seeing the draft, and he scrambled for a receipt.

"Will you please tell Gordon that my cousin is on his way to Juneau, and that we will be settling my uncle's accounts?" I added as he handed me a receipt of the bank draft.

His eyebrows peaked at that news. "I'll tell him," he replied. I could see that I had whetted his curiosity even more, but I said nothing further. Feeling smug, I left the bank, aware that his curious eyes followed me out the door.

Perhaps this would quiet the murmurings about Uncle Joshua. At least no one could say they were left with his debts. When I stepped onto the board sidewalk, Zarnoff's cold blue eyes met me. He was seated in his wagon, parked before the bank.

"I'm ready to leave," I said, climbing in the wagon.

As usual, he had nothing to say as he loosened the reins on his horses, and we left town. I was feeling jubilant about my cousin's arrival, and the relief of being able to pay off my uncle's accounts. It was one of those rare moments when I was willing to go out of my way to be friendly to Zarnoff.

"Mr. Zarnoff," I turned and looked at him, "did my uncle owe you any money?"

His head spun toward me so quickly that his fur cap dipped crookedly over his left eye. He shot an impatient hand up to dash it in place on his bald head.

"No," he answered gruffly.

It occurred to me that he could have said yes and taken advantage of my gregarious nature at that moment. I appreciated his honesty.

"Well," I said, as he continued to stare at me, "I'm taking care of his debts. I thought if he owed you anything . . ."

"He did not owe me money," he said staring straight ahead.

Was there an emphasis on the word *money?* Did he owe him something else? My imagination was running away again; I took a deep breath and tried to remain rational.

As we passed the totem pole, I remembered the trinket on my uncle's grave. While Zarnoff was not one for conversation, I decided to make another attempt.

"Mr. Zarnoff, did my uncle have many Indian friends?"

This question seemed to surprise him even more than the one concerning my uncle's debts. Now, as his blue eyes shot to me, I read a different expression on his face, one I could not easily identify.

"What do you mean?" he asked bluntly.

Now it was my turn to stare. Was the man completely devoid of manners?

"I mean," I replied pointedly, "did you notice any Indian visitors to his home?"

A muscle clenched in this broad jaw as anger flared in the blue eyes that shot from the road to me, then back again. Was he prejudiced against Indians? I wondered, or had I defamed the sacred dwelling by calling it a home?

Like one who has accidentally uncovered a secret, I realized that I had struck a nerve and brought him out of his impassive state. I ran the sentence back through my mind, trying to decide which word had sparked anger in him.

Feeling bolder than usual, I decided to press on. "Occasionally, someone comes to visit my uncle's grave," I said, watching him carefully.

His eyes were fixed determinedly on the road, as though he

dared not look at me again. "I'm not sure if it is always the same person who comes, but now an Indian trinket has been left beside the tombstone."

"When?" he barked.

"Just recently."

He set his jaw more sternly than ever and glared down the road.

I sighed. Apparently the conversation had come to an end once more. My mind wandered on to Tom's arrival and the consolation that we could leave Juneau before the winter set in.

"The man they call Lonesome Bill has Indian friends," he said after a silence. "They often came to visit."

"Oh? Who are these Indians?" I asked.

He shrugged. "I know the man called Bill, but I do not know the others. I have only seen them around town."

As he related that bit of information, a host of new possibilities surfaced in my mind. I thought of the Indian ceremonial mask on the wall, the blanket on the bed, and now the trinket on his grave.

Mr. Zarnoff had answered me honestly about my uncle not owing him money. I had no reason to believe that he would lie about his visitors, a matter less important. I pondered what he said as we rode on in silence.

By the time we reached home, I had thought a great deal about Lonesome Bill, and I had arrived at a definite conclusion. He had not told me enough about Uncle Joshua. Surely a man whom people said was his closest friend would know something about the woman in Uncle Joshua's life. Surely Bill remembered more than he had told me about that last night with my uncle at the saloon, and then later when he brought him home.

Once before, when I had sought Bill out in the saloon, I had believed he could shed some light on my uncle's mysterious behavior. That feeling was now stronger than ever.

I recalled what he had said to me as he'd left the house. "If you need me, just send the Zarnoff boy to fetch me. He knows where I live."

Impulsively, I turned to Zarnoff.

"Mr. Zarnoff, your grandson Jamie offered to run errands for me. I would like to talk with Lonesome Bill. He said Jamie knows where he lives. Will you please ask Jamie to go and tell Bill I need to speak with him?"

Zarnoff stared at me, his eyes filled with questions.

"I will be leaving soon," I explained hastily, improvising my reason for seeing Bill. "I need to clear out the house, do something with Uncle Joshua's possessions."

At that explanation, the look that crossed Zarnoff's face seemed to be one of relief, but why?

"Mr. Zarnoff, would you want anything here?" I asked suddenly.

"No!" he blurted. "I would not take one thing from in there." The harshness in his voice took me by surprise.

I hardly knew the man, but I thought I detected a note of fear in his voice, for the first time since we had met.

"Just thought I would ask," I mumbled as I paid his fare.

"My grandson will run your errand in the morning. He has gone fishing today."

"Yes, I know." *With Scott Morgan,* I remembered.

He said nothing more as he put the lash to the horses, a bit too stoutly, I thought, and the wagon shot off down the road.

I unlocked the door and entered, then stood for a moment staring around me at the lonely house. *What was I doing here?* That question often popped in my head, for this was such an absurd setting for me. Well, it would soon be over, I told myself. As soon as the steamer returned!

The fire Lonesome Bill had built for me was still burning low, and now I hurried to the stove, lifted the poker, and prodded at the coals. Then I placed the kettle on the burner. Rubbing my fingers over the heat, I glanced back at my handbag on the kitchen table, suddenly remembering Uncle Joshua's letter.

I waited until I had a strong cup of tea and a slice of bread for sustenance before I opened the envelope.

As Mother had stated in her letter, there was something sad yet tender about reading Uncle Joshua's last correspondence to us. I took a deep breath and unfolded the ruled sheet.

"It has been a bitterly cold winter," he wrote. "Just when everyone returned to outdoor work, another heavy snow shut us down again . . ."

I read on as he detailed a friend's misfortune. But then, the next paragraph was a jubilant account of a stream he had found that contained some promising gold nuggets. Then the snow had come, temporarily freezing the streams and ending his work.

"But I have marked the spot and drawn a map," he wrote. "After the snow melts and the stream thaws, I will go back. Finally, my dreams will all come true!"

I stared at that sentence . . . haunted, tormented.

Was this the final letter of a man who, in less than a month, would end his life? I stood and began to pace the room. From the beginning I had sensed that something was wrong, but then I had almost convinced myself to accept my uncle's suicide. Now, fresh doubt returned.

Why would a man on the brink of finding the gold he had longed for, the gold that had driven him from one adventure to another, lose hope so completely? I stopped pacing and stared again at the letter on the table. Perhaps the weather had broken, and he had returned to the lucky stream only to find that he was badly mistaken; that, in fact, what he had discovered was only fool's gold. I sighed. That must have been it.

I felt tired, bewildered, depressed. I drained my tea, had a light supper, and went to bed early, wearied by the long day and the disturbing letter. Despite feeling perplexed, I fell asleep rather quickly. It could have been minutes, or hours, when the sound of footsteps on the stairs finally penetrated my deep sleep.

I bolted upright, suddenly wide awake, every nerve in my body attuned to another presence in the house.

This time I was better prepared than before. I reached to the nightstand for the gun, and I waited, my breath jerking in my chest.

The steps continued. I lifted the gun and fired into the wall, a shot that was too far off course to kill anyone. I only wanted to scare the prowler away.

The sound exploded through the night silence; footsteps scrambled down the stairs. The bedroom was swathed in darkness as I crept across to the stairway and listened for steps across the board floor downstairs. I froze, waiting for a door to slam. There was only silence.

I might have chased him from the stairs, but he was still in the house! I groped across the cold floor to the window and peered out.

Eventhough the moonlight was bright, I could see no one in the yard, or along the road.

Still clutching the gun, I fumbled for my robe, then my slippers, listening and hoping for the sound of someone leaving the house. Silence.

If I cowered in my room, he would think he could get away with frightening me, that the one shot was only a warning. However difficult it was, I knew I had to summon every ounce of courage and go downstairs with my gun. I had to let this person know he could not keep coming in this house, frightening me half to death.

Unsteadily, I moved toward the stairs, gripping the stair rail with my left hand, holding the gun in my right. The silence was vast and deep. I felt as though I were descending into a well of darkness, but I forced my feet, stiff with cold and fear, to keep plodding down the stairs.

The gun! I had the gun, and I was safe. I must let him know he could not prowl about without suffering the consequences.

When I reached the bottom step, I heard nothing.

The stairs had been built into a narrow passageway, with one wall forming a partition, so that the living room was not visible. As soon as I turned the corner, I would be in plain sight to whoever still lurked beyond the wall.

I stared into the gray light seeping around the partition and realized the house was not completely dark. There was no obvious light, as there had been before when the lantern was lit; no, this was a more subtle penetration of the darkness. A pinpoint of gray. A lantern in the back of the house?

I reached the bottom step. Then, with both hands on the

gun, I forced myself to take another step, a step that would lead me into the big room. I could see a faint light coming from the kitchen as I stepped around the partition and looked across the huge room. Then I bit back a gasp of terror. My eyes met two red glowing eyes across the room, and a horrible face framed by long black hair that hung in wisps. It was suspended in space, *a face without a body!*

My teeth ground my bottom lip and I began to tremble. Then suddenly I realized what I was seeing, and I almost moaned with relief.

I was looking at the face of the ceremonial mask! Someone had hung the mask back on the wall. Anger surged through me, giving me a boldness I could never otherwise have summoned.

I scanned the room. The furniture crouched like so many predators in the gray light. I stared into the farthest shadows. There was no one.

"Who's here?" I called. "Step out right now and tell me what you want!" My voice bounced off the cold walls, echoing eerily into the recesses of the house.

"I have a gun," I shouted, although this could hardly be news to the one who had scrambled down the steps after the shot was fired. "I intend to shoot you if you set foot in this house again."

There! My voice sounded forceful, convincing. My threat, backed up with the gunshot, should send him scurrying, if he was not already beating a path up the road. If he knew I would not put up with his pranks, or whatever motive had brought him here, maybe this would be the last encounter.

Just when I was beginning to feel confident, the closet door creaked. I lifted the gun, aiming directly at the door, waiting. The tinge of light in the kitchen did not reach the depths of the closet, so I could see nothing in the darkness beyond the cracked door.

The door moved again, opening slowly, ever so slowly.

I squinted across the gray room to the moving door.

The crack in the door began to widen. I lifted the gun, waiting. The door stopped moving.

My skin felt cold. There was a draft in the house. Was the back door open?

Yes, that was it. Whoever had gone inside the closet, found the mask and hung it on the wall had left by the kitchen door, failing to close it completely. Now a draft from the cracked door was seeping into the house, moving the closet door.

I stepped slowly into the room. Then, to my shock, the closet door flew back and banged against the wall.

I froze. No draft had that kind of force!

"Who's there?" I shouted hoarsely, fighting panic. "Come out of the closet this minute!"

In answer to my command, a figure emerged. This time I could not bite back the scream of terror. What I saw turned my blood to ice.

Fortunately, I was still near the back wall, and now it was that wall that held me up.

He stepped into the gray light and stood for a moment near the kitchen door, where the light was distinct. I had a clear view of him, and that view set my teeth to chattering as he stood silently watching me.

Was he capable of speaking? Was he even human?

The face that met me across the room was very much like the face of the ceremonial mask. It was a hideous face, one that looked a hundred years old. Wispy black hair fell to his shoulders above a dark cape. Sunken eyes glittered. He took a step forward. The gun was trembling in my hands, but I pointed directly at him and fired.

Again the sound of the shot was an explosion in the silence, but I had missed him completely. He took another step toward me, and I fired again. I could not believe I had missed him a second time!

A wild, blood-chilling sound gurgled from his twisted lips, a shriek that was not human.

I fired again. And again. The black cape swirled as he turned and lumbered from the living room into the kitchen.

Terror unlike any terror I had ever known seized me. This time I could no longer stand. My knees buckled, and I hit the cold floor. The room swirled about me. My stomach lurched.

My vision blurred. The gun hung uselessly in my hands, which were shaking so violently that I laid the gun on the floor for fear of shooting myself.

It was not fear of the prowler that had defeated me, but rather the knowledge that my bullets had no effect on this sinister being.

The back door slammed, and I jumped and cried out.

Silence stretched, overwhelming me as I sat in a stupor, trying to pull myself together. I sat gasping for breath, and when I heard the horse hooves, I felt a sense of relief. He was leaving. But the horses did not belong to the monster that had left my house; they were thudding steadily toward my door. And then there were voices in the yard.

I might have remained slumped on the floor, frozen in fear, until daylight, if not for the horses, the voices, and then the steady pounding on the front door.

Chapter 10

"Miss Martin?"

The deep voice was familiar, but it was seconds before I could place it.

"Miss Martin? It is Ivan Zarnoff!"

Zarnoff?

Slowly, I pulled myself upright and stumbled to the door.

"Mr. Zarnoff?" I called through the door, wanting to be certain that I had heard correctly.

"It is Ivan Zarnoff," he repeated.

I managed to drag back the chair and unlock the door, even though my hands were still frozen and shaking.

Bundled in a mackinaw, Zarnoff stood on the steps, peering at me curiously. Beyond him, another man sat on a horse. In the darkness I could not make out his face.

"You are all right?" he asked.

I clutched the doorway, trying to steady my trembling knees. "I . . . don't know. Please come in."

"No! I do not wish to enter," he said, his face holding that same expression I had seen earlier when I had asked if he wanted any of Uncle Joshua's possessions.

The rider had dismounted and was now walking to the door.

"What happened?" he asked. It was Zarnoff's son.

I swallowed, trying to find my voice. "There was a . . . prowler," I answered, unwilling to tell everything at first. The younger man brushed past his father and stepped inside.

"Do not go in," his father ordered.

James ignored his father's command and entered. Then his steps faltered in the darkness.

"I'll light the lantern," I said, groping for matches at the coffee table.

"Allow me." He took the matches and quickly lit the lantern. As the light flared over his face, I was struck again by his resemblance to his father. Yet there was a gentleness to the features which I doubted had ever touched the older Zarnoff.

He straightened, and his eyes moved slowly over the living room. I glanced back at Zarnoff, who had taken a step closer and now stood in the doorway. The frigid air engulfed me, chilling me to the bone.

"Who was shooting?" the younger man asked.

"I was. But he . . . got away."

His dark eyes flew back to me, mirroring his surprise. "Did you wound him?"

I shook my head, wondering what their reaction would be if I told him the creature that stood across the room leering at me could not be stopped by bullets.

"Father, either come inside or close the door," James called impatiently. "The woman is freezing!"

The door slammed, and Zarnoff remained on the outside.

James looked at me grimly. "He is very superstitious."

I did not comment, for I feared that I, too, might become superstitious, considering what had just taken place. I hugged my arms around me and tried to think of something to say.

"I'll check the other rooms," he volunteered, and began to explore. I watched as he opened the closet door from which the creature had emerged.

"He was . . . in there," I said, my teeth chattering again.

"Do you think anything was taken?"

I swallowed. "I don't know."

He turned and peered into the kitchen. "How did he get in?" he asked, glancing back at me with a puzzled expression.

I trudged across the room and stood beside him. To my astonishment, the kitchen door was closed; the chair was still propped under the latch.

"I'm not sure," I said weakly.

He walked over and dragged the chair back and tested the latch. "It's locked," he said with a frown as he stared at the door for a moment. Then his eyes shot over my head to the front door. We both remembered my dragging back the chair and turning the key in the lock. Automatically, I turned and stared blankly at the chair standing only a few feet from the door. Then I groped my way to the sofa and sat staring into space.

How could I explain to anyone what had happened when I didn't understand it myself?

"Is it possible you had a nightmare?" he asked, striding back across the room to stand before me.

Slowly, I lifted my eyes to meet the dark eyes of this stranger. I was not prepared to try and convince him of what I had seen. If it had been anybody but the Zarnoffs, I would have spoken my mind; but I knew they resented my being in their sacred place. They would declare evil spirits had come to haunt me, and while I might consider that myself, I was not about to admit it, especially to Zarnoff. Without replying, I dropped my eyes again.

"Is everything all right upstairs?"

I nodded.

He lumbered across and opened the door where Zarnoff stood waiting out on the stoop.

"What has happened?" Zarnoff barked.

James dropped his voice and mumbled a reply. I imagined they were both thinking what a hysterical woman I was. He turned and looked at me again.

"You should be more careful with a gun, Miss Martin."

I glared at him. "I thought I heard someone downstairs. I'm still not sure."

I looked from one face to the other and saw the doubt in their eyes. Indignantly I stood and hobbled to the door.

"Thank you for coming. I . . . am sorry to have bothered you."

"No bother," James said shortly, as the men trudged back to the horses.

I slammed the door and locked it, then heaved the chair

against it again, wondering as I did so why I bothered. Apparently the creature could walk through the wall, if he chose.

My eyes flew over the rooms as my mind grappled with the enormous possibility of a supernatural being. When my eyes met the wicked red eyes of the ceremonial mask, I ran across the room, tore it from the wall, and threw it back in the closet.

My head was pounding. This was a *real* nightmare. What was I going to do? I hurried into the kitchen and slammed the kettle on the stove, trying to think clearly. Maybe I should have asked to go home with the Zarnoffs for the remainder of the night. No! Of course I would not do that! But I would gladly pay Jamie to come and sleep on the sofa.

I began to pace the floor, trying to think. At daybreak, I would pack up and move to town! I would not stay another night in this haunted abbey.

The kettle began to sing, and for a moment I merely stared at the steam rising from it, trying to call forth the horse sense I thought I had inherited from my father.

I did not believe in spirits. There was no such thing. So what had I seen? My eyes fell on the table where Uncle Joshua's letter still lay. Was this what had driven my uncle to madness? I grabbed a cup and made tea with steadier hands. All sorts of possibilities flooded my mind as I sat down at the table, thinking. I had been staring absently at the white spot on the table, the missing chunk of wood that had held the bloodstain before Mrs. Zarnoff had carved it out. Belatedly I realized I had taken the seat where Uncle Joshua had sat on that fateful night. I bolted to the other chair.

I gulped the hot tea, relishing its fiery trail down my throat, while wondering if I would ever feel warm again. I reached for the letter and reread it. This was the letter of a happy man, I decided. What had happened?

Puzzled, I folded the letter and placed it back in the envelope. My eyes moved slowly to the closet door, recalling the horrible visitor that had emerged from there. What had he wanted? If he had intended to harm me, he could have. Either I was a terrible shot, or he was invincible. Perhaps he did not want to harm me, I thought; perhaps he only wanted to frighten me.

I turned in the seat and glared at the locked back door. There was no explaining or understanding it. I took my tea and wandered back into the living room, seeking the gun. It lay on the floor near the stairs. Somehow James had missed seeing it when his eyes swept the room, but of course the lantern light did not reach all the shadows. But that was not something I needed to ponder now.

I knelt and picked up the gun. My only consolation was that I was not harmed; and if he had wanted to harm me, he could have.

A line from an old children's book popped into my mind, and I thought of how appropriate it was now.

But I am a friendly ghost . . .

No, he was not friendly. The evil mouth, the eerie scream . . .

With gun and tea, I climbed the stairs again. Surely he would not return tonight. I must get some rest so that I could face tomorrow—whatever it held.

I don't know how long she had been knocking when finally I was conscious of someone downstairs at the front door. Perhaps she even called to me, and it had been her voice that finally rousted me from a deep sleep. I was curled in a ball beneath the covers in the big Mallard bed. I came awake slowly, blinking sore eyes against the glaring daylight.

The knocking continued.

I stumbled from the bed to the window and peered down. I could see no one, but I heard her voice clearly now.

"Miss Martin? It is Nona Zarnoff."

Nona? Jamie's mother.

"I'll be right down," I called out, doubting that she could hear me. I was still wearing last night's robe and slippers, ready for flight, if necessary. Stiff-legged, I hobbled down the stairs and across to the front door. The chair was still in place, and I dragged it back, then fumbled with the key to unlock the door.

The cold air swept in as I cracked the door and peered at the dark-haired woman bundled in a colorful Tlingit blanket that had been converted to a cape.

"Good morning," she said with a faint smile. "May I come in?"

"Please do," I said hoarsely, stepping aside for her to enter.

I recalled how desperately I had longed for a friendly face the night before, and now her presence was as welcome as the morning sunlight.

"How are you today?" she asked, studying me curiously.

I sighed and wandered to the sofa, motioning her to a chair as well.

"I suppose you heard about . . . the incident last night," I sighed.

She took her seat and removed the colorful cape, then looked across at me. Again I was struck by the kindness in her dark eyes as she lifted a hand to smooth back a strand of her coarse dark hair. Silver bracelets jangled softly from her tiny wrists before she folded her hands in her lap and regarded me with an expression of concern.

"I am sorry for your trouble," she said earnestly.

"It's kind of you to come," I began, thinking she had walked the distance to offer help. I soon learned, however, there was another motive for her visit.

"This morning I overheard James and his father talking," she said. "You want my son to find the man they call Bill and have him come here?" she asked.

Thinking she was concerned about such an errand, I hastened to explain my reasons.

"I need to see the man in order to ask him something."

She nodded, her eyes fixed intently on my face. "You want to ask him about the Indians who once visited here."

"That's right," I said, sensing I was about to learn the answer from her.

"There is no need to ask him," she said. "I can tell you what you want to know."

"Oh?" I scooted to the edge of my seat and anxiously waited for her to continue, but she seemed to have lost her voice. She was obviously an Indian, possibly Tlingit. Were the people who had come friends of hers? Relatives?

"What exactly do you want to know?" she asked quietly.

I took a deep breath. "Someone comes to visit my uncle's grave. I believe it is a woman." As soon as I spoke the word *woman,* I knew, as our eyes met and locked, who the woman was, for I saw the glimmer of tears in her eyes. I bit my lip, sensing there was no point in asking more questions. I had found the answer.

She nodded slowly. "Yes, I came to his grave and left flowers. I had a key to the house, and I entered while you were away and claimed my glove . . . and a picture of Joshua. I am so sorry," she rushed on, "I know it was wrong. It's just that I wanted to keep something. . . ." Her voice faltered and she dropped her eyes.

"I think I understand. So you were the woman my uncle . . ."

"Loved. And I loved him," she said, withdrawing a handkerchief from her pocket to dab her wet lashes. "I know what you are thinking," she said in a rush as her eyes drifted back to me. Her face was pale, tense; her lips trembled. "But it was a thing that could not be helped. Your uncle was interested in the art of my people, and I am an artist. That's how it began." Tears streamed down her cheeks.

I sat staring at her, stunned by this news. And yet it should not have come as a surprise.

"He was such a gentle, tender man," she said in a voice filled with yearning. "And he was interested in so many things. I had never known a man like Joshua. I was drawn to him at once, and he to me. We tried so very hard to stay away from one another, but finally we could not. My husband," she swallowed, "is a rather stern man, like his parents. He does not show emotion; he is not affectionate. It was so heartwarming to meet a man who was not afraid to voice his deepest fears, who could talk openly with me. I was able to tell him things that I could never tell James. I did not know there was such a void in my life until I met Joshua." She paused and dabbed her eyes again.

My mind was racing on, imagining the Zarnoffs' reaction to this affair, if they learned of it. "Did your husband find out?" I finally asked, afraid of the answer.

"He never found out, so to speak, but he suspected. It was the real reason we moved to Sitka."

"I see." There was another question I knew I must ask. "Was that . . . before or after my uncle's death?"

She sighed. "We had already found a place to live, and James had gone into business with another fisherman there. But we had not yet moved when . . ."

I stared at her for a moment, unable to ask the question foremost in my mind.

"So you see," she continued before I could ask, "if you start asking questions about your uncle's companions, it can only cause more pain. There is nothing to be gained by it now."

"Perhaps there is," I said, as I stood and began to pace the room. "Do you believe he committed suicide?" I asked, pausing before her chair and staring down into her face.

Her head jerked back; her eyes met mine, and I saw the fear there. She shook her head quickly. "I do not know, but I had told him only the day before that we could not see one another again. He had asked me to go away with him, but I could not bring myself to do that. Too many people would be hurt."

I listened intently to her explanation, studying her eyes, her gestures, searching for the truth while trying to find a flaw to her story. Nevertheless, I knew in my heart she was telling the truth.

"I must go." She rose to her feet, pulling the cape about her as she swept across the room to the door. "I let my son go for Bill, as you asked. I did not want to arouse suspicion, but now that I have told you what you want to know, please do not press the matter."

I reached out and touched her hand. "Thank you for telling me this. It couldn't have been easy."

"No, but I have told you the truth." She opened the door and stepped out on the stoop. "Is there anything I can do for you?" she asked, glancing back.

"Perhaps." I hesitated, wondering if I should relate to her

what I had seen. If she was as superstitious as her in-laws, she would not allow Jamie to stay here with evil spirits about. However, I was not totally convinced that the creature I had seen was a spirit; and certainly I was not going to positively accept it as such. "The steamship will be arriving soon, and my cousin will be on board. At that time, I will be leaving. For the next night or two, I was wondering . . ."

"Yes?"

"If perhaps Jamie could stay here with me."

"You are afraid?"

"Well . . . the nightmare," my voice trailed off.

"I would not want him to stay if you will be firing the gun."

"You won't have to worry about that," I answered quickly. "I will not be using the gun. Please be assured I would never be careless with your son in the house."

"I will discuss it with my husband," she nodded. "Good day."

"Good day," I said, watching her go. I saw her head turn toward the cemetery, and I looked at the crosses and thought of Uncle Joshua.

Now I knew why he had committed suicide.

After she had gone, I wondered if having Jamie stay was the right thing to do. Shouldn't I just pack up and move into the hotel? It was a question I was unable to answer. Something kept holding me here. I had no idea what.

I made breakfast, dressed, and was thinking of taking a walk when I looked through the window and saw Jamie running up the path. I hurried over and unlocked the door.

"Good morning," I called as he bounded up the stoop.

"Morning." Red-cheeked from the cold, he grinned in his charming manner. I could see the resemblance to his mother in the dark, glowing eyes. "I couldn't find Lonesome Bill," he said.

"You couldn't?" I opened the door and stepped back as he dashed inside.

"I went to his cabin down at the wharf," he rushed on. "He wasn't home. Then I went to Marie's café, and she said he hadn't been in. She doesn't know where he is. Marie said she was worried about him, that he eats there every day, but he's missed two days in a row. Mr. Walling was having breakfast, and he said to tell you he'd come up to see you today." He broke off to catch his breath.

"Good. I need to see Gordon." He was the only person I felt that I could tell about the creature I had seen. Or perhaps I could tell Scott Morgan. I looked back at Jamie. "Did you have a nice time fishing with Mr. Morgan?"

A smile broke over his face. "Yes'm. We caught a bunch of rainbows. He did better this time."

"I'm glad." I tilted my head and looked at him. "What do you think of Mr. Morgan?" It was a question I probably should not have asked.

"I like him, but . . ."

"But what?"

"Nothing." He shoved his hands in his pockets and started pacing the room.

"I wish you would tell me what you were going to say."

He glanced over his shoulder. "My grandparents think maybe I shouldn't fish with him."

"Why?"

He shrugged, continuing to pace a restless circle about the living room. "They said they don't know him that well."

They don't know anyone that well, I thought. They won't let themselves! But then I remembered how Zarnoff had come to my rescue the night before, and my heart began to soften toward him.

"What do your parents say about him?"

"My father calls him a *cheechako*."

"A *what?*"

"It means 'foreigner.' I think it's an old word the first people used."

"Oh. And I'm a cheechako, too," I said, teasing him.

He grinned. "I have to go."

Since he hadn't mentioned staying overnight, I assumed his parents had not decided, and so I said nothing about it. I paid him for running the errand and he thanked me and bounded out the door.

I was puzzled about Lonesome Bill. If Marie was concerned, I felt certain there was reason for me to be as well. Perhaps after stopping off at my door yesterday morning, he had gone on up the inlet. I hadn't noticed the direction he had taken when he'd left.

On my way to the kitchen to stoke the fire and make tea, I heard the distant clomp of horse hooves and peered through the window. Gordon was approaching in his fancy buggy.

I smiled, hurrying to put the kettle on. I was wondering if I really should tell him about the awful-looking creature I had seen, but I had no choice. I had even begun thinking of going into town and speaking to the deputy about it.

"Good morning," I called to him as he hurried up to the door.

He was wearing a dark, tailored suit and a light topcoat. His blond hair gleamed beneath a black felt hat, and behind his spectacles his blue eyes revealed an eagerness to see me. He is an attractive man, I told myself. Why couldn't I feel a tug at my heartstrings . . . as I did with Scott?

"Good morning, Abigail. I hope I'm not coming to visit too early in the day, but I have a meeting later on."

"I'm delighted to see you, Gordon. Please come in."

He stepped inside, removing his hat and glancing quickly about the big room. His eyes returned to me, and he shook his head slowly. "I'm afraid this place works on my nerves. Can't say why."

"It is working on my nerves as well. Here, let me take your coat."

I hung his coat and hat as the kettle began to sing. Then I hurried to the kitchen for tea.

He took a seat on the sofa, studying the white fur cover. "This must be from a mountain goat," he called to me.

A mountain goat! I winced at the thought as I poured tea in the kitchen, then returned with our cups.

"I suppose. Do you take sugar?"

"No, thank you. Well, how have you been, Abigail?"

I took a seat, biding my time before launching into the

sordid story. "Not so well."

"Why not?" he asked, gingerly sipping the hot tea.

I sighed. "Gordon, I had a very strange visitor last night." It was hard for me to go on, to relate to him the horrible thing I had seen. Automatically my eyes moved toward the closet door, remembering.

"What sort of visitor?" he asked, his pleasant smile fading.

I hesitated. "You'll think I'm being overly dramatic."

"I doubt it." He set the teacup on the table and adjusted his spectacles while his eyes slowly roamed the big room. "Nothing that occurred here would surprise me, Abigail."

"But *why?* Why does everyone seem to feel that just because this building was intended to be a Russian church, whoever lives here is automatically doomed?"

He sighed. "Not doomed—just, well, spooked. I don't know. I've heard strange things."

"For example?"

"There's no point in repeating gossip that was probably unfounded. What were you going to tell me?"

I took a deep breath. "Gordon, what sort of gossip did you hear? If you would tell me that, maybe it would make it easier for me to describe the, er, visitor I had."

His brown brows peeked over his spectacles, and for a moment he regarded me rather curiously.

"This was once the campground of a small band of Tlingit. There are silly tales that the area is haunted by the first Tlingit who refuse to give up their ground."

I set the teacup on the table as the cup and saucer began to rattle in my hand. Then I stared at the untouched tea, unable to look at Gordon as I recalled the face. The creature I had seen was an old Tlingit; that was exactly who it was! I swallowed, unable to go on.

"You've probably been listening to the Zarnoffs when you shouldn't have," Gordon said, in an attempt to be reassuring. "You can't put too much stock in their superstitions."

I looked across at him. "I thought it was the Indians who were supposed to be superstitious, not the Russian immigrants."

"Well . . ." his voice trailed off, and he shrugged again.

"Gordon," I swallowed, "there was someone or something here in the house last night. I was awakened by footsteps. I felt protected with the gun you had given me, until . . ."

I was lost again in the awful nightmare, the terror that had gripped me like an iron vise, the utter horror of the creature's face.

"But what?" He was leaning forward, his elbows resting on his knees, his eyes intent behind the spectacles.

I shook my head slowly, looking back at him and trying to dispel the hideous memory.

"But when I came down here . . . and saw him . . . and shot at him . . ."

"What's that? *You shot at him?* There was actually someone down here in this room?" He bolted from the sofa, walked over, and placed a hand on my shoulder. "You're pale as can be, Abigail. Tell me what happened, if you can."

I was staring at the closet, remembering. "He was in there."

Gordon turned, following the direction of my eyes toward the closet, to the left of the door leading into the kitchen.

"When I came downstairs, I could see the closet door cracked, and then . . . finally he stepped out. He had lit a lantern in the kitchen," I said breathlessly, "so that I could see him rather clearly." I paused, looking into his face, automatically reaching up to touch his hand.

"Yes?"

"He was the most horrible-looking creature I have ever seen!"

He was speechless as he stared at me and squeezed my hand.

"I . . . fired the gun . . . two or three times, but . . . the bullets did not faze him. At first, I thought I had just fired carelessly, but I know after three shots pointed directly at his chest, one should have hit!"

He did not answer. He merely stared at the closet.

"You probably think it was all just a nightmare, as the Zarnoffs did," I finished weakly, dropping my hand, and leaning wearily against the chair. Relating the story to him had drained me of my strength.

He began to walk toward the closet, glancing into the kitchen before he opened the closet door and peered inside.

"There's nothing out of order in there," I said, "except that ridiculous ceremonial mask lying on the floor."

He closed the door and turned to face me. "Abigail, I want you to come back to town with me. I insist upon it."

I nodded. "Yes, I'm ready to do that. I just wanted to go through some of Uncle Joshua's things and pass them on to Lonesome Bill, whom I gather was his best friend. But now Bill seems to have vanished. Have you seen him?"

"No, but I wouldn't worry. I heard the Zarnoff boy asking Marie about him, but Marie is easily excited. I imagine Bill has just gone up the inlet to hunt game or scout for nuggets. He's like your uncle; he never gives up on finding gold."

That statement jogged my memory about the other matter that had been nagging me. "Gordon, when my mother wrote to say Tom is on his way, she also enclosed a letter from Uncle Joshua that had been misplaced in the mail." I got up and went to the kitchen table to fetch the letter. "I want you to read it and see what you think."

He took a seat by the window where the light was clear and read the letter I had handed him. When he looked back at me, he did not seem surprised.

"What is bothering you about the letter?" he asked.

"Why, his reference to the gold, of course. Gordon," I walked over to stand beside him, "do you think he got carried away by some fool's gold, perhaps?"

He laid down the letter and smiled sadly. "It's very likely. As I said before, he never mentioned anything to me." His eyes wandered over the big room. "Have you found any nuggets tucked away here? Or have you seen this map he refers to?"

I shook my head. "No. And if there were any nuggets or a map those should be here, shouldn't they? Unless, of course, he took the nuggets to an assayer."

"Which would have caused talk in town. That way, someone could back up his story abut finding gold. But no one ever saw any evidence of gold. At least, not that I know of," he said, looking away.

I recalled the sizable debt, and again I felt a prick of anger toward my uncle for not taking care of his accounts.

As I looked at the letter, something occurred to me.

"Do you suppose he gave the map to someone?"

I could see I had sharpened his curiosity. "Who would he give it to?"

"Lonesome Bill." I said quietly. The question hung in the air for a moment as we stared at each other, our thoughts racing in the same direction.

"If Bill had the map," Gordon finally broke the silence, "he would have turned up some nuggets by now, don't you think? And he would be flashing them around in Juneau."

"Possibly," I said, staring into space. And yet I felt that I might be stumbling onto something important, something I might have overlooked in all the confusion. "Unless he still hadn't found the stream," I said, voicing my thoughts as they came to me.

Gordon was studying the letter again, a frown rumpling his round face. "Perhaps we should have a talk with Bill."

I nodded slowly. "I intend to do that as soon as I see him. He was here yesterday."

Again, I had the feeling that Bill knew more than he had told me. Certainly, he must have known about Nona. If he could keep that a secret, it was quite conceivable that he could keep quiet on something far more important to him personally.

"What did he want when he came to see you?" Gordon asked. I could see that he was beginning to understand my suspicion about the letter.

"Well," I scratched my head, trying to recall the conversation, "he came to tell me he had not learned anything about the woman my uncle was seeing." I hesitated, not wanting to reveal Nona's identity. "I'm really not concerned about that anymore," I said, "but while he was here, I asked him again about my uncle's behavior on that last night they were together."

"What did he say?" Gordon leaned forward, listening intently.

I sighed. "He didn't remember that night due to his own inebriation. He does remember that my uncle was boasting of gold, as usual, but he doesn't remember any details."

Gordon sat back in his chair, sighing. "Well, when you see him he may be more truthful, once you've shown him this letter."

"More truthful? Gordon, do you think the man is being honest about that last night he was with Uncle Joshua?"

Gordon was studying his gold watch, checking the time. I didn't like the lengthy pause that preceded his answer. "I'm not sure, Abigail. He may not be as dumb as he seems. In my business, I've learned manners can be deceiving." He gave a short laugh, even though I did not find the situation very amusing.

"I really must be getting back to town. Will you come with me?"

I glanced around. I wasn't ready to leave just yet. "I have to finish sorting through Uncle Joshua's things. At any rate, I'm not afraid to be alone during the day; it's the nights . . ."

"I understand. There's an amusing play at the theater in town. Perhaps we could go tonight."

I smiled at him. "Yes, I'd like that."

"Shall I come back for you?"

I was staring at the letter again as my mind drifted back to Lonesome Bill. "No, I'll have Mr. Zarnoff drive me into Juneau."

He lifted my hand to his lips and pressed a kiss to my fingers. I thought of how he was always such a gentleman. It was a great contrast to Scott Morgan's bold kiss and probing eyes. I swallowed and forced my mind back to Gordon. "I'll be looking forward to the evening," he said.

"Yes, so will I." I followed him to the door and retrieved his hat and coat from the wall peg.

It was a clear, sunny day, and considering Juneau's tendency toward rain and fog, I knew the sunshine was a blessing. I could not have endured another day of fog and gloom. I closed the door and turned to glance about the room. Today, I would sort through the boxes and clutter. Perhaps Scott Morgan would want the books, and after that, maybe Gordon could suggest some families who would have need of the furnishings. No doubt a Tlingit family would appreciate some of the art . . .

I recalled Nona's sad face. Had she designed the blanket? The ceremonial mask? But I could hardly offer it back to her, considering her circumstances.

Squaring my shoulders, I entered the closet and began to sort through the boxes. I kept thinking of the map Uncle Joshua had mentioned, and I kept an eye out for it, but I never found it.

At noon I stopped for fruit and a sandwich. Since the weather was pleasant, I decided to have my lunch outside. I located a broad stump in the side yard and sat down, munching my sandwich and staring up at the clear blue sky.

The sun, spraying gold over the channel, offset the nip to the breeze as I breathed deeply of the fresh salt air. Perhaps Lonesome Bill had been mistaken about a blizzard rolling in. But if he feared a snowstorm, why had he headed into the high country? Or had he?

As I stared out into the channel, I spotted a boat bobbing along. I watched it as it covered the distance. Then I could see a dark-haired passenger wearing a familiar flannel shirt. Scott!

I caught my breath, wondering if he would stop. Perhaps he was going into town; that possibility was eliminated when the boat turned toward the shoreline.

With a flash of irritation, I realized my heartbeat had accelerated at the sight of him. I turned and tried to regain my composure. One could be deceived by a handsome face and charming manners, as Gordon had reminded me.

Gordon. I remembered how the very mention of his name had put Scott on edge. Well, there was no point in mentioning Gordon, or wasting my time thinking of Scott. I had to close up the house and prepare to leave Juneau.

"Hello," he called out as he anchored the boat.

"Hello. Lovely day, isn't it?" I said, glancing quickly toward the clear blue skies.

"Marvelous. How have you been?"

I looked back at him, trying to ignore the strange joy I felt just being near him. "Not so good. I'm leaving here," I said.

"Why?" he glanced toward the house. "What's happened?"

"Last night," I took a deep breath, "there was someone . . . something . . . in the closet."

"Something?"

"I don't know how to describe what I saw," I blurted. "It was like something inhuman, it was terrible." I covered my face with my hands, trying to shut out the horrible memory.

Strong hands were gently pulling my fingers away from my eyes—eyes that were rapidly filling with tears. Until now, terror or anger had kept those tears at bay; for some strange reason, Scott's presence had evoked them. Or perhaps one source of the tears was the deep awareness that I was strongly attracted to the man, and it was so hopeless!

"Wait a minute," he said, placing my hands between his and rubbing them gently. "Tell me exactly what you saw. Tell me everything."

I sniffed, blinking back the tears. "After I had gone to sleep, I heard footsteps on the stairs. I had the gun . . ." I broke off, remembering our argument over the gun.

"And?"

"And I went down the stairs and called for him to come out of his hiding place. He . . ." I swallowed as Scott lifted a hand to brush a tear from my cheek, "came out of the closet. I saw a very old Indian, Scott. Something ancient, something that had died years ago! He was laughing, only it wasn't a natural laugh. It was a shriek."

I could see his chest rising and falling rapidly as I told the story.

"I fired several shots, but he just kept coming, as though trying to prove to me that bullets would not stop him. It was terrible!"

I finished miserably, then studied his expression. I could see disbelief and doubt, and I didn't blame him. It was a story *I* would not have believed if I had not seen the creature with my own eyes.

I cleared my throat and continued. "Then the Zarnoffs came."

"The Zarnoffs?" he repeated, his tone sharpening.

"They had heard the shots . . ."

"They heard the shots from *that far away?*"

"Well . . . yes." I frowned, as he began to shake his head. For the first time, I considered the distance and felt a stab of doubt as well. "They came right away," I said quietly.

He turned his head, staring down the road.

I looked in that direction as well as I continued to relate what had happened.

"The old man would not come in, but James entered and searched the house. I could tell," I sighed heavily, "that they didn't believe there had been a prowler. And I began to feel stupid. I couldn't bring myself to describe the creature I had seen. You know how superstitious they are? I imagined they would make the creature out to be an evil spirit, which is . . almost what I have come to believe." I finished the story in a voice so low I doubted he had even heard me. But he had.

"Abby, you can't think like that," he scolded softly. "I'm not saying I don't believe you saw someone, but . . ."

"But *what?* You see, you *are* doubtful. And the worst part is, the doors were locked, with chairs pushed against them." I paused, took a deep breath, and sighed heavily. "So much has happened. A letter from Mother came yesterday. She informed me that my cousin is on his way here with more money. I'm going to pay off my uncle's debts, then leave with Tom. Mother also forwarded a letter from Uncle Joshua, one he had written shortly before he died, but which had somehow been lost in the mail. It was a cheerful letter. He told of finding a stream with nuggets. He said he had marked the spot, drawn a map, and would go back when the ice and snow melted . . ." My voice trailed off as it suddenly occurred to me that I was revealing a lot to this man, still a stranger in many ways.

Scott shoved his hands deep in his pockets and glanced down the road again. "I'm on my way to Douglas Island to interview a miner who has just returned from Yukon country. He claims to have found gold there. When I return, I'll see what I can find out for you. Abby, it's possible that someone is trying to frighten you off."

"But who would do that? And why?"

"I'm not sure. But I don't believe in spirits who walk through walls. Someone has a key to this house."

The words hit like small pebbles, stinging my brain with an important fact I had stupidly forgotten.

Yes, someone did have a key.

Nona Zarnoff!

Chapter 11

I don't know why I didn't reveal the news of the key to Scott. Perhaps it was my womanly intuition that Nona had done nothing more harmful than fall in love with my uncle. I could see that Scott was suspicious of the Zarnoffs. If I told him about Nona, he would start thinking . . .

What?

That perhaps a jealous husband had followed my drunken uncle home that night, and in a rage, shot him? Or that old man Zarnoff had taken up the task himself?

My mind was racing so fast that I could scarcely keep up. "When you leave the house, where are you going?" Scott was asking.

"I'll stay at one of the hotels until Tom arrives. The Occidental, I suppose." I had to get off to myself and think this through in a place where I felt safe.

"I think that's a good idea," he agreed, still staring thoughtfully down the road.

"Incidentally, have you see the man they call Lonesome Bill?" I asked.

A curious expression touched his features. "No. Why?"

"I had planned to give him some of Uncle Joshua's things. Also, I wanted to ask him if he knew anything about the map Uncle Joshua refers to in the letter."

Was it my imagination, or did Scott's eyes slide away from me at the mention of the map?

"Lonesome Bill is usually easy to find," he said, without

referring again to the map. "I'll have a look around town while I'm waiting for the ferry to Douglas Island."

He looked back at me again, his eyes filled with an expression I could not read.

"I'll find you when I return. In the meantime, take care, Abby." His voice was filled with concern.

"Yes, I will," I answered, watching as he turned and strode toward the boat. It felt as though my heart was going with him, and again I wished that the heart hadn't a mind of its own, for I feared it had not made a sensible choice.

Take care, he had said. It was the same advice the steamship captain had given me when I'd arrived in Juneau. I *would* take care, I decided, and the best way to do that was to *leave.*

I tossed the remainder of my sandwich to the birds and hurried back to the house. All the while I was thinking of Nona Zarnoff and the key. It had not been Nona who had emerged from the closet, I argued with myself. And yet she was Tlingit; perhaps she had given the key to a Tlingit friend—an ancient friend!

I paused in the yard, glancing across at the distant cemetery.

There was no explaining what I had seen, and so I must push last night's nightmare from my mind. Perhaps in town I would speak with Deputy Wilson, although I could imagine how such a wild tale would sound to him. If he started checking, the Zarnoffs would tell him the doors were locked and reinforced with chairs. Then it would be Crazy Abigail, legacy of Crazy Josh!

The key, I told myself, trying to cling to something logical.

When I entered the house, I looked around the room, too bewildered to think what to do next. The steamer was due in a few days. I would only need to pack a couple of dresses to wait out my stay at the hotel. When Tom arrived, we would return to pick up my trunk and make a decision about the house.

I climbed the stairs to the bedroom and began to sort through my clothing. Then suddenly my eyes fell to Uncle Joshua's tablet of poems on the beside table.

I sat down on the bed, picked up the tablet and riffled through it again. I would take the tablet home with me. We would publish some of the poems in the newspaper as a tribute to Uncle Joshua.

I looked over the poems briefly, then hesitated on the final one, amazed again at how little sense it made.

Then I turned the page and looked at the clean sheet of paper that followed it. My eyes moved to the top of the tablet, expecting to see a ridge where the sheet of paper had been torn away, the sheet of paper on which he'd written the suicide note.

The top of the tablet was smooth, however; no sheet had been ripped from the top, leaving the usual frayed edge. Puzzled, I flipped back through the tablet, finding several tears at the top. Slowly, I worked my way from front to back, finding six tears to indicate missing sheets of paper. The first one was near the front of the tablet, the second and third were spaced between several poems. The fourth and fifth were consecutive. The last tear was the sheet before the final poem, the poem that had made no sense at all.

I sat staring at the tablet, sensing there was a message here. Had he simply skipped a sheet of paper when he'd written the strange poem? And then on that fatal night, had he opened the tablet, thumbed through to the first blank page, and ripped it out to pen his final words?

I cannot go on

My eyes lifted to the sun rays dancing through the bedroom window. He meant he could not go on without Nona. She had told him she could not see him again, that they were moving to Sitka. Then, after a night of drinking, he had come home, slipped into a deep depression, and finally decided he could not go on without her.

I closed the tablet and laid it on the table, sick at heart. If only Uncle Joshua had come back to San Francisco, if only he had remembered he still had a good life there with family and friends.

I chose a couple of dresses and some undergarments and packed them in a satchel. I added my jewelry and an extra pair of shoes. Then I went back downstairs and checked the fire, already dwindled to mere coals.

I did not bother to lock the doors. If anyone wanted to come inside and help themselves to whatever was here, I no longer cared. I reached for my cloak and set off up the path to the Zarnoff cabin.

Halfway there, I came upon Jamie.

"I was coming to tell you I can't spend the night," he said drearily.

This news did not come as a surprise. "It's all right; I've decided to stay at the hotel," I replied.

His dark eyes swept over me, then shot up the road. I imagined he was staring at the house behind me.

"Are you afraid?" he asked quietly.

What was the point of pretending anymore? "Yes," I admitted. "I don't like staying there by myself. I plan to stay at the hotel until my cousin arrives."

"Then what are you going to do?" he asked, tilting his head to study me curiously.

"Then we'll pay my uncle's debts and return to San Francisco."

It was no secret that my uncle owed everyone in town; perhaps Jamie could spread the word around and relieve some worries.

"What are you going to do about that house?" he asked as his eyes darted back up the road. He had fallen in step with me and now we were clipping along at a brisk pace.

"I don't know," I sighed. "Do you have any suggestions?"

He was silent for a moment, watching the flight of an eagle across the sky. "Maybe they could turn it back into a church."

I cast a sharp glance at him and thought about that. "That's a possibility, Jamie."

I looked into his dark eyes and thought of his mother again. I recalled her tears, the pain in her voice, the words she had spoken. It was all so sad. I took a deep breath and studied the Zarnoff cabin as we approached.

"Do you want me to walk to town with you?" he asked.

"I hadn't planned to walk," I smiled. "I was going to ask your grandfather to drive me to town. Is he at home?"

"Yes'm. He and my father are sanding down the fishing boat around back. I'll get him!" He shot across the yard to the back of the house.

My nose twitched as I shifted from one foot to the other while I stood waiting, breathing the smell of dried fish which still permeated the yard. A door slammed, and Mrs. Zarnoff stood on the porch. She was wearing a man's shirt and pants and the usual black rubber boots. Her eyes fell to my satchel and widened curiously.

"I'm going to stay at the hotel in Juneau until my cousin arrives," I explained.

She nodded and she glanced up the road, to the house I had left. I decided to let her think whatever she wanted; I was beyond making excuses or explaining anything to anyone.

"What will you do?" she asked, tilting her head to study me again.

"I'll go home to San Francisco after I pay my uncle's debts."

"And the church will be empty once again." She spoke in a hushed tone, as though we were standing now in the center of the church and regarding it with reverence.

I stared at her. There was no mistaking the fact that she was pleased to know the *cheechako* was leaving.

"That's right, Mrs. Zarnoff. The house will be empty. And for all I care, you people can have it back!" I had spoken the words hastily, impulsively, but now I realized that Jamie's suggestion made sense. It was not suited for a normal home, nor would it ever be.

Her eyes widened; her mouth fell open.

The door was thrown open, and Zarnoff stepped onto the porch, wearing his work clothes but missing his fur cap. His huge bald head gleamed as though it had been polished.

"You are ready to go?" he asked curtly.

"Yes, if you can spare the time to take me."

"I'm ready."

Without saying more to Mrs. Zarnoff, who leaned against the door, watching me carefully, I climbed up into the wagon. As we set off for town, I glanced back over my shoulder and saw that she had shaded her eyes with a plump hand and stood watching us as we drove out of sight.

Zarnoff's eyes dropped to the satchel but he made no comment. I pretended a keen interest in a bird over the channel, hoping to avoid any further conversation, not that there was a chance of it, considering Zarnoff's nature. I was still embarrassed about the incident the previous evening. I imagined the Zarnoffs thought I was a hysterical woman given to nightmares and weird visions. Unless, of course, they knew more about those *visions* than I did.

We passed the trip in silence, until finally the rattling wagon approached the outskirts of Juneau.

"You can drop me off at the Occidental Hotel," I said.

"For how long?" Was his voice less gruff, or had I imagined it?

"Until I leave for San Francisco in a few days."

When I glanced at him, I could see a question on his face, but of course he was too proud, or too stubborn, to ask for details. I decided not to provide any; since he was the champion of silence, perhaps he would appreciate mine. Let him figure things out for himself until he returned home, when his wife would be more than happy to relate good news!

The Occidental Hotel, newly built and furnished with modern conveniences, was a great improvement over a Russian abbey. The desk clerk was pleasant, informing me that for two dollars a day, I could obtain board and lodging. How foolish it now seemed that I had insisted on staying out at Uncle Joshua's place!

The second floor contained a reading room, a billiard hall, and a parlor for ladies. However, once I reached the privacy of my room, I had no desire to socialize with the guests. I needed privacy and safety, and I would have both here.

I wandered across the small room, and looked out the window facing the theater across the street. I was looking forward to going there tonight with Gordon.

Removing my hat and placing it on the dresser, I sat down in a chair beside the window and flipped through the newspaper I had purchased in the lobby. An article on the front page related the latest gold news from the Yukon country, and I recalled that Scott had gone to Douglas Island for an interview.

I sighed wearily as I imagined an exodus of miners in that direction now. Thoughts of Uncle Joshua began to nag at me once more as I laid the newspaper aside and stared at the Brussels carpet.

For some reason, his last poem bothered me now more than ever. That and the order of the missing pages in the tablet. Father had often said, when referring to business matters, that he sometimes found it necessary to get away from the newspaper office for a day or two in order to think a problem through. I understood that. Away from the house, and no longer caught up in the eerie spell it cast, I could think more logically. If there had not been so many different problems, it might have been easier to deal with one at a time. Instead, I could never focus on anything long enough to find an answer.

Feeling safe and secure, I allowed my mind to wander back to the night before, to see again in my memory the wild creature that had frightened me half to death. While the creature still seemed to be an enigma, there was an important fact to consider: someone had a key to the house, and that someone was Nona. Certainly it was not Nona I had seen, but perhaps it *was* a Tlingit relative or friend who had come to prowl in the closet for . . . something.

The map?

No, the face was inhuman. And why had my bullets failed to stop him?

I sighed, closing my eyes. I had never fired a gun, and my hands were trembling so badly that it was quite likely that I had merely fired off-center enough to miss.

Scott had suggested that someone might be trying to scare me, but he hadn't seen, as I had, the creature . . . which was not a *someone.*

I pushed aside that problem for the moment, for there seemed to be no way to solve or understand it.

I glanced at my satchel, wishing I had brought along Uncle Joshua's tablet. I would feel more inclined to study it here; maybe I could discern something new.

I glanced back through the window to the rowdy town perched precariously above the channel. Plank walks climbed from the waterfront to the townsite, overlaying potholes in the streets, in places. Some of the boards were splintered, and I could see why as I watched the iron-shod hooves of a dray horse pulling a cart.

My eyes fell to the swarm of people below, and I found myself searching for the long, lanky frame of Lonesome Bill. He held a missing piece to the puzzle. I was certain of it! Before I left Juneau, I would find him. This time I would persuade him to tell me the truth—even if I must enlist Deputy Marshall Wilson's help.

What if Lonesome Bill had left town? What if he were one of the sourdoughs already heading to the Yukon?

What if he had the map in his pocket?

My eyes returned to the theater across the street, and I squinted to read the bill of tonight's play. "Loon's Cry." I frowned. That did not sound like the amusing performance I needed. I got out of the chair and began to unpack my satchel, thinking whatever the performance, it would divert my mind for the evening.

As I hung the last dress, a low knock touched the door, and I jumped as though it were a gunshot. I had to get a grip on my nerves. Otherwise, all my bravado about being self-sufficient would dissolve before Tom's eyes when he arrived.

"Who is it?" I called.

"It's Gordon."

With a sigh of relief, I unlocked the door.

"I'm so glad you're here," he said, smiling, "but I'm sorry to say we cannot attend the theater tonight. An important meeting of the town commissioners has been called. I'm sorry," he said, shaking his head. "Perhaps later . . ."

"It's all right, Gordon," I replied, forcing a smile. "I'm planning to go to bed early anyway. I haven't slept well lately."

"I understand. Well, you can take your meals downstairs."

"Yes, I will. Please don't feel responsible for me. I'll be just fine."

He reached forward and squeezed my hand. "Then I'll see you tomorrow."

After Gordon left, I paced the room, feeling frustrated and alone. I decided to go downstairs for dinner. I had met several people in Juneau, but when I reached the dining room, I found myself alone in a roomful of strangers.

Then, after I was seated and had ordered a meal of chicken and rice, Edna Vanderhoof appeared in the doorway, glancing around.

She was wearing the gray woolen suit and matching feathered hat she had worn upon our arrival, and this helped me recognize her quickly.

"Miss Vanderhoof!" I called to her.

"Miss Martin!" She rushed to my table with a friendly smile.

"Please!" I reached out and gripped her hand, "won't you join me for dinner?"

Her eyes widened at my exuberant response to her. Obviously, my mood had changed since she'd last seen me. During that time I had been polite yet reserved; now I was practically begging for friendship.

"I'd love to join you," she said, her eyes sweeping over me then darting back around the room, "but I'm meeting friends here. Since I don't see them, I assume they've already gone upstairs to the card room. They play cards here every Tuesday evening. Would you like to join us?" she asked suddenly.

I repressed a deep sigh. "No, thank you." My mind was too frantic to concentrate on a game of cards. "Do you have time for a cup of tea?" I pressed.

"Well, perhaps just a quick one," she relented, dropping into the chair opposite me.

"I neglected to ask who you were visiting," I said. "I don't know many people here."

"Oh? Well, the couple I'm meeting for cards came here from Portland several years ago. They're the William Wrights, and he owns the jewelry store. You must meet them. Won't you. . . ?"

"Some other time," I interrupted gently. Now I must think of an excuse to keep refusing her invitations. Through the window I could see the lights of the theater. "I'm going across the street to see a play this evening."

"Oh, yes," she nodded comprehendingly, " 'The Loon's Cry.' We saw it last night. It's a delightful little play about a crazy bird." Her eyes swept over the room as she sipped her tea. "I cannot believe a lady as lovely as you is dining alone."

"A friend was to have joined me, but he had a business meeting at the last minute."

She lifted an eyebrow and grinned conspiratorially. "Ah, so you have found a young man here!"

Two, I almost blurted. "Just a friend," I smiled. "He's helping me take care of my late uncle's business."

"I see. Well, I trust you're having an enjoyable stay."

"Well . . ." I began, then broke off. Why go into details? She was not likely to understand or be of help. "It's been rather hectic," I explained. "I was disappointed when I learned that my uncle's debts were rather extensive, and then . . ." I broke off, upon realizing I had lost her attention.

She was looking toward the door, smiling and waving.

"Oh! There's Mary now," she said, waving wildly.

A plump middle-aged woman dressed in a dark woolen dress with lace collar and cuffs sauntered over to the table.

"Mary, here's Abigail Martin. Remember I told you about the nice young woman I met on the ship?"

"Oh, yes, of course! I'm Mary Wright," she said, her plump face wrinkling in a wide smile. "Why don't you come over and have tea with us in the morning?"

"I . . ."

"Yes, do that!" Edna insisted, hopping to her feet. "It's three streets over, the fourth house on the right."

"The one with the little birdhouse on the front porch," Mary laughed.

"Enjoy the play," Edna called over her shoulder, "and don't let that crazy sound rattle your nerves."

"Crazy sound?"

"The loon's cry," she answered rather impatiently. "You've probably heard loons here in the evening. They make a wild, nerve-racking sound if you're not accustomed to it. Well, see you later." She tapped my shoulder and flew off.

I leaned back in the chair, thinking. No doubt it was a loon I had heard in the evenings. Still, I would like to know for sure, and perhaps I would learn at the theater. I paid the bill and hurried out of the dining room and across the street to purchase a ticket for the play.

The fact that I was alone brought a few suspicious glances my way, but most were eager to get inside the theater. I hurried down the narrow aisle and settled comfortably into a back row just as the lights dimmed and the curtain went up.

The narrator came onto the stage dressed in a colorful Indian costume. Then, to catch the attention of the audience, a tall creature lumbered behind him and marched around the stage, also in a colorful garb. I bolted to the edge of my seat. Several people around me must have heard my loud gasp. I imagine they thought it was merely a response to the wild creature on stage.

I stared in disbelief.

Quite clearly, the actor was wearing a mask . . . and I had seen that mask only the night before! My heart was hammering as I continued to stare while he leered at the crowd who jeered back at him in fun.

Yes, it was the same face I had seen at the house! Yet this was a very tall man, much taller than the one who I thought had walked through the walls. One thing was perfectly clear: the person who stepped from my closet was not inhuman after all . . . he merely wore a mask.

He—or she?

Chapter 12

I stumbled from the theater in a daze. No doubt I was a subject of discussion to the theater employees later, since I had come alone, remained no more than ten minutes, then rushed back into the lobby as though I had seen a ghost.

Of course I felt, for a moment, that I had. Quickly I crossed the street to the hotel and flew up the steps to my room. It was not until I was safely inside, with the door locked, that the wild beat of my heart began to subside.

My mind was still spinning with the image of that horrible face, the mask. However, as I sank into a chair and caught my breath, the mystery of the midnight visitor, which had engulfed me like a fog, began to clear.

Someone was deliberately trying to frighten me. Who?

Unfortunately, the suspicious trail led back to Nona Zarnoff.

She was an artist, a craftsman. She could create a mask like the one the actor wore. She might have designed that very mask. And the Tlingit blanket that she had fashioned into a cape for herself was similar to the narrator's cape.

I turned in the chair and stared blankly at the theater across the street. I didn't want to believe that the woman my uncle had loved was capable of such trickery and deception. Why would she do it?

The Zarnoffs wanted the church back. Perhaps they were all in cahoots to frighten off *cheechakos!* Or had she been lying about her love for my uncle? Was his money the true source of her interest? The Zarnoffs were obviously poor; quite likely, her husband was as well.

I lowered the shade and began to undress as the weight of weariness crept over me. I needed a good night's rest; my nerves were strung wire-tight.

As I pulled on my flannel gown and slipped into bed, my mind still lingered on Nona Zarnoff. She was the one person to whom my uncle was most vulnerable, the one person who could easily have taken advantage of him.

And if there was, in fact, a map, was it possible that Nona Zarnoff had it as well?

I awoke haunted by the silly poem Uncle Joshua had written. All of his poetry had a special meaning; what meaning did his final poem have?

Silver spurs. The words returned to haunt me, and I thought of Scott again. His were the only silver spurs I had seen. Perhaps I should start looking around.

Like one caught up in a game, I found that each person I had met suddenly became a character in that game. Zarnoff. Mrs. Zarnoff. Nona. Lonesome Bill. Gordon. Scott. All had dealings with my uncle, but only Scott wore silver spurs.

But Scott was not a murderer! He had no reason to kill my uncle, so I must disregard his silver spurs as merely a coincidence.

I got out of bed, pulled on my dressing gown, and walked to the window to stare out at the theater. I was not certain which one of the Zarnoffs had worn the mask, but their efforts to scare me away had finally paid off.

I sighed. What did it matter now? I was much better off here at the hotel, for I could now appreciate heat and electrically lighted rooms.

It was a dreary day. My eyes moved from the theater to the people on the streets below. They were dressed in heavy coats, and I could see the weather was changing.

I reached into the wardrobe and withdrew my blue woolen dress with black braid trim and matching blue hat. It would be pleasant to have tea this morning with Edna and

Mary, who did not regard me suspiciously. After I had dressed and netted my hair, I tossed my cloak about my shoulders and hurried downstairs.

As I crossed the lobby, I noticed a few well-dressed men seated in chairs, reading newspapers. I remembered the article that Scott had written, and suddenly those thoughts of Scott brought a sad twinge to my heart. I had to stop thinking of him; or if I thought of him, it would be to investigate those silver spurs. I would soon be leaving; I would never see him again.

Mary Wright's house was located three blocks from the hotel on a street of small frame houses. All had a similar appearance with their steep-pitched roofs and tiny chimneys busily puffing smoke. I searched for the one with a birdhouse on the porch and quickly found it.

As I climbed the narrow wooden steps, the door flew open, and Mary Wright smiled and bade me good morning.

"Do come in out of this gruesome weather," she said, opening the door wider for me to enter.

"Good morning," I responded, enjoying the warmth of the cozy little house where crocheted doilies, overstuffed sofas, and chairs added a sense of home.

"Here, let me take your cloak!" she offered, just as Edna popped through the door.

"My, but don't you look pretty!" Edna exclaimed. "Mary and I were just talking about how lucky you are to have natural blonde hair."

"And that fair skin and blue eyes don't hurt a thing!" Mary said, her round face crinkling in a wide smile.

"Who was that young man you were talking about," Edna inquired, "the one who was supposed to take you to the theater?"

"Oh, he's just a friend," I explained with a smile. "It's Gordon Walling."

"Well, be glad you have him on your side," Mary called

over her shoulder as she hung up my cloak.

I fought the blush that threatened. She was obviously referring to Uncle Joshua's debts. Was there no escaping that shadow?

Edna patted my shoulder. "I'm so glad you came this morning. I told Mary, I said, Mary . . ."

As Edna lapsed into another of her lengthy accounts, Mary interrupted with a comment. Both ladies, talking simultaneously, drew me into the dining room, where a pot of tea and a loaf of freshly baked bread sent up a heavenly aroma.

I took the seat she offered and stared appreciatively at the golden-crusted bread.

"You look as though you've lost some weight," Edna said, perching on the chair next to me.

"I'll bet you aren't eating right," Mary said, as she took her seat at the table and poured tea. "But then you've probably had no appetite, what with staying all alone up at that old abbey."

I glanced quickly at her, hopeful for information.

"I assume you know about my uncle's house," I said, unfolding the napkin and smoothing down my full skirt.

She shook her head sadly as she handed me a cup of tea. "I'm afraid everyone knows about your uncle and that abbey! No one could comprehend why he would buy that place and try to make it into a home! Why, there were plenty of places to live right here in town!"

"What's that?" Edna interrupted, leaning forward in her chair. "He bought a church and tried to make it into a house?" she cackled, tilting her head to look from Mary to me.

I was beginning to feel annoyed by their narrow views, but my mood changed when Mary placed a thick slice of her homemade bread on a china plate and set it before me.

"Here, dear; have some of my berry jam." She indicated a cut-glass jar filled with dark red preserves.

"Thank you. Mrs. Zarnoff brought me some jam, but I

believe I was allergic to it."

"Well, my jam won't hurt you," Mary said firmly, as she handed a plate to Edna. "I am very careful in my preparations. As for Mrs. Zarnoff," she sighed, "God only knows what she might have put in *her* jam!"

Or in mine, I thought grimly.

"Who are you two talking about?" Edna inquired, her mouth full.

"A strange Russian lady who lives up the inlet," Mary explained, looking back at me. "She's your neighbor, isn't she?"

"Yes. And they *are* strange people. May I ask what you know about them?"

"Very little," she replied, offhandedly. "The Russians are rather clannish. Every now and then one comes into the jewelry store, but few have any money. Except for Nona Zarnoff, that is."

"Nona has money?" I asked, surprised.

"Well," Mary shrugged lightly, "she does well with her jewelry and art. As a matter of fact, we sometimes take her bracelets on consignment at the store."

I remembered the silver bracelets she wore, with the intricately carved designs.

"She does other things as well," I said, deciding to test my theory. "Doesn't she make masks, like those they wear at the theater?"

"I believe she does," Mary nodded, sipping her tea. "She's quite versatile. Now Edna," she looked at our friend who was helping herself to another slice of the tasty bread, "you asked me to help you watch your weight this time."

I glanced at Edna while thinking over this news of Nona. I had to learn more.

"Mary, may I ask why you think Nona has money?" I asked. "I mean, I wouldn't have thought an occasional piece of jewelry or a few masks would bring much money."

"Why, I'm judging from the way she spends money around town," she answered quickly, obviously chagrined that I would question her opinion. "And she always seems to have money in her pocket," she continued. "Whenever I see her, she's making a purchase somewhere. I *assume* she does well on her jewelry. Of course, her husband is a fisherman, but that sort of work is seasonal and undependable, even though . . ."

"My late husband tried fishing right after we married," Edna interrupted, staring out the window. "But it was not dependable work, and he wanted to make a good living for me. I remember he said, 'Edna,' he said. . . ."

My eyes met Mary's over the cup as Edna launched into a detailed account of her late husband's millinery shop. Mary's plump face held an affectionate grin as she glanced back at Edna. Obviously she had been a sounding board for Edna since her arrival.

While Edna droned on, I assembled my thoughts for the next question. When she paused to draw a breath, I quickly spoke up.

"Mary, did you know my uncle?" I asked quickly.

Her brows peaked. "Not very well, actually. We were never introduced, that is. He did come in the store one day when I had taken William his lunch. I remember he bought a handsome stickpin," she said, her expression thoughtful. "But that was a long time ago." She turned and smiled at me. "I think it must have been when he first came to Juneau. I never saw much of him after that. Oh, except for that night at the hotel when we were going to play cards, and . . ." she hesitated.

"And?" I leaned forward, eager to hear.

"And he was having dinner in the dining room with that Morgan fellow from Portland. I wouldn't have noticed, except for their argument."

"They were arguing?"

"Who was arguing?" Edna interrupted, coming back to the moment, and catching only the last words of our conversation.

"Joshua Martin and that young man, Morgan," Mary explained with an edge of impatience.

"Scott Morgan?" I repeated the name, wanting to be sure we were discussing the same person, although I doubted there was another young Morgan from Portland in a town the size of Juneau.

"Yes, he's a bit of a rogue," she said off handedly. "Anyway . . ."

"Rogue?" I repeated, my spine stiffening.

"Oh yes," she lifted a hand airily. "He's from our hometown."

"Did you know him in Portland?"

"No, but we knew of his family. I understand he's the grandson of Templeton Morgan, who is quite wealthy," she explained, brushing a crumb from her lap. "Apparently, this young man was disinherited."

"Why do you say that?" I pushed aside my cup and plate, my appetite vanishing.

"Well," she looked back at me curiously, "why else would he strike out up here with no money, and then chop wood for a living?" She surveyed me suspiciously. "Have you been associating with him?"

I cleared my throat. "He brought firewood to me. However, since he was a friend of my uncle's, I have not bothered to avoid him." I could hear the defensive note in my voice, and I looked at Mary and forced a smile, trying to revert to a more casual manner.

"Firewood?" Edna asked, staring. "You mean you had to build fires up there?"

"It's up in the wilds, Edna," Mary explained hastily, clearing away the plates.

My smile was beginning to stiffen as a sort of condescending attitude had overtaken Mary. The attitude change had begun with Scott, I realized. She obviously did not have a favorable impression of him.

I lifted a hand to my forehead, where a dull ache had begun; I tried to return to the matter we had been discussing. "He was arguing with my uncle, you say?"

"Yes." Mary frowned. "Rather heatedly, as I remember. And they seemed unaware that they were making a scene."

"What were they arguing about?" Edna asked, sneaking another bite of bread.

"Oh, how should I know?" Mary said breezily. "We didn't stop to listen; we just glanced in the dining room as we passed, after we heard raised voices."

"Did you see them together often?" I asked.

"No. Morgan seems to be a loner. Your uncle was usually surrounded by other friends." She glanced back at me, her eyes sympathetic now. "It's too bad things ended as they did for him."

"How did they end?" Edna blurted.

I saw the warning glance that Mary sent in Edna's direction. Nevertheless, Edna remained oblivious, being either too dense, or too nosy, to take a hint.

"What happened to your uncle?" she pressed, her head cocked sideways, her blue eyes fixed on me curiously. Once again, she reminded me of a bird, a bothersome blue jay.

I took a deep breath. "It seems he enjoyed the gaming tables more than he should have. And," I hesitated, then decided on total honesty, "he drank too much toward the end." I hoped that explanation would be sufficient. I couldn't bring myself to recount the death.

"Well," Mary said, shaking her head and staring at her cup, "we mustn't be too harsh in our judgments. He had some bitter disappointments, I understand."

"What exactly do you mean?" I asked deliberately.

"Well, the gold . . ."

"The *gold?*"

"Perhaps I shouldn't mention it," she hesitated, looking contrite.

"Please go on," I insisted.

"I know the townspeople thought Mr. Martin was a bit of a . . . well, a braggart," she replied slowly, choosing her words with care.

"What did *you* think?" I asked, steeling myself for what I

assumed would be another negative response to my uncle's character.

She pressed her lips together firmly and thought for a moment. "My husband believed him," she finally answered. "William happened to be at the assayer's office having a gold watch appraised when your uncle came in with the nugget."

I caught my breath, swallowed, then tried to speak in a normal voice.

"The nugget?" I repeated.

"Yes. The one he found up at his stream."

"Then he *did* find a nugget!" I blurted.

She shrugged. "Well, that is . . ."

"Mary, why don't you just speak your mind?" Edna burst out. "You're making me nervous."

"Oh all right," she snapped, glancing hotly at Edna. "The town gossips said he never found any gold, that he . . . well, that he lied a bit when he was drinking. But my husband saw the nugget!"

I was frozen in my chair, tensely awaiting each word she spoke. To think I had debated about coming for tea! Now I felt as though I had once again stumbled onto something very important.

"What else did your husband say?" I asked carefully.

Her plump face rumpled in a frown. "As I recall, he just said that Mr. Martin brought in a small nugget as William was leaving the assayer's shop. William did not wait to hear the assayer's report, but he said it looked real to him. It was, mind you, a small nugget," she conceded.

"I understand. And which assayer's shop was it?"

"It would have been Clarence Holman's place, there on Front Street. That's where William goes."

I folded my napkin and placed it on the table. "Thank you for telling me that." I stood, looking from one woman to the other. "And thank you for inviting me over. Now I really must get on with my shopping this morning."

Edna lurched to her feet. "Must you go?"

"Well, I have errands . . ."

"My dear," Mary said, laying her hand on my arm, "I hope all this talk about your uncle hasn't been upsetting to you. I can imagine this entire situation has been most distressing to you and your family."

"Yes, but the trip hasn't been a complete disappointment. Juneau is an interesting place," I said with a smile. "And I've enjoyed having tea with you."

"Are you going out on the steamer this week?" Edna asked as they followed me to the door.

"Yes, I plan to. My cousin is on his way to accompany me back to San Francisco."

"Then we'll be traveling companions again!" Edna clasped her hands before her, her blue eyes twinkling.

"Yes, we will," I said, swallowing a sigh as I threw the cloak around my shoulders and tied the strings under my chin.

"Well, the tide is right," Mary said. "The steamer should be on time; perhaps it may even come early."

I nodded. "Thank you so much for tea. Well, good day, ladies." I waved and hurried down the sidewalk, heading directly for the assayer's office on Front Street. Obviously, settling the score for Uncle Joshua was not yet over. In fact, it might have just begun. . . .

Chapter 13

I found the shop easily enough, but obtaining information from the assayer was quite another matter. He was a tiny man with a beak nose and thin face framed by wispy black hair. He put me in mind of a raven.

"I'm Abigail Martin," I began, upon entering the tiny, cluttered shop. "I'm Joshua Martin's niece."

The dark eyes snapped wide before he pretended a sudden interest in a small rock lying on the counter.

"What can I do for you?" he demanded abruptly.

"I wanted to ask you something," I said. "My uncle brought a nugget here to be assayed back in the spring. Would you please tell me the value of that nugget?"

With infinite precision, he laid the rock aside and slowly, carefully, wiped his hands. He seemed to be stalling for time.

I watched him closely, for I sensed his hostility, and that had put me on guard immediately.

His sharp eyes drifted back to me, and he shrugged. "Miss Martin, do you have any idea how many miners have brought nuggets to me, most of which are worthless?"

"No, I have no idea, and I'm afraid I'm not interested in other miners' nuggets. I'm only inquiring about the one my uncle brought to you."

A caustic grin worked at his thin lips. "It's impossible to remember all of the nuggets, particularly if they are worthless."

I drew myself up and fixed an unwavering stare upon him.

"What is your name?" I asked abruptly.

He blinked in surprise. Obviously he was not accustomed to a woman who called his bluff.

"Clarence Holman."

"Mr. Holman, I would hope that you have some sort of business procedure here. An accounting system . . . perhaps even a set of books. Naturally I wouldn't expect you to remember every nugget that was brought to you; but I am certain that you must make some sort of notation."

"Yes, I have a ledger," he answered stiffly. He turned and opened a desk drawer and withdrew a thick tome with yellowed, dog-eared pages.

I fought back a deep sigh when I looked at it. Obviously many, many people had come to him with nuggets. I had a flickering sense of why he had become jaded after so long; still, I was determined not to be outdone.

"When did you say your uncle might have come in?" he asked over his shoulder, as he began to flip back through the pages.

I took a wild guess. "Sometime last fall. I understand you had a bad winter. Do you recall when the first snow came?"

He glared at me, scarcely concealing his irritation over being put to the trouble of tracking down my uncle's visit. "That would have been October, I believe." He scanned through the pages, heaving a disgusted sigh.

"There's nothing in either September or October," he said, his voice muffled as he lowered his head, tracing each column of names with a long, bony finger.

I felt a temporary stab of defeat, but held on stubbornly. The last letter was dated March. Perhaps he had just located the spot and drawn a map!

"Would you please check the month of March? I'm sure you're very busy," I continued determinedly. "If you don't mind, I'll just take a seat over there and look back through the ledger."

At that veiled threat, he clasped it tightly against his chest, as though the ledger itself was precious gold.

"I do not allow *anyone* to go through my ledger!" he snapped.

I had had quite enough of him. "Not even Deputy Wilson?" I narrowed my eyes and glared at him. "Mr. Holman, I intend to go directly to the deputy's office upon leaving here, unless you decide to be more cooperative. After all, I don't believe that I have made an unreasonable request, considering certain, er, circumstances." At those last words, his eyes darkened. He obviously knew what I meant.

"Just time consuming," he said huffily, as he laid the book down on the counter and began to flip slowly through the dog-eared pages.

"Well, you don't appear to have anyone standing in line," I said, glancing innocently around the empty office.

I knew I had made an enemy, but I didn't care. I would be leaving soon, and I intended to pursue this last, important link to Uncle Joshua's life . . . or death!

I placed my elbows on the counter and watched him closely, deliberately, silently confirming that I would not be put off again.

The pages fluttered beneath his fingers as he riffled back to a page with "March" scrawled darkly across the top.

I strained to read the names in the columns, where ink was smeared like dark footprints in the margin. Even though I was pressed flat against the counter, I was still unable to read each name. When his eyes shot back to me and a scowl crossed his face, he obviously thought I had spotted my uncle's name, for he threw the ledger down before me.

"He was here in March," he pointed.

Eagerly, my eyes flew to the crowded column of names. I read "Joshua L. Martin," then an inscription beside the name.

"What does it say?" I glanced at him.

He shrugged. "Just that it was a sizable nugget. *But it was not gold,"* he announced, watching smugly as he delivered the bad news.

I stared at the notation, then glanced at the other names. There was no such notation by the others. There was merely a figure. He slammed the book and I looked at him in surprise, unable to dispel my lingering suspicion.

"My uncle wrote to say he had found a stream with gold. He was very enthusiastic. Is there another assayer's office in Juneau?"

"I'm afraid not. As for your uncle being so certain his nugget was gold, that's not surprising. That's how the term *fool's gold* originated," he said with a smug grin.

"Perhaps not everyone is as foolish as you think," I said coldly, watching his jaw drop before I turned and swept out of his musty little shop, slamming the door behind me.

My temper was in full blaze as I made my way up the scarred plank walk leading to the center of town. A cold breath of wind blew over the channel and flirted with my hat. Grabbing the brim, I turned and looked across the deep blue water. Somewhere far south of here the steamer was chugging dutifully toward this destination. I had much to do before it arrived.

Knowing my cousin Tom, he would not favor a delay to investigate one gold nugget, or, for that matter, even Uncle Joshua's death. Unfortunately, like so many others, he too had lost respect for my poor uncle.

I had almost reached the hotel when I saw her.

A dark-hooded cloak enclosed the small woman as she stood idly staring into a shop. She turned, and I could see her profile, small and sharp, against the fringe of black hair creeping from her hood. I had suspected it was Nona Zarnoff when she lifted a hand to brush back a strand of hair, and the silver bracelets jangled. Now I was certain.

I quickened my steps, trying to reach her before she entered the shop.

"Nona," I called out.

She whirled at the sound of my voice, and I caught up

quickly. Her startled expression softened to a smile as she said hello.

"I'd like to speak with you," I said matter of factly.

Her dark eyes widened. "I haven't long," she said.

"It won't take long! We can have a cup of tea in the hotel dining room while we talk."

She relented, seeing there was little choice. We hurried through the front door of the hotel and into the lobby, which fortunately was uncrowded at this early hour.

Once we had taken our seat in the dining room and ordered tea, I folded my hands on the damask cloth and looked into her thin face. She was pale, her features drawn; and now that paleness increased as I stared at her.

"I'll come right to the point," I said. "Do you know why anyone would come to the house and try to frighten me?"

She opened her mouth, then hesitated.

"Before you draw any conclusions about me being overly anxious, easily frightened, or stupidly naive, let me explain why I am asking. The person wore a mask exactly like the one the actors are wearing in the play going on now at the theater!"

I watched her expression turn to shock, then to something else I could not define.

"I do not know," she said. "If you are accusing my family, we were all at home on the evening we heard the shots."

How did she know precisely which evening I meant?

I drew a deep breath and tried to think of another approach. If someone in her family was the villain, she was obviously determined to remain loyal.

"Then may I ask if you know anything about a gold nugget my uncle found?" I rushed on. "Or a secret stream? Or a map he drew indicating that stream?"

She caught her breath. Obviously she had not expected or anticipated this.

Her bracelets jangled as she lifted a hand to sweep the hood off and straighten her long black braid. Suddenly I recalled the night I had seen her leaving the cemetery in this cloak. This time, I would not be put off by her affection for my uncle. I still believed that she loved him, but I believed that loyalty to her family was much more binding.

I regretted the arrival of tea at this precise moment, for it gave her a few seconds to compose a reply.

"Well?" I prompted as soon as the waiter was out of earshot.

"Yes, he spoke of a nugget that he believed was gold. He told me he had marked the spot and drawn a map. A snowstorm came late, and he had to give up his work for a few weeks. It was during that time that we . . ." Tears sprang to her eyes before she dropped her head.

"Yes, I understand." I took a deep breath, trying to think what else I could ask that might help to illuminate the dark mystery surrounding my uncle's last days. The poem!

"Nona, my uncle left a rather strange poem in his tablet. The one about mosquitoes and silver spurs . . ."

She lifted her head and a puzzled expression crossed her face. "I did not see that one. He wrote one or two special poems for me," she replied softly, and the damp eyes grew dreamy for a brief moment.

"This one made no sense," I explained. "I am beginning to think that it contained some sort of message."

A tiny frown rose between her dark brows. "What did it say?"

I sighed. "I should have brought his tablet with me. It went something like this:

Climb the trail to the dark totem poles,
There the one-eyed Indian resides,
Safe from mosquitoes and silver spurs
and death in the Alaskan night.

"Dark totem poles?" she repeated, a blush creeping over her face.

"That's right." I watched her carefully. "That has some meaning for you, doesn't it?"

She dropped her eyes. "The unusual bed." She paused for a moment before her glance flew back to me. "The rest makes no sense, except I do recall he once mentioned a one-eyed Indian as a sort of joke." She lifted a hand to her forehead. "I believe this was mentioned in a conversation I overheard between Joshua and Lonesome Bill. . . ." Her voice trailed as her eyes rounded on something behind us.

I glanced over my shoulder and saw James Zarnoff framed in the doorway. His narrowed eyes and flushed face hinted at a terrible anger. I caught my breath as I looked at him, for I was seeing the face of a man whose fury might conceivably lead him to . . . murder!

"I must go," she said, coming quickly to her feet. "Thank you for tea."

She hurried across the room to meet her husband, and I stared after them as they quickly disappeared through the door.

So! Lonesome Bill had known about her all along—which made him a liar! Now I suspected he had lied about other matters as well.

Frustrated and angry, I paid the bill and hurried out of the dining room. I had planned to go upstairs and rest for a while, but I found myself too restless to do that. Despite the cold weather, I went back outside and stood on the sidewalk, staring up and down. Fewer people milled about in the chilly air, and all the faces I saw were unfamiliar.

I began to walk, uncertain where I was going. The restlessness within me was building, building, building, until I felt I would explode if I didn't get some answers.

If I was any judge of character, the assayer was lying. So what if the nugget *was* real gold? The cold wind blew over me, and I stared idly in the windows of shops, where fires blazed in potbellied stoves. There really had been a woman in my uncle's life. What if there had really been a map? And what if the nugget had come from a secret stream that was enough to prompt a murder? Lonesome Bill was becoming more suspicious all the time.

Thoughts swirled around in my head like a Juneau fog. I found myself marching determinedly toward Deputy Wilson's office.

I pressed the wooden latch, but it held stubbornly beneath my gloved hand. Locked! I glared at the closed door, incensed that such an important office would be locked at midday. What a careless way to run an office of law and order!

"If you're looking for Hank, he ain't there," a man called from the next doorway. "They found a body floating in the channel up the inlet. He took off to investigate."

I turned and stared at the shop owner. "How far up the inlet?"

"Don't know. Just up past that old Russian church somewhere!"

I stared at the man, dumbfounded.

Scott! Could it be Scott? He was the only person I knew who lived up the inlet from me.

I turned and fled down the walk, my cheeks burning against the cold. Now what was I going to do?

Gordon! I would find Gordon.

I was breathless by the time I pushed the door open and hurried inside the bank. I started toward Gordon's office, then drew up quickly as the clerk blocked my path.

"Good morning, Miss Martin!"

"I need to speak with Gordon," I said brusquely.

"He'll be sorry he missed you," he said, his eyes sweeping me curiously. "This is his morning to go to Douglas Island."

"When will he be back?" I asked.

"Late afternoon, I imagine. May I be of assistance?"

Hardly! Douglas Island . . . That was across the channel. Or *up* the channel?

I thought of the body and felt another tremor racing over me.

"Have you heard anything about a body being found up the channel?"

He frowned and regarded me as though I had just emerged from the theater and was babbling about a play. "No, I have not," he said stiffly.

"Please tell Gordon I need to see him when he returns," I said, turning on my heel to leave.

"You're staying at the Occidental." It was a statement, not a question.

I glanced sharply at him. Apparently, the townspeople knew of my every move.

"Yes, I am," I called, hurrying out.

I was walking the cold street once more, uncertain of what to do next. I decided to return to the hotel until I heard from Gordon. Or perhaps the sheriff would be back in his office later on in the day and I could speak with him about Lonesome Bill.

The body!

It continued to haunt me. Scott, where was Scott?

I knew I was working myself into a frenzy, but I couldn't seem to control my frantic thoughts. I had never in my life felt so tense and anxious, so certain of evil hovering just out of sight. Something seemed to be pulling me back up the inlet. I knew it was my concern for Scott that tugged at me, until I felt compelled to go up and see for myself exactly what had happened. I was terrified that the body was Scott's!

Once I reached the hotel lobby, I purchased a newspaper, hoping to divert my mind from a whirlpool of emotions. As I started for the stairs, however, a familiar voice reached me.

"Miss Martin!"

I turned to see Jamie Zarnoff dashing across the lobby. A tweed coat and matching cap jostled with his bouncing stride.

For the first time in a long while, I felt a rush of tenderness. It was pleasant just to look at someone young and happy. Apparently he had not heard of the body, and I decided not to mention it. Nothing could be accomplished by spreading terrifying rumors until we knew all the details.

"Hello, Jamie." I tucked the newspaper under my arm and smiled at him.

"I have to give you something," he said, reaching into his coat pocket. He produced an envelope with my name written across the front. "From my mother," he said, and his grin faded. His eyes were serious now, his expression one of concern. "She asked me to bring this note to you."

"Oh." I took the note and stared at it for a moment. "Well, thank you very much."

I reached into my bag to pay him, but he waved the money aside. "No ma'am. I did this for my mother," he said. "Well, good-bye."

"Wait, Jamie!" I said, touching his shoulder. My hand rested there for a moment, and the nubby tweed of his coat felt cold against my palm. "Where are you going now?"

"Me and Grandpa are going back home."

"Where are your parents?"

"They're visiting some of their friends here. They won't be coming home till this afternoon."

I bit my lip. I was torn with indecision. Then suddenly my concern for Scott overode all else.

"I think I'd like to get your grandfather to take me up to the house," I said impulsively, without thinking the matter through.

"It'll be cold up there without a fire," he frowned at me.

"Then perhaps you'll build one for me," I said hastily.

He grinned. "Yes'm. I can do that," he replied, as though pleased to be of service. "I'll go tell Grandpa to stop by here as we leave town. We're almost ready."

"Good. And I'll grab an extra coat."

I hurried upstairs, wondering why I had behaved so irrationally. Still, I felt it made sense to investigate a death near my house; furthermore, I wanted to retrieve Uncle Joshua's tablet, which I had foolishly left behind. The tablet held an important message; I was certain of that now. If someone had, in fact, come to his kitchen as he sat at the table drinking, if that person had harmed him, I knew my uncle well enough to know he would have tried to leave a clue, particularly if the tablet and pen were within reach. Why had I stupidly overlooked this before, I wondered? Because I had never fully believed he was murdered . . . until now. In my heart, I knew he had found gold, had drawn a map . . . and that someone had wanted that map enough to kill him. I still suspected that *someone* was Lonesome Bill, even though James Zarnoff's angry expression loomed threateningly in my memory.

While so many trails led back to Nona, I still believed she would not have killed the man she loved, not for money, nor to keep the affair a secret. After all, she had been very open with me even at the risk of my telling her family.

These thoughts were uppermost in my mind as I climbed the stairs, tightly gripping the envelope.

Once I had reached the privacy of my hotel room and bolted the door, I opened the envelope and found not one letter, but two. My breath caught as I spotted the familiar handwriting of my uncle in a second note, but first I forced myself to read Nona's letter.

It was written on ruled white paper in a neat, precise script.

> Miss Martin,
>
> Please believe me. I did not deceive either you or your uncle. Nor did I try to frighten you from the house. I have kept in the lining of my handbag the last letter your uncle wrote. I now entrust it to your care, so that you can see your uncle's affection for me was genuine. And I can only give you my word that I felt the same. Never would I have harmed him, or allowed anyone else to do so, if I could have prevented it.

If I could have prevented it! I hesitated on that one sentence, which seemed to jump before me.

With a pounding heart I read on.

> Please do not continue to seek me out or ask questions. It is causing problems with my family. The

Zarnoffs have been more than understanding. Even my mother-in-law insisted on going in my place to clean house on that terrible morning when she found Joshua.

I stopped reading and thought back to my conversation with Deputy Wilson. Mrs. Zarnoff cleaned house for your uncle, he had said. Either he hadn't known which Mrs. Zarnoff, or he hadn't bothered to elaborate.

On the day before Joshua died, I sent him a note, begging him to understand my situation. If he did not, and if, in a weak moment, he took his life, I will bear that burden forever. But I do not wish the Zarnoffs further embarrassment. I want to assure you again that I never saw the gold nugget or the map you mentioned.

There was a directness about Nona Zarnoff that convinced me of her honesty. I sank onto the bed and unfolded the letter my uncle had written to her, his last letter.

Dearest Nona,

I fear I cannot go on without you, but I know that I must try. I must tell you that these past weeks have been the happiest of my life. Never had I imagined that I could find a woman who filled my life so completely that all else dimmed in comparison. But you have.

I will not tempt you with promises of wealth, for I know you are a good woman, bound more strongly by loyalty than by love. I respect you for that. But if anything should ever change, please come back to me. . . .

Tears blurred the last words, and I swallowed heavily, trying to find some consolation in the fact that he had been happy for a while. Happier than ever before in his life.

I folded both notes and put them in my handbag. Nona was right; there was nothing to be accomplished by digging up the past and hurting her and her family. If, in fact, it had been one of the Zarnoffs who wore the mask and came to scare me off, perhaps this was one more reason for doing so—a desire to protect Nona. And I imagined that person might have been her husband. As Scott had said, James Zarnoff and his father had heard the shots and arrived amazingly fast, considering the fact that it was late at night and they lived a quarter mile away.

I sat for a minute, staring into space, absorbing what I had read.

It had been Nona who'd cleaned house for my uncle; Mrs. Zarnoff had tried to protect her by claiming that it was she. Or had she ever claimed that?

Suddenly, other possibilities occurred that I had not considered. If my uncle had been expecting Nona, rather than Mrs. Zarnoff, would his strange poem have had more meaning? Would he believe Nona might understand it?

I jumped from the bed and paced the room. That was one of the missing pieces to the puzzle. The poem, which had seemed so distorted in meter and logic, might have made sense to Nona, but of course, she had never seen it!

I grabbed an extra coat and my rubber boots and hurried back downstairs to await Zarnoff and Jamie.

I had to see that tablet again! And I had to find out about the body.

Somehow I had managed to keep at bay my feelings for Scott throughout the past hour, but now as I stood at the front of the hotel, waiting for Zarnoff, I felt tears welling in my eyes.

What if Scott had drowned? I swallowed. No, I had to believe it was someone else until I knew for certain. He had gone to Douglas Island for an interview. Had he crossed the channel by a different route? Or had he returned home the previous evening?

The wagon rocked to an abrupt halt before the hotel, and I dashed out the door. Jamie hopped down to give me his seat.

"I'll ride in the back," he offered.

"I hate to put you out," I said, hesitating.

"It's okay. I ride in the back a lot."

My eyes crept up to meet Zarnoff's, but this time, to my utter surprise and immense relief, he did not regard me with the usual cold, hard stare. Instead, he tipped his fur cap rather politely and bade me good morning.

I was almost too shocked to respond but finally returned his greeting as he tapped the horses with the frayed reins. We lurched ahead.

"Mr. Zarnoff," I said, once we were on the outskirts, "I just heard that a body had been found up the channel." I tried to lower my voice, thinking for some foolish reason that Jamie should be spared this news.

It was Jamie, however, who enlightened me on the situation.

"Yes'm," he shouted above the clatter of wagon wheels. "The deputy's gone up to see who it is. They think it's just an old miner."

I glanced curiously over my shoulder. Jamie was dashing up a hand to secure his tweed cap as we jostled along.

"I heard them talking about it at the general store," he continued calmly. "Did you hear anything about it, Grandpa?"

"No, I do not know."

I cleared my throat. "This is one reason I wanted to make a quick trip back. The shop owner next door to the deputy's office said the body had been discovered up near . . . my place."

Zarnoff's dark blue eyes shot toward me as a muscle in his hard face clenched. There was never any understanding his thoughts or moods.

While he made no comment, he tapped the reins with more force, and the old horses shuttled into an accelerated trot.

By the time we reached the house, the wagon had gained enough speed to force me to hold onto my hat while the wind bit my face and lifted my cloak. Finally the wagon lurched to a stop, and my head snapped back as I looked at the desolate house. My eyes rose up to the glass pane of the bedroom window, then on to the enclosed tower with the broken glass. I recalled the old bell I had seen on the Zarnoff hearth, an oddity in their cabin. It belonged up there in the tower, and I knew it. A sigh escaped me. Now that I was back, I felt the old apprehension creeping over me once more as I sat on the wagon seat, reluctant to climb down.

"How long you will be here?" Zarnoff's stern voice broke through my thoughts.

"I'm not sure," I replied. "I wanted to see about the body that was found near here . . ."

Then we were all three staring up the channel, which looked perfectly still and peaceful in the cold half-sun.

I turned and looked back at Jamie, who had hopped down from the wagon.

"Have you seen Mr. Morgan today?"

Jamie's face grew serious as he whipped his head about and shot a worried glance north. "No'm. I haven't. Grandpa, maybe we oughta ride up there."

"We will wait and see," he said firmly, still staring north.

"You want me to go inside with you?" Jamie asked.

"Oh yes, please do!" I blurted, then bit my lip, glancing at Zarnoff. "I have some tidying up to do here before I leave. If Jamie could stay on and help me for a while, I will pay him. Then I would like to hire a ride back to town late this afternoon."

Zarnoff frowned, studying the sky. "We will be getting snow very soon."

"How can you tell?" I asked curiously. There were a lot of scattered clouds, but none that looked severely threatening.

"I feel it in the air," he said gloomily. "I smell it."

Smell it? "Then I won't ask you to take me back to town if

the weather is too unpleasant. I'll just . . ."

"I will take you," he said firmly, "if you need to go. The grandson can only stay for a while; the wife has a job for him."

"Tell her I'll be home in a little while," Jamie called, waiting for me on the stoop.

I fished into my purse and found the key, almost spilling out Nona's letter in the process. I glanced nervously over my shoulder, but Zarnoff had already turned the wagon and was rattling off down the driveway.

"I'll build a fire for you," Jamie said. "Then I can come back later. I promised to scrub out the smoke shed for my grandmother. She's canning fish," he explained, as I inserted the key into the lock.

He pushed the door back for me, and we stepped inside. The frigid air enclosed us immediately, but Jamie strode quickly toward the kitchen.

"I'll build you a fire right now," he said.

"There's wood behind the stove, and old newspaper and coal oil in the cabinet."

"Yes'm," his voice echoed through the rambling house. Shivering into my cloak, I threw the extra coat around my shoulders and set my rubber boots down beside the door.

Cautiously, my eyes swept the room. Again, I felt no sense of home whatsoever, but then I had never tried to make it so. I walked about the room, satisfied that everything was as I had left it. When I opened the door and peered into the closets, nothing had been touched.

I looked into the kitchen. Jamie was busily at work at the stove, and I could see he knew what he was doing. My thoughts flew to Scott, who had patiently and generously built the fires, and I was again filled with a sense of alarm.

"Jamie," I said, "after you build the fire, do you think you could . . ." I hated to ask him to do something to which his grandfather would object.

"Could what?" he asked. He turned to face me, and I saw a smudge on the front of his coat and winced, imagining his stern grandmother's reaction. "Well . . ." I tried to think of a job other than the one I had really intended.

His face was tilted, quizzical.

"Actually," I sighed, "I was about to ask you to make a dash up to Mr. Morgan's cabin, but I have no right to ask that. I would pay you, of course." Coming from a wealthy family, I always had an inclination to offer a bribe. Perhaps it was a bad habit, but I had inherited my father's philosophy of paying for requests with the belief that the job would be done more thoroughly.

"Oh, I'd like to go to Scott's place," he said, stuffing the last newspaper in the stove's black interior. "Yes'm, I'm kinda worried about Scott myself. There aren't many other cabins up there."

We both fell silent, deep in thought. Jamie finished building the fire, lit the match, and waited for the blaze. I walked over to stand beside him, appreciating the healthy flame that consumed the oiled paper and then licked at the sticks of wood.

"Now it's going," he said, closing the lid.

"Jamie, I appreciate the fire," I said, smiling at him. He was a good boy, and again my thoughts were moving back to his mother and father. I wondered how strong their love for each other had been before my uncle had come along.

"You're welcome. Want me to go to Scott's cabin? I can run up there and back in an hour."

I bit my lip. "I really hate to ask. I'm afraid your grandfather wouldn't approve."

He grinned. "He doesn't have to know about it." With that, he bounded toward the front door. "If he's there, what do you want me to tell him?"

I stared at Jamie, framed in the open door, the cold air sweeping in. "Tell him to come here, please. And pull your cap down around your ears," I called after him, thinking I must sound exactly like his mother.

The door slammed and I sighed, rubbing my hands together and hurrying back to stand before the stove. Through force of habit I filled the kettle with the small amount of water remaining in the bucket, and put the kettle on for tea. While I waited for the water, my eyes strayed back to the kitchen table, lingering on the space where the bloodstain had been.

My mind was racing again. I imagined Mrs. Zarnoff coming into the room and discovering my uncle slumped over the table. Why had she come to clean in Nona's place? Nona had told him she could not see him again. Yes, that was it.

Or had Mrs. Zarnoff already volunteered to come in Nona's place, determined to put an end to the affair that was threatening her son's happiness? Threatening to destroy his family?

A chill ran over me as I thought of how fierce the Zarnoffs could be, how rigid. I recalled the strong woman's abrupt manner and remembered she rarely softened, except where her family was concerned. She had not wanted to enter the kitchen on the day she had brought the jam; I had assumed it was because of her superstition. Could it have been because she had, in reality, discovered my uncle seated at the table, writing a letter or a poem, and had shot him? Guilt could have kept her from the kitchen until . . .

My breath caught as I remembered the ease with which she had grabbed a knife and heartlessly carved out the wood of the table.

The kettle began to whistle, startling me from my macabre thoughts. I made tea with an unsteady hand, thinking that everything was happening too fast. I felt as though I were on a runaway horse, viewing bits of scenery in a blur, and powerless to slow down.

I sat at the table, sipping the tea, relishing the warmth radiating from the stove. I would calm myself, try to think logically.

The tablet!

I leapt out of the chair and ran through the living room. The heat from the kitchen stove had not yet reached the upper floor, and I was enveloped in cold, stale air as I climbed the steps. When I reached the top step and looked into the spacious upper room, I gripped the stair rail, reeling with shock. The room looked as though someone had set out to turn every single article upside down. The drawer to the nightstand lay on the floor, the contents strewn about haphazardly. The covers were torn from the bed, the mattress heaved on its side, and a long, jagged tear in the center of the mattress sent stuffing trailing in clusters.

Stunned, I picked my way over the debris to the armoire, where the door hung open. My dresses had been rudely snatched from the hangers and now lay in a colorful heap. Even Uncle Joshua's winter shoes, hauled from the bottom of the closet, were sprawled before me, the linings ripped out!

I could scarcely believe the gross destruction. Even his fiddle had been cruelly broken; one string dangled uselessly. Every box of books had been overturned, the contents spilled onto the floor and trampled over, pages carelessly torn.

The dresser drawers stood ajar, my lace-trimmed pantalettes dangled on the edge of a drawer.

Hadn't I stupidly left the door unlocked? But this was not simply a mischievous deed! I brushed back a trailing wisp of hair and swallowed, trying to think what to do. It would take hours for me to put everything back in order, and at the moment I was in no mood for that.

Then I remembered why I had come upstairs in the first place.

Where was Uncle Joshua's tablet?

My eyes flew over the clutter as I began to seek the tablet in earnest. It was nowhere in sight.

Already frustrated to tears, I now felt another sickening wave of disappointment as I searched behind the bedside table and then under it; then I heaved up a corner of the heavy mattress and looked under the bed.

Puzzled, I lifted my skirts and hurried unsteadily down

the stairs.

I hesitated, glancing quickly over the big room. Nothing was out of place here, and that seemed very strange indeed. I hurried about, opening and closing drawers. Breathlessly I straightened up and glanced curiously about the room. I peered inside the closets, then went to the kitchen. I even opened the cabinet door and looked on the shelves, although I knew, despite my frantic state of mind, I would not have put the tablet in a kitchen cabinet.

No, the tablet was not here! *It was gone.*

I sank into a kitchen chair and began to gulp the tepid tea. My last important clue to Joshua's death was the tablet, his final poem. And now it *had vanished.*

Chapter 14

I began to pace the kitchen floor, my anxiety mounting. I soon turned to the living room, seeking a larger area to pace.

I would not be outsmarted!

If I had finally collected my wits enough to decide the poem was a link to . . . *something,* someone else had as well!

I stopped pacing and stared blankly through the window. The sunlight had disappeared. Now there was a gray, ominous look to the air, one that matched my mood to perfection.

Had Nona Zarnoff tricked me again? She was the only person who knew that I was concerned about that final poem. I had quoted it to her and asked for her interpretation, and apparently she had found an all-important clue that only she could decipher!

I pressed my hand against my forehead, hoping to spark my memory. What had the poem said? The dark totem poles . . . silver spurs . . .

Scott! At the mention of silver spurs, I was tormented again by my concern for Scott. I hurried to the window and stared across the bleak gray channel. Jamie should be back soon; he could help me straighten the upstairs. Perhaps he would have news of Scott.

My thoughts were bouncing from the tablet to the poem, to the map, back to Scott. The body . . . the murderer . . . the thief who had come once more. . . . The trail led back to Nona Zarnoff! I turned and grabbed my handbag from the coffee table, rummaging haphazardly through it for the envelope.

Though it was early afternoon, the lost sun left behind only a heavy gray light. I went to the window and took a seat to take advantage of that scant light. I withdrew both notes from the envelope. The parchment crinkled coldly in my hands as I read Nona's letter again. If she had lied to me, she was the most convincing liar I had ever met.

I laid her letter aside and grabbed Uncle Joshua's letter. I opened it up, smoothed it out in my lap, and reread every word.

The tablet seemed more precious than ever; why had I so stupidly gone off without it? I glanced back over his love letter again. Then suddenly my eyes, and my thoughts, came to rest on that very first sentence.

I fear I cannot go on without you.

I looked up, glancing idly toward the desk, thinking. The suicide note, how was it worded? I leapt out of the chair and hurried to the desk drawer, withdrawing the small note that I had refolded and placed in the drawer, doubtful that I would ever read it again.

But now I carefully opened that note and hurried to the kitchen, where I spread both notes on the table, smoothing the crinkled places. There was no question that both were the same handwriting, but one all-important fact jumped out at me now.

I cannot go on, the suicide note read.

I fear I cannot go on without you, the love letter read.

I looked back at the suicide note. *I cannot go on*

There was no period!

Then suddenly it came to me! The two sheets that had been torn out before the final poem were these two. If only I had the tablet, I could match the frayed tops of the letter to the upper edge of the tablet. Even without the tablet, however, one thing was perfectly clear to me now. *The suicide note had been the beginning of his first letter to Nona.*

I cannot go on

Absently, I reached for my tea, needing its bracing strength.

Uncle Joshua had rewritten the letter to Nona. He had begun with *I cannot go on.* Then he had stopped writing, thinking that this statement was too hard for Nona to accept. He had then started another letter which read, *I fear I cannot go on without you.*

I looked at the suicide note again, and now I suddenly realized why something had always seemed amiss in this note: there was no period; the sentence had not ended. And yet he had taken great care in signing his name, *Joshua L. Martin,* a detail which seemed unnecessary after his hastiness in writing only four words. Being the precise man that he was, Uncle Joshua would have ended the sentence with a period—particularly if he knew it was the last sentence he would ever write.

The tablet! If only I had the tablet! If the poem was the last thing Uncle Joshua wrote, then I was certain that poem held the clue to his death!

I sighed heavily, dropping my head to my hands. Someone else had figured this out as well.

An abrupt knocking at the door sent me flying from the chair, practically running across the big room as I glanced toward the window. Zarnoff's wagon was not in the drive. Jamie must be back. Hurriedly I unlocked the door and found a muddy, weary Jamie leaning against the wall.

"Come on in," I said, stepping aside.

As he entered, he began to shed his mud-caked rubber boots just inside the door. Then he hobbled on in, moving at an uncharacteristically slow pace.

"You must have run all the way there and back," I observed as he flopped into a chair.

"Near 'bout. He isn't at his cabin," he said, catching his breath.

"Oh." My heart sank. I was thinking of that mysterious body again.

"Can I get you something?" I asked, concerned that I had asked him to cover so much distance. "How about an apple?"

He nodded, still conserving his words until he had regained his strength. I hurried to the kitchen and extracted the last apple from the meager supply I had bought.

"But he's been there," he said as I returned. "I just missed him."

I was in the process of handing him the apple when he delivered this news. My hand froze in space; my fingers tightened on the apple.

"How do you know?" I asked.

"The door was open. If he's gonna be gone for a while, he locks the door. And the fire's still warm in the stove. And I smelled coffee."

"Oh." I sank onto the sofa, absently watching him eat the apple.

"Was his boat there?" I asked, dreading the answer.

"No'm. It was gone. But Bering was there, and Bering usually goes fishing with him." He bit into the apple, and it made a loud crunch in the ensuing silence.

I frowned. "He wouldn't be out fishing in this weather, would he?"

"Shouldn't be. Fishing's no good."

The old worry began to gnaw at me again. The body . . . "You didn't see any sign of Deputy Wilson, did you?"

"Well," he paused, wiping his mouth on his sleeve, "way across on the other island, I could barely see a crowd of people right there at the edge of the water."

"Do you think," I looked earnestly at him, "that could mean . . ."

"Yes'm. Something was going on. Maybe that's where they found the body."

"Perhaps that's where Scott has gone," I said, hopefully. "I'm sure he would be curious as to what was going on over there. Then when Deputy Wilson was summoned, perhaps there had been a mistake about the location of the . . . body."

"Did you want me to do anything else before I go home?" Jamie asked, tossing the core in the wastebasket.

I remembered the disaster upstairs.

"Well," I sighed, "if you don't mind, I do need some help. It seems I've had another visitor while I was away. Someone came in the house, went upstairs, and tore the place apart."

"What?" His eyes darted to the doorway of the kitchen. "Just upstairs? They didn't bother anything down here?"

I shook my head. "Apparently this area has already been searched. Come on, I'll show you. By the way, Jamie," I said as we crossed the big room, "would you happen to know why someone keeps coming here to rummage around?"

His expression became more solemn.

"What are you thinking?" I asked as we reached the stairs.

"Nothing."

I didn't want to dispute his reply, but something had crossed his mind; that was obvious. As he darted up the steps, I could see the heels of his woolen socks had been darned, which led me to recall that Mary Wright had said Nona always had money. I doubted that now.

Jamie gave a loud whistle as he reached the top of the stairs and surveyed the disorder.

"I've never seen such a mess!" he said, wide-eyed.

"This couldn't have been spirits," he said.

"Why would you even mention spirits?" I asked wearily, as I leaned down to gather up a leatherbound volume of Shakespeare.

"I don't know," he mumbled, dropping to his knees to scoop up an armload of books.

"I think *I* know," I replied. "Your grandparents believe there are spirits in this place. That because it was intended to be a sacred dwelling, humans should not inhabit it." I straightened, replacing the books on a table between two overturned bookends. Then, as the words I had spoken rang through my ears, an important fact occurred to me.

Old Man Zarnoff would not cross the threshold into this house, and although his wife had entered the house, she had clearly been on edge, anxious, and superstitious. With that in mind, it seemed unreasonable to assume they would come here and prowl. Nona, on the contrary, had shown no such apprehension. She had, in fact, used her key and come in alone for her glove and a photograph of Uncle Joshua. Or had she really come for those items on that day? Had she actually come for the map?

I had been standing in one spot, staring at the leatherbound Shakespeare. The thudding of objects behind me drew my attention back to Jamie, who was dutifully replacing the drawer in the nightstand.

I turned and stared at the frame of the Mallard bed, the large mattress tilted against the bedposts.

It would take a strong person to heave the mattress from the bed, and a vicious one to take a knife and slash it open. Vicious . . . or desperate.

Had her husband done it? Did James Zarnoff know about the map? Either in a weak moment or in an effort to redeem herself, had Nona told him about the map? Did he believe that finding the map, and then the gold, could make him a rich man? And win Nona back again?

I remembered that he had no qualms about entering the house on the night they heard the gunshots.

"What are you staring at?" Jamie asked.

I came back to the moment, and glanced at Jamie. He was gathering up a handful of mattress stuffing, then poking it back through the slit in the ticking.

"I was just wondering," I said, watching him closely, "why anyone would do this." Did he turn his back to me on purpose, or was it merely a convenience in restuffing the mattress? "Do you have any idea?"

"No'm. Did they steal anything?"

I glanced around, bewildered. "It's difficult to know just yet." I lifted my skirts and tiptoed over a squashed hatbox, some shoehorns, and a pair of riding boots. "Maybe together we can shove the mattress back on the bed," I said.

The Tlingit blanket lay at my feet in a hideous heap, the faces crookedly jeering. I kicked it aside, and with Jamie's help, angled the heavy mattress back onto the bed. In doing so, we had a good view of the mattress and the bed slats. Nothing was hidden here.

My shoulder bumped the bedpost, and suddenly my memory was jarred back to that moment when Nona had flushed and mentioned the unusual bed.

I frowned, trying to recall the conversation.

We had been discussing the map!

I was trying to trace that line of thought as the old suspicion against Nona surged through me anew. I had quoted the poem to her, and something had sparked her memory about this bed.

"I've never seen a bed like this," Jamie commented.

I looked back at him. "It's called a Mallard bed. It was designed by a Frenchman named Mallard, whose trademark is an egg carved in the center of the bed frame there. Do you see?" I pointed. "I'm afraid my entire family took a liking to these beds. Uncle Joshua even had his bed frame shipped up here. Wasn't that absurd?" To say nothing of the fact that it had cost him a fortune. I still remembered the confusion when two men from the dock had appeared at our door with an order to ship Uncle Joshua's bed frame to Juneau, Alaska. We kept a key to my uncle's house, and they had come for the key.

Jamie was still studying the bed curiously. "My uncle wrote to say that the mosquitoes were bad here," I continued. "There's netting kept in these posts." I lifted the top of the post, but the pocket designed to hold the net was empty.

"Mosquito season is over," Jamie said, examining the post.

I frowned. Such trouble and expense for my scatter-brained uncle, particularly if he had now lost the netting!

"But mosquitoes here can be real critters! My mother's people have a legend about mosquitoes."

"What's that?" I asked.

"Once there was a huge giant who had magical powers. Arrows couldn't stop him because he lived on human blood. Then, a noble warrior learned there was one spot on the giant's body that was not magic. It was his ankle. The brave warrior fired an arrow into his ankle one day, but as the giant was dying, he put a curse on the Indians. He told them he would come back for their blood. The Indians built a big fire and burned the giant to ashes. Then they scattered his ashes over the land, but the ashes turned to mosquitoes!"

He finished his tale with a lopsided grin, but while I thought the legend humorous, I could not alter my worried mood enough to laugh. I was thinking about the night my mystery prowler came with the horrible mask. When my misfired shots had missed him, I might have believed the old legend if I had heard of it then—that the magical giant had come back to haunt me!

"Why are you staring at me?" Jamie asked.

I blinked. "I'm sorry. I'm not really staring at *you.* I'm just thinking."

Actually, I *had* been staring at him, for when I looked in his eyes, I could see Nona, his mother. And I was still troubled by that reference to the bed.

"I know someone who wanted your uncle's books," Jamie spoke up, as his eyes moved over the extensive collection tumbled about.

"Who?"

"Well . . ."

"Who?"

He sighed. "Scott and your uncle used to argue a lot. I know he wanted some of those books," he inclined his head toward the leatherbound volumes I had stacked on the table.

"Maybe so. But that would hardly prompt him to rip the mattress," I glanced around, "or tear up Uncle Joshua's fiddle. Scott Morgan isn't destructive." Why was I defending him? How could I be sure?

"Well . . ."

My nerves were pricking me like pinpoints, and my patience had completely disintegrated. I turned on my heel and glared at him.

"Jamie, if you know something, I insist that you tell me!"

"I have to be going," he said, turning toward the stairs.

"You *do* know something," I called after him. "We've been friends," I reminded him, hurrying to follow. "Furthermore, my uncle may not have taken his life," I said emphatically as we reached the living room.

Jamie stopped at the front door, reaching for his boots. Wide-eyed, he turned back to me, startled by the last words I had spoken.

Now that I had his attention, I pushed on, determined to learn his secret.

"He may have been murdered," I said, looking at him

pointedly.

He caught his breath, a loud hiss in the sudden silence.

"If you know something, you must tell me. Otherwise," I hesitated, then decided to bluff, "the deputy may ask you to come to his office. I went there today, seeking his help. That was when I discovered that he was investigating the, er, body up the channel."

Jamie was sitting on the floor, rapidly tugging on his boots. His eyes had not left my face as I related this shocking news to him. "Murdered?" he echoed, as though he had heard nothing else.

His face had begun to turn pale, accenting the freckles along the bridge of his nose. Did the secret he was trying to conceal involve someone close to him?

He stood up, his eyes fixed intently on the muddy toes of his boots. He was obviously locked in a mental struggle between loyalty and honesty. He lifted his head and his eyes circled the room as tiny lines bunched on his forehead in a perplexed frown.

"My mother asked me to bring a note here one night," he said quietly. "I could hear loud voices when I came up the front steps," he paused, looking back at me. "Just before I knocked on the door, I heard him say, 'Damn it, Josh you should give it to me.' "

"Him?" I repeated.

He nodded.

"I had to knock a long time before your uncle answered the door. When he finally opened it, I saw Scott Morgan sitting over there." Jamie's eyes moved to the sofa, and he blinked and stared for a moment.

"Anything else?" I asked, hating the question, dreading the answer.

"Well, they had some stuff piled out on the table there," he nodded.

"What stuff?"

"Books, and that tablet, and I don't know what else. It was all jumbled up. They didn't have much to say to me. Then I handed your uncle the note, and a funny look came over his face. He put the note in his pocket, gave me a coin, and patted me on the shoulder. He didn't seem mad any more, but Scott's face was all red, like he was still angry. He looked like he does when a big fish gets off the hook. He just kept staring at something there on the table." Jamie looked back at me, his face filled with confusion. "Then I left," he finished quietly.

I nodded, absorbing his words, feeling worse by the moment. I had asked for the truth, I reminded myself, as I reached into my handbag.

"Thanks, Jamie," I said, pressing a bill into his palm.

"I don't know if I should take this much," he said, staring at the crumpled bill.

"You've earned it. Now run on home, before your grandmother gets worried about you."

He bolted for the door, then glanced back over his shoulder.

"What time do you want to go back into town?" he inquired.

"I don't know," I said distractedly, automatically glancing at the coffee table, wondering what had fascinated Scott Morgan so much. "Whenever your grandfather is ready, I suppose," I added wearily. There was no cause to linger; the tablet was gone. Scott was probably safe. Those were my reasons for returning, although I wished now I had remained in Juneau.

He bolted through the door, slamming it behind him. I jumped before I could stop myself, as I crossed the room and sank onto the sofa, feeling the thick white fur against my back.

I felt as though every ounce of energy had been drained from my body. Something important had been revealed to me; I didn't want to hear it. I didn't want to accept the cold truth nagging relentlessly at me. But I must!

I dropped my head in my hands and listened to the wind wailing around the house, tugging at a loose board somewhere. The room was warm and cozy, however, thanks to Jamie's robust fire. It was even reaching upward now, warming the bedroom which I did not intend to sleep in again.

Well, I must explore the truth concerning the one man who had fascinated me more than anyone I had ever met. A man who—if I would admit it—had absolutely stolen my heart. He had sat here, argued with my uncle about something on the table. *It.* Not books. Not the great writers of the century, as he had once said.

You should give it to me. It could mean only one thing: the map.

I opened my eyes and looked over the board walls of this strange abbey. Yes, it was an abbey, not a home, and I would not think of it as a home, not ever again. If only the walls could talk, if only the idiotic bear's face on the rug below me could relate the secret, for it was here. The abbey knew the truth; the abbey knew the murderer.

Something drifted to me above the moan of the wind, something different. I frowned. It was something pleasant, something lighthearted. Someone was whistling!

I leapt from the sofa and turned to the window.

He was walking quickly across the tidal flats, his arms swinging, his hooded mackinaw half shielding his handsome face. Despite the angry, blustering wind, he seemed comfortable, a part of nature, even energized by it.

Scott was whistling contentedly as he broke into a trot, and loped up the path to the front door.

Chapter 15

I watched him curiously, suspiciously. He was still an enigma to me. *That* was the fascination, I argued with myself. Perhaps when the mysterious side of his nature came to light, my attitude toward him would drastically change. But until then . . .

My heart was beating faster as I heard his light steps approaching. Suddenly all the accusations and dark suspicions of others were screaming through my memory again.

"I think he was disinherited," Mary Wright had said.

"A sourdough," Gordon reported. "A ladies' man."

Mary Wright's tone had sharpened at the mention of Scott's name, and Gordon hadn't bothered to hide his condescending attitude. Now there was Jamie's revealing statement to consider.

"They were arguing," he had said. "Scott's face was red . . ."

He was knocking on the door, and I froze beside the sofa, staring worriedly at the closed door. I must trust the opinions of others who knew him. I must not be charmed into clouded judgment.

I drew a deep breath and slowly walked over to unlock the door, having no idea whatsoever how I would react to him. He had probably seen me from the window; I could hardly pretend not to be at home.

I gripped the doorknob tightly and pulled. That simple

gesture seemed to require enormous strength, for I was suddenly weak from anxiety. Scott didn't know I was suspicious of him, I reassured myself. Perhaps I could use that to my advantage.

"Good morning!" His face was clean shaven; his green eyes glowed above the wide smile. He looked as innocent and charming as a schoolboy.

"Hello," I said, behind a tight smile.

Belatedly, I stepped back, realizing I could not leave him standing out on the steps. He dashed into the room, quickly removing his mackinaw and dropping it on the peg by the door.

"I've been worried about you," he said, taking a step closer.

"Let me get you some tea," I hedged, hurrying toward the kitchen just as he reached out to embrace me.

"I don't want any, thanks. Say, are you all right? You seem a bit edgy."

"I *am* edgy," I replied, crossing my arms. "I was worried about you. Did you find out anything about the body?"

His smile faded as a quizzical expression touched his features. "What body?"

My mouth went dry. "I heard in Juneau that the deputy had come up here to investigate a body, that someone had been found . . ." I broke off, swallowing. "I was afraid . . ."

"That it was me?" His eyes softened as he looked at me. "It was kind of you to worry, but I just returned from Douglas Island. I haven't heard anything about a body," he said, glancing through the window to the turbulent channel. "Quite likely it was a fisherman who should never have gone out in rough water."

Suspicion, then fear, knotted my stomach, and suddenly I felt sick.

"He wasn't out in the weather," I said tightly. "Someone

had already found him this morning. What time did you get back?" I asked, hearing in my own ears the shrill edge to my voice. I prayed he wouldn't notice.

"Just now," he replied. "I stayed overnight. When I stopped in at the hotel, the desk clerk said you were here. Come sit down with me," he started toward the sofa, "and tell me what's happened."

I looked at the sofa as Jamie's accusation tormented me anew. I turned to Scott again, seeing more clearly than ever a man whose charm and intelligence could be as threatening as the Taku wind.

"I . . . I haven't time," I answered stiffly. "I'm just gathering up a few items to take back to the hotel. Mr. Zarnoff will be coming any minute."

"You're going back in?" he asked, glancing from the window back to me.

I swallowed. "Yes, for the time being."

We stared across the room at one another, but now there was far more than the small distance separating us. My heart wrenched as I looked into his handsome face. I heard the howl of the wind above the hammering of my heart.

"Scott," I began, then swallowed. How could I possibly learn the truth? Was there a question I could ask that would quiet my suspicions—without his being aware of what I was doing?

"Scott," I said carefully, "while I was in town, someone came here and ransacked the upstairs looking for something."

"Looking for what?" he asked, his brow knitting. "Did you leave money or jewelry?"

I shook my head. "No. But I don't think they were looking for *my* possessions."

He studied me for a moment, then turned his back and walked over to look out at the wind-tossed channel. The fact that he had averted his eyes and walked away from me did nothing to allay my suspicions.

I took a deep breath and tried another approach. "I need to talk to Lonesome Bill. There are some things I want to ask him."

He did not respond, but merely continued to stare out the window.

"No one has seen him in a couple of days," I added, thinking again of that body.

Now I had his attention. He turned quickly, his lip clutched between his teeth. I could see that he was considering something.

"I found out he was not completely honest with me," I continued. Should I tell him about Nona Zarnoff? Did he know that as well? He crossed the room and pulled me into his arms before I was prepared to resist.

"You should leave this place, Abby," he said. His words were warm and persuasive against my ear, and for a moment I felt myself slipping back into that romantic spell he so easily cast. For one split second I wavered, tempted to throw my arms around him and tell him everything.

When I tilted my head back to look up into his face, however, the words I might have spoken were lost in my throat as he lowered his lips and kissed me urgently. I felt myself melting against him, forgetting that I must leave *now;* forgetting that this could be a very dangerous man!

"Scott," I burst out, stepping back from him, "tell me what you know about my uncle's death. About everything!" I said breathlessly, my eyes imploring him to speak the truth.

He shook his head slowly. "I can't! Not yet. Trust me, Abby," he said, reaching for my hand and pressing it to his lips. He kissed each finger, then turned my hand over and brushed his warm lips across my palm.

I fought against a swift longing as I stared at his lowered head, the dark, shining hair that waved in ridges at his collar. I wanted so much to believe him, but there were other important things weighing against his feeble explanations.

"Why don't you come home with me?" he said huskily. "You will be safe there. The storm . . . "

"No, I can't." I said, hastily withdrawing my hand. I was vulnerable to his presence, to his kiss, to the look in his eyes that did crazy things to my senses. I drew a deep breath, looking away from him, trying to find a deeper strength.

"I believe that my uncle did find gold and that he drew a map to a special stream somewhere," I said, strangely calm now. "And that map, I believe, is what got him killed!"

My voice was small yet decisive in the sudden quiet as Scott's dark brows shot up on his forehead, registering his surprise.

"Someone came here," I continued "and ransacked the upstairs looking for that map. I wonder if they found it," I finished deliberately.

His eyes snapped with sudden anger. He had read my suspicion as clearly as if I had spoken it aloud.

"Is that why you asked me if I had just returned from Douglas Island? There was something different in your voice when you asked me that." He took a step toward me, and my breath caught in my throat. "Abby, could you possibly think that I . . . ?"

"I don't know what to think," I burst out. "You say you haven't been home at all."

"No, of course not! I just got back."

He was lying. There was no doubt of it. He had no way of knowing that I had already dispatched Jamie to his cabin, that I had learned Scott had come home; that he had made coffee and built a fire. He must have returned home the night before . . . perhaps after he had gone through the house!

"Do you want me to do anything for you before I leave?" he asked more formally. "Shall I put things back in place upstairs?"

"No, Jamie helped me do that," I said, looking at him through a cloud of disillusion.

He looked silently at me for another second as a muscle in his jaw clenched. Then he turned for the door. "If you believe a map is hidden here, and that someone is still searching for it, then obviously it has not yet been found," he said, staring straight ahead. "You must leave."

"Yes, I will."

The door opened and closed, and I sprang forward and turned the key in the lock. Then I bit my lip to silence an angry cry. He was lying to me; possibly he had been lying to me all along. Why?

Money, of course. The map. The promise of gold. It was the lure that seemed to drive all men mad.

I hurried toward the kitchen, willing myself not to peer through the window, not to watch him as he crossed the yard to the flats. Was he traveling by boat? I hadn't even bothered to look. And I would not go back and look now, I told myself stubbornly.

Unsteadily, I poured a cup of tea, trying to clear my head.

"Uncle Joshua," I burst out, as the tears I fought to suppress now rushed to my eyes, "what did your silly poem mean? What were you trying to say?"

I sobbed into the silence of the kitchen, frustrated almost beyond endurance by the fact that I had already unraveled much of the puzzle on my own. Why couldn't I be smart enough to decipher the rest?

Well, I simply must go to the deputy with these suspicions. Let *him* question Lonesome Bill, or Scott, or the Zarnoffs. Or even Gordon, the banker. And where was Gordon, anyway?

The body, I remembered. The crowd gathered across

the channel, across at Douglas Island, where Gordon had gone!

I prayed the body belonged to a careless fisherman, as Scott had suggested. Not Gordon, and not Lonesome Bill, who had mysteriously disappeared. There were questions I needed to ask these men. I only hoped that Bill, or Gordon, would be able to answer my questions!

A pounding on the front door brought me quickly through the living room. I glanced at the window in passing and gasped.

Millions of snowflakes darted and danced and swirled, transforming the dismal gray background to a world of white. I could dimly make out Zarnoff's horses and wagon out in the yard.

I rushed over and unlocked the door. "You are ready to go?" he demanded abruptly, his scowling face a reprimand when he saw that I was not ready. He was wearing a fur coat and cap and thick mittens.

"I'll just be a second," I said, my eyes moving over his head to the wild dance of snowflakes. The warmth of the room felt cozy and comforting as the wind shrieked through the woods, across the yard, battering the house. As I witnessed the unpleasantness of an Alaskan storm, I had a sudden change of heart. "On second thought, I'm not going," I replied. "I'm quite comfortable here. And it's unfair to ask you to take me to town in a blizzard."

"The road will be dangerous in places," he conceded, his gruff tone softening at the prospect of not having to make such a difficult trip to town.

"I'll wait until the storm is over. Until tomorrow, if necessary."

"You are warm?" his eyes took in the room.

"Your grandson built a strong fire, and I know how to keep it going. I have firewood."

"You have food?"

I nodded. "Yes, enough."

"Then you will be all right," he said, before bending his head against the cruel wind and plodding through the thickly falling snow to his wagon.

I closed the door against the raging storm, quickly turning the key in the lock. Then I hurried to the kitchen, checking the fire, which was still burning brightly. I peered at the firewood stacked in the corner. This was the last of the large supply which Scott had brought to me, but certainly there should be enough to last until tomorrow.

Food . . . that might be a problem. I opened the cabinets and rummaged about. I still had a supply of tea, two or three tins of soup, and two stale pieces of bread which would do in an emergency.

Feeling content, I wandered back to the living room and snuggled up on the fur sofa, watching with fascination as the snowflakes continued to fall. While I had sworn never to spend another night here, I now felt perfectly safe. No one would come out in this blizzard to torment me.

Suddenly, in the midst of the monochromatic world, something stirred. It was almost as if a clump of snow moved right before my eyes, but upon studying the object more carefully, I saw that it was a ptarmigan.

The lonely little bird cocked its head, surveying me with two dark eyes, the only contrast to its surroundings, for its plumage was as white as the snow, serving as a camouflage. It began to move across the yard, in that humorous sort of rolling gait, finally disappearing around the corner of the house.

The sight of the bird had cheered me momentarily, allowing me to feel that I was not quite so alone.

While I had imagined the snowstorm would last for hours, the flakes began to subside within the hour. The sky was filled with low-hanging clouds. It seemed if I reached out I could almost touch one of those clouds.

The world beyond the frosted pane was monochromatic, enclosing me in a nest of gray. I felt oddly safe, cozy. The wind had died down, as though promising no further disasters, and I gave over to the weariness that claimed me. The fur of the sofa brushed warmly against my cheek as I stretched out and closed my eyes, feeling relaxed for the first time in days.

A steady persistent knock finally penetrated my deep sleep. I sat up, rubbing my eyes, groggily wondering where I was. My eyes crept over the big room, as a rush of memory placed me. I realized that I was back in my uncle's house, and now I remembered everything that had happened.

The knocking continued, and I jumped to my feet, squinting through the snow-framed window.

A sturdy dark horse stood in the drive, his head lifted, his nostrils flared, sniffing the air. Since I had never seen the horse, I was reluctant to open the door, despite the continued knocking. I pressed my face against the cold window, trying to peer around the corner of the house, but the front stoop was concealed.

"Miss Martin? It's Hank Wilson!" the deputy's deep voice called through the door.

Deputy Wilson! I hurriedly unlocked the door and found the large-framed man bundled in a fur coat.

"Please come in," I invited, quickly opening the door for him.

He hesitated, scraping the snow from the soles of his big boots before entering.

"Can't stay long," he said as he stepped inside.

"Won't you take off your coat?"

Slowly he removed it, and I placed it on the hook by the door.

"Never could figure your uncle buying this place," he

said, removing his gloves and rubbing his hands together to warm them. "Stopped in here once." He paused, looking around. "He seemed happy enough."

"Yes, well . . . ," my voice trailed in frustration when I thought of my uncle's unusual life. "Deputy Wilson, I'm so glad that you've come," I continued, trying to organize my thoughts. "I have some things I need to discuss with you."

"Yes'm. Harold, next door, told me you were looking for me earlier."

I swallowed. "He said you had found . . . a body," I broke off, hating the sound of that word. "Up near here," I added feebly.

"Yes'm." He heaved a sigh and lumbered across the room to take a seat in the arm chair. In the process he cast a frown toward the bear's face at his feet. "Hell of a rug," he commented.

"Who was the person you found?" I blurted, dropping to the edge of the sofa.

He began to shake his big head, which looked odd without his ten-gallon felt hat. "Hated it. Thought everybody liked him."

"Who?"

"Lonesome Bill."

"It was Lonesome Bill?" I repeated with a gasp.

"Yes'm."

"Wh . . . where?"

"Fisherman found him out in the channel."

"How far from here?" I managed to ask, although I felt as though I were losing my voice.

"Well," he scratched his head again, "he was about halfway across the channel. Between Scott Morgan's cabin and Pirate's Cove, on the other island. We had to pull him out over there."

I sat back, horrified.

"Been dead a day or so, I'd say."

"Do you . . . know what happened?"

"Not sure. But I intend to find out," he said emphatically.

I cleared my throat. "Speaking of unpleasant subjects, I want to talk with you about my uncle's death."

He frowned. "What is it?"

"Well, my mother forwarded a letter to me that had been lost for months. It . . . I don't know . . . it must have been placed on the wrong ship leaving Portland. In any case, it was a letter from my uncle, postmarked shortly before his death." I leaned forward, my hands clasped tightly. "Deputy Wilson, it was not the letter of a man about to take his life! Uncle Joshua's letter told of a stream he had found, one he believed would make him rich." I hesitated, watching his thoughtful frown turn to an expression of surprise.

I took a deep breath, trying to think of a clear, concise way to explain all my other suspicions.

"I know Lonesome Bill kept secrets about some of my uncle's activities." I rushed on, hoping the big man with the speculative frown would not ask me to elaborate. "Since Lonesome Bill was with my uncle on that last night," I cleared my throat again, "the night of his death, I can't help wondering if he knew more about that so-called suicide than he indicated."

Deputy Wilson leaned forward, placing his elbows on his knees.

"What are you getting at, ma'am?"

"My uncle drew a map of the location of his stream. I'm wondering if that map got him killed!"

He bolted upright. "You think your uncle was murdered?"

I threw my hands up in the air. "What else can I think? His suicide note is highly suspicious . . ."

"How's that?"

"If I had the tablet on which it was written, I could

show you. That note was actually the beginning of a letter to . . . someone."

I went after the suicide note and placed it on the coffee table before him. Then I carefully unfolded the letter Uncle Joshua had written to Nona Zarnoff, leaving the salutation covered, so that her name was not visible. "Please read the first two sentences of this letter," I pointed. "Then read the suicide note."

He took both pieces of paper in his large, callused hands and studied each note.

"I don't see what you mean," he said, shaking his head.

"My uncle would have written more than four words as an epilogue to his life, Deputy Wilson. And look—there's no period at the end of his sentence."

His eyes swung back to me, and I saw the skepticism returning. I was losing him again.

"You would have to know my uncle to understand what I mean," I tried to explain, aware of his growing doubts over a mere period missing at the end of the sentence.

"There's still the fact that it was his gun, his bullet," the deputy replied. "And he was here alone."

"How can you be *sure?*" I cried in frustration. "We only have Lonesome Bill's word for that. He *said* that Uncle Joshua was sitting alone at the table, but now Lonesome Bill has suddenly met with a fatal accident. Doesn't that seem highly suspicious to you?"

He chewed his bottom lip, his eyes moving from one note to the other, reconsidering what I had told him.

"In addition to all this, I have another reason for believing my uncle did not commit suicide," I announced.

He laid down the note and leaned back in his chair, crossing his arms. "What is that?"

"A prowler has come here three times!"

"Three times since you've been here?"

"That's right. At first I believed someone was trying to

scare me off. The last time, however, the upstairs was torn completely apart. Someone was looking for something."

I had his attention now. "What do you reckon they were looking for?"

"My uncle's map. I had a prowler on my first night here, but I assumed it was merely a hungry vagrant looking for food. He plundered the kitchen cabinets and scattered tins all over the floor." I hesitated, recalling the second encounter and the terror that had consumed me. It made me angry to think that someone had almost succeeded in running me off before I discovered the real truth. I plunged on, determined to make Deputy Wilson fully aware of what had transpired. "The second time I had a visitor, I was asleep upstairs and heard noises down here. When I came downstairs, someone stepped out of that closet over there," I pointed, "wearing a hideous mask. Of course, I screamed, and I even fired a gun at the man; but I missed him, and he got away."

Hank Wilson was staring wide-eyed at me, obviously trying to decide if I were given to exaggerations or even hysteria, or if I were telling him exactly what had taken place here. With unwavering eyes, I met his curious stare, and in a surprisingly calm voice I continued.

"Believe me," I said, "I am telling you the truth!"

He scratched his head and looked around the room, more carefully this time. "You got any idea who's doing this, Miss Martin?" he finally asked.

"I suspected the Zarnoffs the first couple of times. But then while I was in town, someone came back and tore the upstairs apart! Now I have begun to suspect, well, *everyone.*"

"Was anything stolen?" he asked.

"Nothing except the tablet."

"What tablet?"

"Uncle Joshua wrote all his poems and letters on a

certain tablet. Even the suicide note came from that tablet, but the frayed edges at the top of the tablet prove that particular note was *not* the last thing he wrote."

"What was?"

"A mysterious poem which I believe he wrote while the killer was here. The tablet and pen were on the kitchen table when," I swallowed, "Uncle Joshua was found."

"A *poem?*" he repeated, studying me doubtfully.

"You see," I explained, "this alleged suicide note was torn from the tablet *before* the last poem was written. The poem made no sense, followed no particular rhyme or meter . . ."

"If he was drunk . . ."

"If he was as drunk as everyone would have me believe, he would have been unable to pen even that bad poem; yet the handwriting is perfectly legible. We only have Lonesome Bill's word that he left Uncle Joshua sitting here at the table. Alone. And now Lonesome Bill has suddenly met with an accident!"

Deputy Wilson's bushy brows were drawn together in a perplexed frown as he stared at the note.

"Without that tablet, I cannot match the frayed edges to the top of the tablet to prove my point to you. That last odd poem went something like this:

Climb the trail to the dark totem poles,
There the one-eyed Indian resides,
Safe from mosquitoes and silver spurs
And death in the Alaskan night.

He was staring at me, obviously trying to make sense of it.

"What do you think it means?" he asked finally.

I shrugged. "I don't know."

He shook his head slowly, his lips pursed. "Miss Martin, I'm afraid the law can't place too much credibility on a poem, or a note that had no period at the end of the sentence."

"What credibility do you place on Lonesome Bill's death?"

He heaved a deep sigh as though he were very tired. "Don't know yet. But I promise you this, Miss Martin. We're going to check out his death the best we can. And if there's a link to your uncle's death, I'll do my best to find it."

He stood, apparently considering the matter settled for the time being.

"Deputy Wilson," I persisted, "my cousin is on his way here to accompany me back to San Francisco. My family would like some satisfaction that my uncle's death is being investigated thoroughly." I realized as I spoke that my words sounded more like a threat than a request, but I didn't care. I needed his help.

"I'll do my best," he said stoutly, then lumbered toward the door. "Thought I heard you were staying in town."

I nodded. "Yes, I am. I just came up here to pick up . . . some things. The tablet, for one. I found the place torn up and the tablet missing, as I said. Then I got caught by the storm. I'll be coming back into town tomorrow."

He pulled on his coat, then lingered, his eyes sweeping over me, and then the large room.

"Might be a good idea for you to come back into town today," he said abruptly.

I glanced out the window to the horse. I didn't fancy riding behind the deputy on his horse all the way back to town. Zarnoff did not favor the roads, and Scott . . .

I did not, for a minute, want to think of the man.

"I think you're right," I replied. "Would you be kind enough to ask Gordon Walling to come for me in his buggy, provided you find the road passable when you return?"

He nodded. "I'll do that. Until then, you just sit tight." He turned for the door, then hesitated again. "Might be a good idea not to open your door to anyone else."

"I hardly think I'll be having company in this kind of weather, do you?"

When he looked back at me, there was no mistaking his concern for my safety. "I wouldn't be taking a ride from anyone else either. Just wait for Gordon. I'll send him right back with that buggy. The temperature's dropping. It'd be an awful cold ride for you, but you're welcome to double with me. Buck's a strong horse."

Visions of a freezing ride on the back of a horse held no appeal.

"No, I'm not quite ready yet. But thank you just the same."

"You're welcome. If I don't locate Gordon, I'll borrow a buggy and come back for you myself."

"That's very kind of you."

He bade me good day and stepped back out into the cold. I pounced on the door, locking it swiftly behind him. Then I walked to the window, hugging my arms to warm myself against the blast of cold air from the door. Through the window I watched the tall man lumber back through the snow to his horse. He swung into the saddle, turned the horse's head, and loped off down the road. He had left a trail of large footprints, the only indentation in a thick white carpet. The snow had piled up incredibly fast.

As I stared at the peaceful setting where all the sharp angles had been softened by the pristine snow, my mind became more tranquil. I felt remarkably safe. And I was relieved that I had finally convinced Deputy Wilson that Uncle Joshua's suicide note should not be written off as that of a man who was down on his luck and inebriated on that fateful night.

Encouraged, I walked back to the kitchen to check the

fire. The flames had begun to burn down, but I would not add more wood, since I would be leaving soon.

I wandered back to the living room and up the stairs, making plans for a return to town.

The heat had risen to the upper story now, but despite the warmth of the room, a chill ran down my spine as I thought of someone coming here, tearing up the room looking for the map.

I looked across at the big bed whose mahogany posts stood like . . . dark totem poles!

Climb the trail to the dark totem poles
There the one-eyed Indian resides,
Safe from mosquitoes and silver spurs,
And death in the Alaskan night . . .

I walked over to the bed and touched a round bedpost. Nona had interpreted the first sentence of the poem as a reference to the bed. I ran my hand up and down the cool wood, wondering. Curiously, I lifted the top of the post, feeling inside the small pocket where the mosquito net was kept, when not strung over the posts.

It was empty.

Where was the net, I wondered, moving to the opposite post at the foot of the bed.

That pocket was empty as well.

Perhaps the net was stored in the . . .

Stored!

Beware of mosquitoes . . .

Why hadn't I thought of this sooner? How could I have stupidly overlooked such an important thing?

I turned to the headboard and removed the top of the left post. Empty. I scrambled over the pillows to the other post. The top would not twist. My fingers circled the post, seeking a firmer grip. The wood held firmly.

I stared, exploring every angle. The wood was not

simply stuck, I finally realized. There was a dark trace of something on the wood. A stain. Some sort of adhesive?

Was the mosquito net inside this post?

I turned and headed for the stairs, lifting my skirts to speed my flight. My heels made a frantic thudding over the board floor as I flew across the big room, almost tripping again over the bear's mouth and cursing myself for always forgetting.

I flew into the kitchen, yanking open a cabinet drawer. In my reckless haste, the drawer clattered to the floor, scattering knives, forks, and spoons in all directions. I dropped down, scrambling for the knife with the sharpest blade. I seized it, carefully testing its blade against the ball of my forefinger.

Yes, it was sharp enough. It would do the task.

I forced myself to walk back through the living room at a reasonable pace. I would not, despite my eagerness, run wildly up the stairs, knife in hand. I could imagine tripping over my skirts, plunging back down the steps, piercing myself with the knife, bleeding to death all alone. My imagination was getting the best of me, but considering the preposterous things that had taken place here, such an accident was not beyond the realm of reason.

Again I climbed the steps, trying not to think of the person who had preceded me here at some time, who had set upon the room with a fierce determination only to be defeated in the end.

No, the person had not discovered the map, thank God. But I had a strong inclination that I was about to do that.

I approached the bed, trying to maintain my composure, despite a feverish urge to stab open the post. Carefully, I lifted the point of the blade to the seam where the top was joined to the post.

At first, I had no luck in prying through the crack. I

took a deep breath, gripped the knife more firmly, and pressed until I began to pierce the thick adhesive. Whatever my uncle had used to seal the post had worked remarkably well. Only someone familiar with the Mallard bed would know one of its purposes, that the top of the post could be removed for storing mosquito net.

Or perhaps a map could be stored there!

The knife blade bit into the wood, making a light crunching sound, until the crack began to widen. I worked my way cautiously around the circle, pleased to see that the top was loosening, that it would be removable once I reached the back side of the post.

Suddenly the top fell off in my hand and I was staring at a small, neatly folded square of ruled paper from Uncle Joshua's tablet.

Chapter 16

I tossed the knife to the floor and grabbed the crinkled square of paper. Seeking better light, I dashed to the window, where the moaning wind blew frigid air in and around the window casing.

I unfolded the note, handling it with great care, as my heart began to hammer. This was not a poem, not a letter. The crinkled edges opened back, and I was staring at lines and circles and x's. Across the top a humorous title had been scrawled.

The one-eyed Indian.

I remembered the poem.

Climb the trail . . .

The stairs!

To the dark totem poles.

The bedposts!

There the one-eyed Indian resides . . .

Those words had been a mystery until I saw the name of the map. Uncle Joshua had drawn a set of rocks above the stream on his map, and the rock formations formed an unusual pattern. For one with a vivid imagination, I could see how the seams between rocks might resemble creases in an old, weather-scarred face. An Indian face, perhaps.

One particular set of rocks was grouped together oddly, like a single eye . . . a one-eyed Indian. I could imagine Uncle Joshua working this unusual formation into a poem, even a story for the hometown newspaper.

"I remembered hearing something about a one-eyed Indian," Nona had said. "It was in a conversation between Josh and Lonesome Bill."

Lonesome Bill! He had known about Nona—and he had known about my uncle's claim! And, I felt certain, that knowledge had something to do with his death.

I tilted the paper, studying the detailed map. The spot could easily be located by one who knew the area. Uncle Joshua had indicated with an X his house and the back woods, and the stream that began at the base of the woods and climbed a narrow mountain trail.

Lowering the map, I turned and looked out the window. I could scarcely see the snow-covered crosses as fresh flakes began to fall. But now I had the satisfaction of knowing that Uncle Joshua had been put to rest remarkably near the one-eyed Indian. My eyes traced the mountainside, where the snow weighted the tall spruce and hemlock and covered up the rocks. When the rocks were not snow-covered, if one traced the stream to its source, the one-eyed Indian would be there . . . waiting.

I wondered how many times Uncle Joshua had stood at this very window, looking out into the distant woods, longing for the snow to melt, the ice to break, in the stream that held his wealth. I turned and glanced back over the room and my eyes fell on an abandoned gold pan in the far corner. A deep sadness filled me as I thought of my uncle waiting to claim his bonanza. Then something else occurred to me, something that brought icicles of fear spearing down my spine.

It was inconceivable that he had not shared this map with the woman he loved. For a man desperate to hold onto the love of his life, wouldn't the sight of distant wealth from his bedroom window be too brilliant to keep secret?

I don't know how long I stood there holding the map, staring at the snow-covered mountainside. When finally I pulled myself back to the moment, however, I suspected Nona Zarnoff more than anyone else. Nona had related the reference of a one-eyed Indian to my uncle's conversation with Lonesome Bill, which meant that Lonesome Bill had known about the map all along!

Obviously Nona had deceived me from the beginning. I had believed her tears, her trembling voice, her declaration of love, just as my uncle must have believed her.

She alone knew the Mallard bed was a clue to the map. She had not left with her husband to visit friends, but rather to return ahead of me, and she and her husband had torn the upstairs apart, never realizing the bedposts were removable.

I stared at the crinkled map in my hand, amazed that Uncle Joshua had never revealed to her the map, or the secret hiding place. But then . . . perhaps Uncle Joshua had sensed he should not trust her completely. If he had not told her about the map, or the location of the nugget, perhaps he was not as trusting as she believed.

I folded the map back into a small square and placed it inside the volume of Shakespeare. I knew the value—and the danger—of the map. I would not leave it in plain sight.

Beware of mosquitoes and silver spurs . . .

Silver spurs!

I had begun to descend the stairs, and now another startling truth hit me: if dark poles and mosquitoes had specific meaning, my uncle had not simply thrown in silver spurs for poetic effect.

Weakly, I entered the living room and sank into the nearest chair, clutching the book, recalling the boots I had seen on Scott's doorstep. Boots with silver spurs!

Surely others here wore spurs! James Zarnoff, for example. Or old man Zarnoff? Anyone who rode horses was capable of owning spurs. Even Gordon Walling. My mind flew back to his neat slippers, then his rubber boots.

In Scott's case, the silver spurs were strikingly out of place. To my knowledge, he didn't even own a horse! He traveled by foot or used his small boat.

Lonesome Bill. My hopes rose again. Surely Lonesome Bill had owned silver spurs. I rubbed my forehead, thinking back to the times I had seen him. Rubber boots. He wore rubber boots, like most everyone in Juneau.

Lonesome Bill had been killed near Scott's cabin.

I felt sicker by the moment. I had reached the downstairs, and now, as I wandered over to place the book in the desk drawer, I wanted to shut out the droning voice in my head, the voice that incriminated Scott.

But I must listen to that voice. It might save my life!

Why hadn't I expressed my doubts about Scott to the deputy? Why had I neglected to tell him Scott had lied to me about staying at Douglas Island overnight? He had gone back home, built a fire, spent the night, made coffee. At what point had Lonesome Bill stopped in for a visit, perhaps told him he knew of Scott's argument with my uncle just before his death? And that he knew of the map . . . and the one-eyed Indian?

Was it possible . . . I sank into a chair and stared into space as my mind began to fit the puzzle together.

What if Scott had been here when Lonesome Bill had brought my uncle home? What if Scott had bribed him not to tell? What if he had promised to share the gold once he found the map and located the stream?

I bolted from the chair and began to pace the room. I

was furious with myself, furious for being so deceived!

Perhaps I *should* marry Thad when I returned to San Francisco. I had waited for a romantic kind of love, for a man who could turn my heart into a wild drum—and look what had almost happened!

A ladies' man, Gordon had said. Another wild thought darted through my tormented mind. Nona was still a question mark, ever since she had connected the poem to the bed. Was it possible that Nona . . . and Scott . . .

Tears sprang to my eyes as I realized I must go to Deputy Wilson's office as soon as I reached town. I must tell him what I believed about Scott. And, I promised myself, I would never again allow myself to be ruled by my emotions, like a lovesick schoolgirl! If I had stupidly gone home with him on the pretext of being safe from the storm, would I have ended up out in the channel like Lonesome Bill, once my suspicions were voiced aloud?

I sauntered wearily to the kitchen to stand before the stove in an effort to absorb its heat, for suddenly I was cold to the bone, and it had nothing to do with the dropping temperature.

I would simply put the matter in the deputy's hands. Let him do what he was being paid to do, and I would go back home with Tom. Perhaps I would marry Thad at Christmas. And I would not think of Scott Morgan again.

A horse neighed, and I froze. Deputy Wilson had warned me not to open the door for anyone. Could I simply hide inside and pretend not to be at home?

I doubted that would stop anyone from coming in. Window glass could be broken if someone really wanted to get in. Or . . . Nona Zarnoff had a key!

The gun!

It was the first time I had thought of the gun that Gordon had given me. I had placed it in the drawer of the coffee table the morning after that disastrous night when my shots had not deterred the masked caller.

The boards creaked beneath my guarded steps as I moved slowly from the kitchen into the living room, which had never before seemed so large, so heavy with silence.

I inched along the wall, trying to reach a vantage point to see through the window. A knock thudded on the door, as I cautiously approached the window. Gordon's horse and buggy!

I hurried over to unlock the door, heaving a sigh of relief.

"Gordon!" I reached out and touched the cold sleeve of his hooded parka. While the thick parka was fur-lined, Gordon's face was red from the cold, and he was shivering as he stepped inside.

"Oh, Gordon! Bless you for coming. I'll make some tea to warm you up. You must be frozen!"

"Yes, I am," he said through chattering teeth.

"I'm sorry to put you through this," I said, taking his damp parka and feeling guilty for summoning him during a snowstorm.

"It's all right." He was removing his spectacles to clean the mist from the lenses.

"I'll get you some hot tea," I said, hurrying into the kitchen.

"How are you?" he called.

"Not too well. Things are beginning to get out of hand . . ."

"Get out of hand?" He stood in the doorway frowning as he hooked his spectacles around his ears. "What do you mean?" he asked, taking a seat at the table.

I waited until I had prepared his tea before I continued. I wanted to choose my words, rather than babble, as I seemed inclined to do lately. I took a deep breath and set down across the table from him.

"Well, Gordon," I began, folding my hands before me and trying again to ignore the chipped wood, "while you were at Douglas Island, some strange things occurred here."

He nodded, taking a sip of the steaming tea. "I just heard about Lonesome Bill when Hank came with your message."

"Well, that's just one thing," I sighed. "When I came back from town, I found the upstairs in a shambles. Someone had gone up there and turned everything upside down. Even the mattress was slashed in search of the map."

"The map?"

"Yes. Uncle Joshua drew a map to his secret stream, Gordon, and he hid it somewhere in this house. I'm convinced he was killed for that map."

"What?" He set down his teacup and stared wide-eyed.

"That's right. He did *not* take his life, Gordon!"

"How can you be sure?"

I sighed, pressing a hand to my forehead as I began to pace the kitchen. "I discovered the identity of the woman who was having an affair with my uncle," I glanced back at him. "It was Nona Zarnoff."

"No!"

"Yes! And I'm only telling you now because I gravely fear she may have been adversely involved in this whole thing. That last poem in Uncle Joshua's tablet has never made any sense to me. It was completely out of character with Uncle Joshua's style. When I decided to move to the hotel, I neglected to take the tablet along with me. While I was there, however, I started to think about that poem, and about the fact that the suicide note should have been the last page torn from the tablet. It was not. There were two pages torn consecutively from the tablet before he wrote the poem."

"There were?" He placed his elbows on the table and leaned forward, his eyes swinging back and forth to follow me as I continued my frantic pacing, which somehow helped me to think better.

"Yes. The suicide note read *I cannot go on.* The next page was a letter to Nona Zarnoff that began, *I fear I cannot go on.*

"I don't see . . ." he began.

"The suicide note," I interrupted, "was actually a letter he had begun to Nona. When he looked back at his words—*I cannot go on*—this must have seemed too final, too cruel. He began another page that read, *I fear I cannot go on.* The killer looked back through the tablet, probably in search of the map, and found that page."

I paused for breath, waiting for Gordon's response. He said nothing; he was adjusting his spectacles to peer at me more closely.

"When he, or she, found that page in the tablet, the killer ripped out the first letter he had begun and forged Uncle Joshua's name."

Gordon's eyes dropped to his teacup as he sat considering my proposal, which, I suspected, sounded far-fetched to him. "Well, I suppose all of that is possible," he conceded, after a lengthy moment, "but it will be difficult to prove anything without the tablet."

"Of course," I retorted. "That's why someone came in and took that tablet before I figured everything out."

"Was it upstairs?" he asked.

"No, it was down here." I stopped pacing and looked into the living room where I had left it. "It was in there on the coffee table. I've had a prowler twice, but on both occasions, I was upstairs and that prevented a search up there. This time the prowler made the most of my absence."

He pushed his teacup aside and folded his hands on the table. "So did they find the map?"

"No, they did not. But I did."

"You did?" He bolted upright in his chair. *"How?"*

"Well, here's how that final poem read, the one that made no sense:

Climb the trail to the dark totem poles,
There the one-eyed Indian resides,
Safe from mosquitoes and silver spurs,
And death in the Alaskan night.

That poem seemed ridiculous until finally I began to think about each word. You see, Uncle Joshua was expecting Nona Zarnoff to come here that next morning."

"Nona Zarnoff?" he repeated, a strange expression crossing his face.

"That's right. Only she was trying to end the affair, and her mother-in-law came in her place. Apparently Mrs. Zarnoff, in tidying up, closed the tablet and thought nothing of the poem. Nona never saw the poem; if she had, she would have known the dark totem poles referred to the Mallard bed."

"The Mallard bed?" He was beginning to sound like an echo, but I pressed on.

"You remember I told you that my uncle had the Mallard bed frame shipped up from San Francisco. The bedposts are tall and dark, and the tops are removable for storing mosquito net. However," I looked at him pointedly, "there was no mosquito net in the pockets, which seemed odd. After prying loose the top I found the map. I'm afraid I also found a clue to the killer."

He was blinking rapidly as he stared at me.

"Silver spurs." More than any words I had ever spoken in my life, I hated to voice the name, but I did. "Scott Morgan owns a pair of silver spurs," I said emphatically. There was no point in detailing when or where I had seen those spurs. I swallowed, looking away. "I didn't want to believe he could . . . would . . ."

"Well," Gordon leaned back in his chair, "I've always thought there was something suspicious about the man. Did you give the map to the deputy?"

"No." I pushed the chair back and stood. "Actually, I found the map after the deputy left."

I went into the living room and opened the desk drawer to remove the leatherbound volume. "I placed it in Shakespeare's safekeeping," I said.

Gordon was standing when I returned. He lifted a hand to adjust his spectacles.

While the map was important, I could not dispel the dreariness I felt over naming Scott as the possible killer. I remembered Jamie's words and decided while I was telling Gordon the story, he might as well know everything.

"Jamie Zarnoff told me he came here one night shortly before my uncle died," I said. "Just as he reached the stoop, he overheard an angry voice saying, *'Give it to me.'* When my uncle opened the door, Jamie saw Scott sitting on the sofa. They were studying something on the table, but Jamie couldn't see what it was. I now believe it was the map."

My hand began to tremble as the enormity of this horrible thing took hold of my heart. I leaned down to spread the map on the table, and in doing so, my hand accidentally struck Gordon's teacup. It hurtled against his coat sleeve, and he yelled and cursed as the hot tea poured over his arm.

"Oh, Gordon! I'm sorry!" I threw the map down on the table and grabbed a cloth to mop the spilled tea as Gordon peeled off his coat and began to roll up his sleeve.

He whirled back to the table, abruptly shoving me out of the way as he grabbed for the map. "You fool!" he said. "You've spilled tea on the map."

I stepped back, shocked speechless, my eyes frozen in disbelief as he pounced on the map, swabbing at it with the cloth.

I looked at the map, dismayed. The tea had stained one small corner, but the ink had not smeared. The drawing was perfectly legible.

He moved to the far end of the table, smoothing out the crinkles as he intently studied the map.

I stared at his arm. For a second my heart almost stopped beating. He had removed his coat and rolled up the damp sleeve of his white shirt. I gripped the back of the chair for support as my eyes locked on his forearm . . . on the tattoo. A small tattoo of a spur!

I swallowed, trying to collect my frantic thoughts.

"It's not far from here," he mumbled. "It's just up that mountain."

He was leaning over the table now, both his palms flattened on each side of the map.

Before I could logically reason out my suspicions, I began to back away from him. Gordon Walling had turned into a stranger right before my eyes. Gone were the polite facade, the concern, the manners. The man who pored over the map, mumbling to himself after calling me a fool, was as possessed with gold fever as my uncle had been. No, quite possibly this man's obsession went deeper. I was now looking at a man whose darker side was coming to light, and the revelation was stunning.

I was halfway into the living room before it occurred to him that I had left the kitchen. He whirled, staring after me. "Where are you going?" he demanded.

I tried desperately to effect a nonchalance as I made my way to the coffee table, to the drawer where the gun was kept. "What difference does it make?" I replied lightly.

He was folding the map and pocketing it while watching me warily. Then he began to follow me into the living room.

"Abigail, I have a proposition for you concerning the map. If this goes to the deputy, it's likely to end up, well, misused. I believe you and I can come to terms on our own. I'll accept this map as payment for your uncle's debts."

He was almost the old Gordon again. Almost. But I could not forget his rude manner and an odd intensity concerning the map. And now that I had been alerted, I heard the underlying greed in his so-called proposition.

"You'd accept this map as payment?" I repeated. "Why, it may be worthless! No, I don't think I want to do that," I said quietly, testing my theory that his charm was only skin deep, that the darker side of this man was ruthless—and dangerous.

He sighed heavily. "Why do you insist on being difficult?"

I shrugged, taking a seat on the edge of the sofa, placing myself conveniently near the drawer of the coffee table. "I'm not being difficult, I'm merely being honest. I think this is a matter for Deputy Wilson to decide." As soon as I spoke those words, my suspicions were confirmed. I saw his brows lower, and the anger I had glimpsed in the kitchen suddenly returned to his face.

"Don't be a fool."

"I'm trying not to be," I said, still faking nonchalance. I even attempted a stiff smile.

He studied me quietly, for a thoughtful moment. "What do you want, Abigail? I'm not inclined toward marriage and children. If you're looking for a husband . . ."

"No, thanks!" I snapped, then bit my lip, regretting

the hasty words. I should have bluffed him, or I should have dumbly pretended not to notice the obvious. These thoughts occurred to me far too late, however.

"I'm sorry things had to work out this way," he said with a sigh.

"What way?" I asked bluntly.

"To your detriment. It's too bad that Scott Morgan became so greedy that he was willing to kill for a map he'll never see."

"I don't think Scott killed anyone," I replied before I could stop myself.

"But you just said you thought he did." He took a step toward me, standing on the opposite side of the coffee table. He tilted his head, and his blue eyes probed my face through his thick spectacles. "You just said there in the kitchen that he wanted the map, that he killed your uncle. And that is precisely what I intend to tell Hank Wilson. It's just a shame," he said, shaking his head slowly, "that you decided not to come back to town with me."

"But I *am* returning to town with you" My voice was weakening; the bluff I had attempted was slipping away.

My hands lay in my lap; my right hand was only a foot from the drawer of the table. The gun was there, loaded.

"No, Abigail." He said in an irritating monotone. "You've just told me that you don't want to return to town, and so I won't force you." His mouth tightened in a grim line, as he stood there, silently staring at me.

I swallowed, determined to say no more. I could think of nothing to say other than the obvious accusation which I tried to suppress for my own sake.

"It's still snowing," he said, glancing at the window behind me. "It's a very cold afternoon. As a matter of fact, it's life-threatening to be out in this weather."

"Then you'd better hurry home," I said flatly, glaring at him.

"Yes, I will. But first, I think we should walk over to your uncle's grave. Come along."

"Absolutely not! I have no intention of plodding through the snow to the cemetery."

"You really shouldn't have gone over there," he continued matter-of-factly. "A person out in weather like this could freeze to death. In another hour it will be dark. If you were to have a fall over there, strike your head on a rock, knock yourself unconscious . . ." He clucked, shaking his head in an expression of mock remorse. "Why, you could lie there all night before someone discovered you . . . frozen stiff."

My temper snapped. I dived for the drawer, yanking it open, scrambling for the loaded gun. It felt small and cold in my palm, but I felt a surge of satisfaction as I lifted it and pointed it squarely at Gordon Walling's heart. At this close range, I would not miss.

He merely laughed. "Don't count on your toy there. You see," he said with an ugly little grin, "the gun hasn't real bullets!"

It took a moment for that startling information to register. "You mean . . ."

"Of course! I didn't want to get shot at when I came to scare you off."

"It was *you!*"

He heaved a sigh. "Really, Abigail, there's no point in going into the sordid details. You don't want to hear them, and I haven't the time to explain. Let's just say that your uncle made the fatal mistake of trying to deceive me."

"To deceive you?"

"Yes. You see, he *did* owe me money."

"He owed the *bank,* you mean."

"Well, that's a mere technicality. Anyway, I suppose that he might have intended to sell some of his stocks back in San Francisco, but only as a last resort. He wanted to strike it rich, like so many of these other fools. And he needed a grubstake. In the beginning, I considered him just another dreamer. But his story became more convincing when he produced a nugget which Clarence Holman confirmed was valuable."

"So that weasly little man is in cahoots with you!" I stormed, understanding the man's offensive behavior.

"Clarence Holman owes me a few favors," he conceded.

I glared at him, wondering how many other people in town owed him *favors*.

"Anyway, when Crazy Josh came to me wanting a grubstake, I decided why not go along with it? But then, unfortunately, your uncle listened to some bad advice and decided not to cooperate with me."

Suddenly I was drawn into the story, so much that I began to forget some of my fear.

"What do you mean bad advice?" I pressed.

He shrugged. "I grubstaked a few miners who were too poor at handling their finances to repay me. I was forced to take over their claim." A twisted little smile appeared on his face, and for a moment, I felt a surge of pure hate racing through me.

"You probably cheated them out of their claim!" I accused hotly. "I'm just amazed that you've been able to get away with your devious schemes for so long."

"They were fools, I told you. They gave up and left town. Except for that idiot, Lonesome Bill. He hung around."

"And he persuaded my uncle to have no dealings with you?"

"He tried," he said flatly. "Unfortunately, your uncle had already signed some bank notes after too many nights at the gambling tables. The final loan for the grubstake had already been signed when Bill tried to talk him out of it."

"And so my uncle decided not to trust you with the nugget."

"Oh, I got the nugget! I got that as collateral on the day that your uncle came to tell me about his lucky stream, and to borrow money for a grubstake. The problem was," he frowned, "he did not come back as he had promised."

I swallowed, realizing that my uncle must have sensed the danger of dealing with a man like Gordon.

"When I heard he had been boasting of his secret stream at the saloon, I confronted him. He pretended it was merely whiskey talk. Then I met up with Lonesome Bill after he returned from taking your uncle home that night. Bill was drunk enough to be loose jawed," he said, with a condescending grin. "When I pressed him for information, he admitted Josh had a map and that he intended to take Bill to his secret stream the next day."

His face was flushed, his nostrils flared, as he related the story to me, and I sat on the edge of my seat, tensely awaiting the conclusion.

"When I realized how your uncle was planning to trick me, I saddled up and rode to his cabin that very night." He paused, his eyes drifting back to the kitchen. "He was slumped over the kitchen table in there, fumbling with his tablet. I came in and confronted him with what Bill had just told me, but he merely laughed in my face. And then he denied having a map. I knew he was lying. I grabbed his gun and threatened him. But he kept on laughing at me." Gordon's eyes narrowed as he looked at me coldly. "I will not be laughed at. I had enough of that when I was growing up. Your uncle ignored the gun and started scribbling in his tablet."

He paused, glancing around the living room, remembering that night.

"I came in here and searched the desk, the table, everywhere. *'You're wasting your time,' he called to me from the kitchen.* I went back in there and told him I would kill him if he didn't give me the map. He looked me straight in the eye and said there was no map. I shot him."

I gasped in horror.

"Then," he sighed, "as he slumped over the table he said . . . he said, *there is a map here. But now you'll never find it!* And then . . . he died."

I stared at him, scarcely able to believe what he had just told me, yet I had no doubt that it was all true. How stupid I had been! Uncle Joshua had died rather than give this crook the map. Yet I had handed it over freely.

"I've searched this place time and time again," his voice rose in anger, "but I never found it. I began to believe that Crazy Josh was just lying when he died, that he just spoke those last words to torment me. After you came back and moved in here, I started thinking about the map again. I had held onto the place, afraid to let it go in case there *was* a map hidden somewhere. I was afraid you might stumble onto it, and that's why I tried to scare you out of the house. As it turns out, you were even brighter than I thought," he said, glaring at me. "You figured the whole thing out!"

"No," I said on a heavy sigh, "not completely. Not until now. And so you killed Lonesome Bill, too?" I asked, feeling sick to my stomach.

"Bill was one of the few men who could really incriminate me to Hank Wilson and to you. The other miners could be written off as bad loans, but Bill, well. . . ." His voice trailed off, and I could imagine how easily he had taken advantage of the gregarious Bill.

"Was it Bill who warned my uncle about you?" I asked, swallowing.

"Unfortunately. But surprisingly, he believed your uncle's suicide. That was one of the problems with Bill. He was stupid and weak. After he came to see you that last time, it finally began to dawn on him that I could have come up here that night, and that your uncle hadn't killed himself, after all. When he confronted me with that idea, I refused to talk to him, but he kept on. He was too weak to fight me on his own; he had to get help. He said he was coming up to Morgan's cabin the next day to tell him everything. Morgan has always disliked me; Bill knew Morgan was the only one who would believe that I was . . ."

"A crook?" I interjected.

His eyes flashed angrily. "But your boyfriend had gone to Douglas Island," Gordon continued smugly. "I happened to see him boarding the ferry. And so when Bill figured on coming up and getting Morgan to join sides against me, I planned a little surprise for him. Well," he said, drawing a deep breath, "none of these things would have happened if people hadn't set out to trick me."

He reached into his pocket and withdrew a derringer. "And now, unfortunately, you've become too smart for your own good."

I was staring at the derringer in his hand.

"This one works, so don't get any crazy notions," he said, inclining his head toward the coat rack. "Now get your coat and let's take a walk."

My eyes flew from the gun to his face, then back again.

"Now that I know the story, maybe I'll reconsider your offer, after all," I responded.

"Because you know the story, it's too late to reconsider."

"I *do* need the money, Gordon. Maybe we can work

something out." I was merely trying to stall him while my mind searched for an escape.

He shook his head. "You should have accepted my proposition. Now that you've heard my confession, it's too late to reconsider."

"But I'm entitled to something!" I pleaded, concerned for my safety and not the map or the gold. I was merely babbling as I gauged the distance between us and tried to devise a plan.

"No, everything will be mine," he said, arrogantly. "This town will someday be the pride of Alaska! Juneau is a town on the boom. I plan to play an important role in its growth. Someday I will own most of this town!"

"You're obsessed with money!" I cried.

"It isn't just the money, Abigail. It's also the power that wealth brings. You don't know how to appreciate that, having enjoyed it all your life. But it was quite different for me." A shadow crossed his face, and then his eyes narrowed. "I've wasted enough time with you. Get up!"

I took a deep breath, trying desperately to bluff him again. "No, I'm not going out in the cold, Gordon. If you're going to kill me anyway, I prefer to die here in the house. Not out in the cemetery, thank you."

His hand tightened on the gun. A horse neighed. I whirled and looked over my shoulder, desperately hoping someone had come to my rescue, but I saw that it was only Gordon's horse.

When I glanced back at Gordon, I saw that he, too, had been momentarily distracted by the horse. He was still cautiously looking out the window, and, in that split second, with his attention diverted, I sprang forward, knocking the gun from his hand. It arched through the air, clattering across the board floor, several feet from both of us.

I dived for the gun, but a sharp blow struck my shoulder, knocking me away from it. Gordon reached for the gun, but I gathered all my strength and threw my weight solidly against him. He fell backward, his arms flailing.

I whirled for the gun, but he had regained his balance and shoved me down. My back hit the floor, and he stood over me, his arms raised.

I sprang up, clawing at his face, while aiming the sharp tip of my boot to the pit of his stomach. With an angry curse, he toppled back; as he fell, his glasses flew off, sailing through the air, landing conveniently beside my right foot.

I recognized the opportunity, despite my state of panic, and again I put my boot to use, grinding the lenses of his glasses into the floor. I rolled to the other side, crawling away from the broken glass, desperately searching for the gun.

Because of the thick lenses, I sensed he was half blind without his glasses. I dared hope that I now had the advantage.

I could hear him scrambling about somewhere behind me as we both searched for the gun. Somehow I had ended up on the bearskin rug, and now the teeth of the bear's open mouth raked my palm, and I cried out, yanking my hand back.

Then I spotted the gun mere inches from Gordon's foot. I slung my hair back from my eyes and began to crawl toward it. He was standing over me, the breath jerking though his chest as he squinted down, trying to focus. I felt like a helpless animal being stalked by a predator.

But if I could just reach the gun . . . if I could just get my hands on it, then *I* would be the master of this deadly game.

I inched my way toward the gun; still Gordon had not moved. Without risking a glance in his direction, I dived for the gun.

It felt small and cold in my sweaty palm as my hand closed over it. But then his rubber boot shot out, kicking the gun from my hand. I screamed as shafts of pain throbbed through my fingers while he dropped to his knee, fumbling for his weapon.

Pain and fresh rage increased my determination.

I threw my shoulder against him and made another dive for the gun.

But I was not quick enough.

Chapter 17

"You're dead," he said, grabbing the gun, and scrambling to his feet. The stairs were directly behind him. It would take a second longer for him to turn and shoot. If I tried to run out the front door, I would be directly in his line of fire.

These thoughts zipped through my mind like flashes of lightning. He would shoot me if I remained still; he would shoot me if I ran. With a cry of panic, I lunged for the stairs, just as a bullet whizzed over my head and caught the partition that separated the stairs from the living room.

Panic clutched at my nerves and weakened my knees as I stumbled blindly up the stairs.

I could hear him cursing as he lumbered after me. Never had I been so grateful for someone's poor vision. With my heart jumping in my throat, I hobbled across the top step and into the bedroom, slamming the door behind me.

My hands were shaking badly as I groped for the key in the door. It tumbled from my stiff fingers and bounced over the boards. The bottom step thudded with his approach, and I fell to the floor, pouncing on the key, fighting tears of frustration and terror. Somehow I managed to hang onto the key, insert it into the lock, and turn it with trembling fingers as he thundered up the stairs.

The lock clicked.

I whirled, searching frantically for a heavy object to heave against the door. My trunk sat on the opposite end of the room, and I ran for it, stumbling, catching myself, landing on the trunk.

With my heart about to burst, I leaned over the trunk and pushed. It sailed across the room. I stared, so numb with fear that I could not think. It was practically weightless without my clothes, which still hung in the armoire. No, the trunk would not stop him.

I glanced frantically around the shadowed room.

The nightstand!

I bolted for the nightstand and shoved hard. The candlestick smashed to the floor; the candle bobbed beneath my feet as I leaned against the nightstand, pushing it toward the door. It made a loud screech against the boards, then banged against the door.

The nightstand would not deter him for long, however; he was already rattling the door knob, now shaking it viciously.

I ran to the window and looked out. The clouds seemed to be hovering just above the roof as the wind wailed around the window, scattering millions of snowflakes through the gray atmosphere.

I turned back, again desperately searching the room for some sort of weapon with which to defend myself.

There was nothing . . . *nothing!*

A feeling of helplessness began to consume me. I whirled and stared at the door, hearing the heavy thud of his body against it. I turned back to the window.

I have to escape, I have to.

Soon he will break down the bedroom door, charge through and kill me. There is no way he can let me go free. I know too much. Somehow I have to get out of the house.

The window is cold against my trembling hands; the latch is frozen. I heave with all of my strength. It is stuck!

I *must* escape. Otherwise, no one will ever know the truth.

Fear grips me, icing my blood. I shove hard on the latch, and this time it moves beneath my weight. I lean against the window, pushing with every ounce of strength. Suddenly, it flies up, and I lunge forward.

Snowflakes fly on the wind; the arctic air sweeps over me. Leaning out the window, I am praying for someone—anyone!—to appear on the deserted road. But there is no one—no one to help me. A scream for help now would merely be a waste of breath. I have dispatched my last ally, and he has sent back the enemy!

I cast one last furtive glance over my shoulder and see the door shuddering beneath the persistent blows. The door cannot withstand those blows for long.

Any second he will break through. I have to go out on the ledge—there is no other way.

I lift my skirts and yank off my crinoline, then I tighten the strap on my boots.

The wood of the door is splintering!

I must not stop to consider the danger of the ledge. I must get out there . . . now! I will not think of the consequences of the narrow ledge . . . I will simply crawl out there and I will not look down.

Bunching my skirt in my hands, I crawl through the window as the door behind me gives way with a crash.

Like a giant hand, the wind slaps me back against the wall of the ledge. One thing I know, Gordon Walling will not follow me onto the ledge. Only a fool would step onto a narrow, ice-slickened ledge that promises a long fall. And yet I prefer taking my chances with a fall to facing a ruthless crook eager to kill me.

You will not fall, a voice in my brain commands. *You will escape and stop this dangerous man from harming anyone else.*

I can hear him laughing as he crosses the room to the open window. He is certain I will fall, and if I do not kill myself in the fall, he will be down there, waiting for me!

He thinks that now I have made his task easier!

The hem of my skirt is whipping in the wind. The frigid air gusts up my legs, biting, stinging. With tiny, cautious steps, I began to grope along the ledge, inching my way far enough to escape the hand that is flailing from the window, grabbing for my skirt.

Another gust of wind sweeps over me, tossing my skirt toward his outstretched hand. I cry out, inching my way a few more steps on the ledge, just as he extends his arm, almost reaching the trailing end of my skirt. Almost, but not quite.

I want to scream as tears of rage and terror fill my eyes. My vision is already blurring from the cold. I can feel the boards of the abbey trembling. I cannot make it!

Yes, you can.

He leans out the window, peering around at me, laughing. It is a hollow, ugly laugh that will linger in my tortured memory until the day I die.

"You cannot make it, Abigail. Either you will fall . . . or you will freeze in a matter of minutes! Good-bye . . ." His demonic laugh is snatched up on the wind and thrown across the deserted yard.

Then the window slams down.

Against the wind and falling snow, I can see the bell tower above me, an ominous shape in the gray light. The steps? Where are the steps?

The wind-driven snow is stinging my face like sharp needles; my skin has begun to feel odd, different. If I do not act quickly, he is right; I will freeze to death.

For a moment, I consider leaping to the snow-packed ground. But he is probably waiting for me down there, watching from the front window. And I am too cold to run.

Anger, blessed anger, fills me again, sharpening my determination not to be outsmarted by such a man. He has obviously forgotten the old steps, so long abandoned.

I inch my way around the ledge, squinting through blurred vision and whipping snow. *The stairs . . . where are the stairs?*

I can see a vertical line only a few feet away now . . . the stair rail! Only a few more treacherous steps along the ledge and I will reach the stairs. With my right foot, I test the wood, find it solid, then press down, moving my left foot in the same manner. The slickened ledge is a death trap; if I make one step that is not deliberate, that is not planned and negotiated with infinite skill, I am gone.

The stairs are only three feet away!

Carefully, I move my right foot again . . . but there is no wood! With my back flattened to the wall, I slowly lower my head to examine the ledge.

A piece of the ledge is missing!

My heart is hammering; my teeth are chattering. I am beyond knowing how cold I am.

Go on. Go on!

Can I possibly reach the stairs if I jump? If the steps or the handrail on the steps are not secure, I will fall.

I am screaming. I cannot stop myself. If only someone would appear out of the storm to save me! Across the meadow I can see the cemetery. The Russian crosses rise like white fingers in the ghost light. Uncle Joshua is there . . . poor Uncle Joshua, who died at the hands of the killer within the house, the demon who is laughing and waiting for me to die!

I must live to tell what he has done.

I blink away the moisture on my lashes and concentrate on the steps again. Either I jump or I freeze. Steeling myself, I lunge forward out of sheer desperation. The rough wood splinters my palm, a pain that brings a leap of joy. For miraculously my feet have landed on the steps, and the handrail is secure beneath my desperate hands.

A numbness is creeping over me. A warning. Through the swirling snowflakes, I count the steps leading up to the tower. Six steps.

I bunch the hem of my skirt in my left hand and lift it above my boots, while I cling to the rail with my right hand. The Taku wind is wailing louder now. A wind-tossed strand of hair falls over my eye, blinding me until I toss my head back and grip the rail.

The second step.

The third step.

Then the fourth step.

The fifth step is breaking beneath my foot!

I do not hear the wood splintering but I feel it giving way. I am swinging in thin air! The weight of my body is pulling me down, down, down. My hands are frozen to the rail. *I am going to fall.*

Get your footing again, the voice that has guided me on is now the only sound I hear, although the wind rages, and I feel the heave of sobs in my chest. Blood fills my mouth. I must be chewing my bottom lip, but I feel no pain.

One step, only one more step. *Reach for it.* Reach for it now, or you're dead.

My body is still swinging, but my right foot lands on the lower step, gaining a precarious foothold. My left foot follows. I am temporarily anchored.

The top step. I have to stretch for it.

With both feet now secure on the fourth step, I stretch as high as I can reach. The tips of my fingers brush the icy step. If I can touch it, I can reach it. I must!

Something is happening, something strange and wonderful. A strength I have never possessed flows through me, drawing my body upward. First my right hand is moving up the rail, then my left hand, pulling my body with a determination born of desperation.

Finally, by lifting my knee, then my foot, I am on the last step.

I am looking into the tower window, dark and desolate, but promising the shelter that will save me. The window glass is broken, there are only a few remaining shards around the edge. Small, jagged shards.

I wedge my way through the window, too desperate to worry about splintered wood or broken glass. My body strikes the wooden floor, a haven for me, as tears of terror now turn to tears of joy.

The tower is narrow and dark, but beside the window a long shelf holds two blankets and an old mackinaw. The wind is shrieking through the open window, spitting snow and mist into the tower.

My muscles are like iron, unwilling to bend. My hands are awkward and stiff as I reach for the blanket and stuff it into the open window. The howl of the wind is muffled, the frigid air is shut off.

I sag against the window for a moment, almost overcome with relief. Then I turn and glance around me, grateful for the unfinished tower that is only a wooden shell; yet the board floor holds a faint warmth from the heat rising from downstairs. How grateful I am for the big fire that Jamie built for me.

I fumble with the buttons on my soaked dress and then, in frustration, rip them loose in my haste to get out of the dress. The woolen blanket is a haven for my frozen body. The old mackinaw provides a tent for me. I crawl to the farthest corner, my body drawn tightly into a ball beneath the cover. I am safe for now.

Later, he will go outside, expecting to find me in the yard, having fallen from the ledge, frozen stiff. When he does not find me, he may suspect that I am in the tower, but he cannot get to me, not for a while. In the meantime, I shall hope, and desperately pray, that my one true friend will come looking for me.

For now, I must stay warm, keep calm. I will, for a while, push from my mind this day, the worst day of my entire life. Yes, I will think of something else . . . I will think of those first days in Juneau. I will think back to how it all began. . . .

I don't know how long the knocking had been going on before I finally became aware of it. The floor beneath me had begun to vibrate ever so slightly. Puzzled, I began to realize that something was going on. What was I hearing? A muffled sort of thudding.

I sat up, pulling the mackinaw down from my head. I laid my hands on the boards beneath me and felt the vibration. My body had been numb for some time, but now as I stared at the floor in confusion, I realized that I could not think clearly. Then I began to realize that someone was beating on the ceiling of the bedroom directly below me.

Boom. Boom. Boom.

Was Gordon tormenting me again? Yes, that was it. He knew where I was hiding, and he was tormenting me with that knowledge. I concentrated on a voice beneath me. He was laughing at me again. No, the sound was not laughter, it was a word. I leaned down, pressing my ear to the cold boards.

One word. *Abby!*

Gordon had never called me Abby . . . but Scott always did.

"Scott!" I tried to form the name on my thick tongue, but my voice was a mere croak that could never be heard through the heavy floor.

"Scott!" I pushed the name through my aching throat, but it was scarcely stronger than before. "I'm up here . . . in the bell tower!" I tried to scream the message to him, but it was useless.

There was no response. Even the thudding had stopped.

I lowered my face to the floor, cupping my hands around my mouth to enclose and strengthen my words. "Scott!" I shouted against the wooden floor, "I'm up here . . . in the bell tower!"

From far, far away came a muffled reply.

"Come to the window!"

Joy soared through me, warming me, clearing the numbness from my dazed brain.

My body was so stiff that I could scarcely move, but now I was propelled by new strength, new hope. I threw back the mackinaw and hobbled to the window, the blanket gripped as tightly as my cold hands could hold it.

I reached up and yanked the other blanket from the small window. When I did, a gust of cold air blew in, and my body began to tremble. Bleary-eyed, I stared out at the darkening day. The snow had ceased to fall, after creating a soft, white winter wonderland.

"Abby!" I could hear Scott's voice clearly now, for the wind had finally exhausted itself to a mere whisper in the distant woods. *"Abby!"*

"Scott, is that you?" I shouted hoarsely. My throat ached from the effort, and my lungs were stabbed by the piercing cold that engulfed me.

"I'm coming out on the ledge. Just stay where you

are!" he called back, and those words brought shudders of fear.

"No!" I cried. "You can't make it! The ladder is broken."

There was a moment of silence as I clutched the blanket tighter, feeling hopelessly trapped.

"Abby!" he called again. "Go back inside the tower and cover up the hole in the window. I'll chop through from the bedroom floor. Go to the farthest corner of the tower."

I heard the window slam. Confused, I stuffed the blanket back in the hole in the window and hobbled to the far corner where I had been nestled. I drew the mackinaw over me, shivering so hard that my teeth were chattering. The tower was like an icebox now. When I removed the blanket, the frigid air had swept to the farthest corners. Apparently there was no longer any heat rising from downstairs.

Gordon! The memory of the killer rushed back, bringing another wave of panic. *Where was Gordon?* If Scott was downstairs, surely Gordon had left.

He must have gone outside looking for me; he was probably searching the roads this very minute, shocked not to find me lying dead in the front yard.

I huddled into a ball, covering my head with the mackinaw.

Scott had come for me . . . that was all that mattered. Scott had come to save me. It was all that I could think about as I drifted off to sleep.

Chapter 18

It was like a strange, eerie dream, the kind in which one is aware of the dream but is unable to wake. In one part of my mind, I was vaguely aware of a steady, persistent sound, accompanied by distant voices. It was an odd, heavy thud that droned on and on, endlessly. Then the voices grew closer, disturbing me, nagging my deep sleep, but I could not wake up. Nor did I want to.

A heavy crash sounded beyond my little tent, but I could not move. I tried to push my mind to consciousness, to investigate what was happening, but it was useless. I was dimly aware of arms around me, and a sense of being moved.

"She couldn't have lasted much longer," a male voice was saying. Scott's voice?

Far away, another voice spoke a muffled response.

It seemed I was dropping down, down. . . .

"Everything's going to be fine, Abby."

It was Scott's voice. Or perhaps I was only dreaming.

Heat flowed through me. Blessed heat. Voices buzzed in the background. My body was numb, but my sense of smell was still working. I identified the aroma of sizzling resin from a warm fire in the kitchen stove. I felt extremely tired, but with great effort, I forced my eyelids open.

Scott's face loomed before me. A frown furrowed his forehead; his green eyes held a worried expression. I tried to smile, but my lips would not cooperate.

"Just sit still," he said, tucking something around me. A blanket. "I've built a fire in the stove."

I could hear steps moving around in the background. A dark skirt swept by.

"Abby, we've removed your shoes and stockings. You need to put your feet in this pan."

"What?"

His words made no sense at first. Now I was smelling a very strange odor, something unpleasant.

"It's coal oil," he explained. "Maybe it will prevent frostbite."

I blinked at the colorful face on my lap, dazedly realizing it was the Tlingit blanket from the Mallard bed. There was a weight on my leg, and I peered down groggily.

Scott was kneeling beside me, lifting my feet, placing them gently in a pan of coal oil.

I cried out as the liquid enveloped my feet, but then a firm hand pressed my shoulder. "It is necessary," a woman's voice assured me.

I looked up to see Nona Zarnoff standing beside me. Her almond-shaped black eyes were filled with tenderness and concern.

"It will be over in a minute," she said with a gentle smile. "Just try to sit still."

I could feel the friction of Scott's hands as he rubbed the calves of my legs, trying to restore circulation.

Another form emerged from the background. Someone was making tea. A plump, wrinkled hand extended the cup of steaming tea to my mouth.

"Drink very slowly," a matronly voice advised.

I looked up into Mrs. Zarnoff's wrinkled round face.

Surely I *was* dreaming.

As I stared at the tea in the cup, the memory of what had taken place here broke like a dam and flooded through my brain.

"Gordon Walling!" I cried out. "He tried to . . ."

"We know," Scott responded, holding the tea for me. "Don't worry. James Zarnoff and his father have gone to town in search of Deputy Wilson. But don't try to talk yet. You can tell me everything later."

"But he . . ." My tongue was still thick, unable to communicate the horrible thoughts that filled my mind. "He mustn't get away!" I finally blurted.

"He won't get away." Scott's voice was firm and convincing. "Walling is going to get what's coming to him. I promise you that!"

The Zarnoff women had walked around to stand beside the stove, and now they were looking at me with worried faces.

"How did you find me?" I asked, as I began to sip the strong tea, relishing its wonderful taste. "How did you know . . ."

"I had Ivan bring me here to give you some hot soup," Mrs. Zarnoff said.

"He came inside?" I echoed, unable to believe it, given his superstitions.

"He was worried about you," Nona replied softly, smiling at me. "We all were."

"The banker was terrible to Ivan," Mrs. Zarnoff continued, her round cheeks flushing as she spoke. "He called Ivan a stupid old fool," she said, her voice rising in anger. "He told us there was no one home. When Ivan grabbed him and demanded to know where you were, that evil man struck Ivan, then shoved him aside and rushed out the front door. We searched everywhere but could not find you."

Scott touched my arm. "They came to my cabin asking for you. They had seen me coming here earlier and thought perhaps you had gone home with me. Of course I didn't know where you were, but when I heard that Walling was here, I was alarmed. I knew that Josh had never trusted the man."

"He killed Lonesome Bill, too!" I blurted. "He admitted it!"

Scott's glance shot to both women, and their faces paled with this news.

"And he killed Uncle Joshua, too," I sighed, as tears filled my eyes and the enormity of all that had happened engulfed me like a tidal wave. I began to sob uncontrollably. The teacup was removed from my hand, and then Scott's arms were around me, comforting me. I nestled eagerly into the warmth of his shoulder, needing to feel safe.

The spicy smell of spruce clung to him, and I thought it was the most wonderful perfume in the world.

"Go on and cry," he said, hugging me tightly. "It will do you good."

I don't know how long he held me, or how long I sobbed into his flannel shirt; but finally, when all the frustration and terror and sadness had poured from my heart, I wiped my eyes with stiff hands and looked into his face.

"Abby," he sighed, brushing my tangled hair from my face, "I'm sorry for all you've been through. I should have told you from the beginning that I distrusted Walling, but I knew how that would sound."

I nodded shamefully. "Particularly after my wisecrack about his being so respectable . . ."

"And when it appeared that I was merely a drifter!" He finished for me.

I glanced at his face, expecting to see a look of

wounded pride. Instead he was grinning at me, a wonderful grin that crinkled the fine lines fanning back from his eyes.

"I confess to you, Abby, that I would never have to worry about money if I chose. However, I wanted to do something on my own, rather than take the money I had inherited from my grandfather and live a life of ease and luxury in Portland. I want to be a writer," he said slowly. "I wanted to test my talent by living in a place filled with adventurous stories. I knew if I couldn't write stories here, then I should give up the idea of writing, and start learning about stocks and bonds."

"But you've proved your talent," I said, smiling weakly.

He nodded. "I had something else to prove. I wanted to live close to nature for a while, really appreciate the simple life. That's been good for me, but," his eyes moved over my face and he grinned, "I think I've had my fill of playing Thoreau."

"Scott," I sighed, "I'm sorry that I've been so blind and stupid."

"But you haven't been! You just didn't know everything, that's all. And I'm the stupid one for not telling you. The thing is, I had sworn loyalty first to Josh and then to . . . well, to myself, I suppose.

"You see, Josh asked both Lonesome Bill and me never to reveal Nona's identity. He loved her very much," he said quietly. "I confess I didn't understand that kind of love at the time, but now . . ."

My breath caught. What did he mean *now?* Did I dare hope . . . ?

"Josh did not want to cause embarrassment or pain to Nona or to her family," he continued. "Nona wanted to protect the Zarnoffs, although she was riddled with guilt!"

I felt a deep sadness for Nona as I recalled how tearfully she had spoken of her love for my uncle.

"What will happen between her and the Zarnoffs?" I asked, worried.

"She's a good woman, and they know it. She and Josh just . . . well . . ." his voice trailed. "But to use an old cliché, it's an ill wind that blows no good. I think her husband appreciates her much more than he did before. He used to go away on his fishing trips for days. Like the Zarnoffs, he does not show his affection for her. I believe that has changed, now that he realized he could have lost her to another man."

"Did the Zarnoffs know about her affair with my uncle?"

He nodded. "They suspected it, I'm sure. But now she has told them everything and asked their forgiveness. The Zarnoffs have a more compassionate nature than one would think. They know that Nona is a good woman. They were rather prejudiced against her in the beginning, being superstitious about Indians and so on. They may have realized their mistakes as well. Mrs. Zarnoff came to clean for Nona on that . . . that morning when she found your uncle . . . so that Nona and Josh would not see each other again."

"I never understood about the cleaning . . ."

"Well," he shrugged, "Josh purchased the ceremonial mask from Nona at some sort of benefit for artists. Then he started to buy her jewelry and finally the blanket. I think for Josh it was love at first sight. He tried to stay away from her but couldn't. He commissioned the blanket, and when she brought it over . . ." His voice faltered. "He needed someone to clean his house, and the older Mrs. Zarnoff had agreed, but then she became ill, and Nona came in her place. He asked her to come again, but I suspect it was just an excuse."

I shifted and looked over my shoulder, peering into the living room. "I assume we're alone; otherwise, you couldn't talk so candidly."

"Yes, they left after they were assured that you were going to be all right. They decided to let us have some privacy. I'm afraid," he broke off, shaking his head, "that I will have to offer an apology to James Zarnoff when all this is straightened out. You see, at one point I suspected him of your uncle's death. He has a short temper, like his parents. But then," he ran a hand through his dark hair, "I should have realized that none of them was capable of murder."

"I suspected all of them! I knew that Nona had a key, but now that I think back, I remember that Gordon unlocked the door for me on the first day I arrived. Obviously he kept an extra key for himself so he could come and pilfer, and frighten me out of my wits!" I shook my head, thinking back to the horrible encounter with Gordon. "Will he be arrested, Scott?" I asked, worried, "or will he buy his way out of this? There's only my word . . ."

"No, not anymore. A fisherman came by my cabin today and said he had seen Gordon Walling up there with Lonesome Bill. You say Walling admitted that he killed him, and it's obvious he tried to kill you," he said, his jaw clenched angrily. "The Zarnoffs know he is a liar and a cheat. No, I don't think we'll have any trouble putting him behind bars."

I drew a deep breath. "To think that Deputy Wilson sent him up here after me, that he had no idea what an evil person Gordon Walling really is!"

Scott nodded. "Gordon went to great lengths to keep Hank Wilson misinformed. But Hank's a fair man. He'll believe your story, and we'll all back you up."

I closed my eyes, still feeling weak and disoriented. "I can't believe all of this has happened . . . Wait a minute," I said, pressing my palms gently against his chest so that

I could look into his face. "How did you know where I was?"

He reached down and lifted a corner of my skirt, and I saw that at least three feet of ruffle was missing.

"You left a piece of your skirt on the ladder," he answered. "When I came back with the Zarnoffs, I glanced up at the bell tower. I saw that something had been stuffed in the broken window. When I looked more closely, I could see the cloth there on the ladder. We couldn't find you anywhere else, so I dared hope you were up there. I knew it would take a brave soul to make the climb, but then you've been brave from the very beginning. It's one of the things I love about you!"

Love? My heart was soaring again, as I looked into his green eyes.

"It will be hard to say goodbye to you Scott," I said feeling a deep, aching sadness.

"Maybe you won't have to." His arms tightened around my shoulders as his lips brushed my forehead, my cheek, and then settled on my lips. His lips were warm and gentle, and suddenly the nightmare of all that had happened began to fade, replaced by a happiness that was full and complete, surpassing anything I had ever known. My heart had led me to Scott all along, and now that I was free of doubt and suspicion, I could admit to myself that I had fallen madly in love with him.

Someone was knocking on the door. I felt a reckless inclination to ignore whomever was there, but Scott gently pulled my arms from around his neck and smiled down into my face.

"When James Zarnoff went into town, I asked him to bring back a buggy so that we could take you into Juneau."

"But I'm alright," I began to protest.

"Yes, I think you are, but just to be on the safe side, I

think we should take you to Doctor Willis. It might even be a good idea for you to stay in the hospital overnight."

"I don't think . . ."

"I do! Now be a good girl and cooperate with me."

"Alright," I sighed, as he left to go open the front door. I snuggled into the blanket, not thinking of the hospital, or the Zarnoffs, but the words he had spoken earlier.

"It's one of the things I love about you . . ."

Chapter 19

I stood on the deck of the steamer, watching the men load cargo. Pewter gray clouds hung low, masking the mountains in the distance. I felt sorry that I could not depart on a day of sunshine, so that once again I could see the town clearly. But everyone was saying that winter had now come, and that sunshine would be a rarity.

Juneau snuggled in the white blanket of snow, romantic and cozy. The small cabins were now gingerbread houses on stockinged feet. The rough streets held an ermine carpet, although the traffic was rapidly churning the snow to an ugly mush.

The water in Gastineau Channel did not freeze in winter, I discovered, due to warm undercurrents, and now the smell of salt was riding on a light wind.

I traced the winding streets north as far as the eye could follow through the low-hanging clouds. Then my eyes moved to the channel, slate gray in the morning light. Up the inlet the abbey stood alone and silent now, but it is no longer Uncle Joshua's house. I have given it back as a special place of worship for those who desire it. While I did not believe that spirits dwelled there, I was never quite able to shake the feeling that I was trespassing on hallowed ground. . . .

Nona Zarnoff came to see me at the hotel this morning. She delivered a note from the older Zarnoffs, a simple, painstakingly printed note of thanks regarding the church. As for herself, she had another sort of gift for me, an assurance of her happiness despite everything.

"We will not be returning to Sitka," she said, with a smile. "We can make our home here in Juneau once again. Finally we have all faced the truth."

"I'm glad," I replied. "I wish you well."

"Thank you. I should explain to you that in the beginning the Zarnoffs were not very kind to me. James married me against their wishes."

"But why?"

"Because I am Tlingit. Even though I was sent to the mission and educated, I am still Tlingit."

"But I don't see . . ."

"The Tlingits and the Russians fought for so many years. When the Zarnoffs first came here, they heard bad stories. They would have preferred that he marry among his own people. But the heart finds a way," she said with a faint smile.

"The best way, usually." I was thinking of Scott when she spoke those words, wondering about the decision he would make today.

"James and I are a new generation, and now the Zarnoffs have accepted that. I think we have all grown wiser."

Thinking of my new perception about matters of the heart, I touched her hand. "Nona, will you be happy?"

She looked into my eyes and nodded firmly. "Yes. Because of his parents, we have had our problems. But we must put this in the past. Yes, I do love James now, more than before. I never knew he could be so compassionate, so forgiving." She glanced down at her wrist, then began to remove one of her silver bracelets. She placed the intricately carved bangle in my hand. "Please take this with you as a remembrance. I wish I could do something more," she said, looking at me with an expression of regret.

"You can," I answered. "Will you see that my uncle's grave is taken care of? I'm not asking you to do that yourself," I rushed to explain. "I just want you to see that it is done"

"It will be," she said quietly. "The people of the church will see to the cemetery, and no doubt he will always be remembered."

Now, as I stood on the deck, staring out at Juneau, hearing the piano from one of the saloons, watching a husky and his master lope through town, feeling the Taku wind in my face, I had found the adventure I sought here . . . one I would never forget.

As for my uncle, it will take a long time to forget the sadness he must have known in the end, but I must not think of endings, I must think of beginnings. And the middle parts of one's life when there is pride and satisfaction in having followed a dream. I felt certain that Uncle Joshua's years in Alaska were the happiest of his life. He had learned so much about life . . . and love. And he had followed his dream.

As I leave Juneau, I am taking with me a part of my uncle—the tablet of poems. I will see that it reaches the hands of a publisher, and Uncle Joshua's talent will live on. The tablet was found in Gordon Walling's desk at the bank. The man is now behind bars, as Scott had promised he would be.

Deputy Marshal Hank Wilson believed my story, and that story gave others the courage to come forward with their accounts of how Walling had swindled them as well.

It was a surprise to all to learn what a thief he was. However, most of the money he had amassed was in a special account at the bank. William cooperated with Deputy Wilson and the townspeople, and now most of the swindled money has been given back to those who were cheated out of it.

I think Deputy Wilson felt that he had failed these people by not seeing the man Gordon Walling really was. But then I too was taken in for a while.

Restlessly I began to pace the deck, looking over the milling crowd once more. I had been trying to fight the disappointment that threatened to overtake me, but I was on the verge of losing that battle. Slowly, carefully, my eyes moved over each face in the crowd as they waved to boarding passengers. My eyes moved on, anxiously searching the narrow street leading up the hill to the shops. He was nowhere in sight.

I swallowed, fighting the ache in my throat, the sudden rush of tears. I must not cry like a schoolgirl, I must hold up my chin and be proud. And yet I would toss my pride to the wind if only Scott would come.

"Abigail, if you don't get out of that horrible wind, you're going to catch your death of cold!" Tom's reproachful voice was like a stab in the back, and I whirled on him, ready to strike.

My middle-aged cousin sat huddled in his woolen coat, his back pressed against the ship's cabin. I decided it was time for me to take issue with Tom, Edith, and the entire lot of distant cousins, for that matter.

"Tom," I strolled over to his side, "I think that I've grown hardy enough the past month to take care of myself. You won't need to worry about me any more."

"Abigail," he said, exasperated, "I have always had to worry about you."

I looked into his narrow face beneath the fashionable little derby hat, and I wondered suddenly why I had ever let any of them tell me what to do. My character had always been far stronger than theirs; I felt my intelligence was superior as well. Their nagging was about to come to an abrupt end, beginning this very minute.

"No, you haven't always *had* to worry about me," I snapped. "You have enjoyed worrying, both you and Edith. You thrive on worry. Well, let me tell you something, Tom. I don't need your concern, nor do I want it. I could have made the trip back quite capably on my own!"

"You never should have come to this awful place," he replied in a voice that had shrunk from a threat to a whine.

"Maybe *you* are the one who should not have come!" I lashed back. "However, I'm certain that Mother paid you quite well for your trouble."

"Someone had to come with more money to reconcile your uncle's lavish debts."

"This was his money you delivered, Tom. And from now on, I will not tolerate any more of your slandering remarks against Uncle Joshua." I paused, hearing the rage in my voice and recalling how I used to throw temper tantrums as a child. Belatedly my mother had instilled in me a certain amount of respect toward my older cousin and his wife. That respect was now unfounded, I realized, and hereafter I intended to say whatever I pleased to Tom and Edith.

"Tom, I happen to think that Joshua Martin was a wonderful man; furthermore, he has left something of value to this town. He restored a church that had been abandoned, and he did kind things for his friends. His life counted for something!" I continued, my temper in full blaze. "It was a joy to know Uncle Joshua. He was a robust and pleasant man who enjoyed life, who appreciated nature, who was not afraid to take a chance on his own judgment."

I paused to draw a breath. Tom seemed to have flattened himself against the wall.

My temper began to cool as I spoke my piece, and

now I turned back to the deck and once more cast a searching glance out over the crowd as the workers finished loading the cargo.

And then I saw him.

He was running toward the ship, his carpetbag slung over his shoulder. He leapt onto the gangplank, then paused to speak to the ship's captain. As he did, his eyes moved upward as though searching for someone.

I waved wildly. He gave me a jaunty wink.

My heart soared like an eagle taking flight. I felt I could touch the clouds, ride the wind. I whirled on my heel and returned to Tom, who was staring gloomily into the channel.

"By the way, Tom," I said, "I have some good news. Our paper is going to flourish as never before, and you will reap some of the benefits, of course."

His eyes snapped to me, his jaw dropped. "What do you mean?"

I felt myself grow taller before his eyes. "If I can come all the way to Juneau, settle my uncle's business, and catch his murderer in the process . . ." I paused to draw a breath, "not to mention having to defend myself from that murderer, then I believe I have proved that I am capable of running a newspaper. I intend to sit at my father's desk when I return." I was intoxicated with freedom and happiness.

"But . . ."

"And if I continue to encounter resistance, I may have to remind everyone that I am now the *owner* of the newspaper. Contrary to the opinion of those who do *not* own the paper, *I* am the only one who cannot be replaced! You would do well to remember that."

"Your mother . . ."

"Is apt to listen to me now. Furthermore," I said, turning as I heard the approaching footsteps, "we may now have a new writer for our newspaper, the best writer ever to grace a masthead."

Scott had reached my side and was looking down at me, obviously amused, as he quickly interpreted the heated exchange between Tom and me.

"At least I have offered that position to him." I turned and looked at Scott. I am certain my eyes were filled with an adoration that I no longer tried to conceal. "I pray that he has accepted it."

"I think it might be interesting work," Scott replied, "for a while."

"But Thad . . ." I scarcely heard Tom's pitiful plea in the background, but I turned back with a withering stare.

"Thad may find himself suddenly out of a job if he isn't careful," I said. "Since he's always been *your* friend, you might be wise to pass that word along to him."

I turned back to Scott, recalling his words. *For a while,* he had said. Stirrings of doubt began to nag at me, until I realized that a part of Scott's charm was his unpredictability, which might be a well-needed lesson for me. I had grown up, shamefully demanding and often receiving whatever I wanted. I was finally learning that some things must be *earned;* perhaps the most endearing gifts of all must be earned, I thought, with that flash of perception that often comes when least expected.

"Are you sure you want to come back to San Francisco with me?" I asked softly.

A slow grin began to form in the corners of his mouth. He was wearing his favorite parka, one which I imagined Tom was silently condemning. His corduroy pants were clean, however; his boots were polished, his silver spurs gleaming.

"Yes, Abby, I want to come," he answered. "Why not? Remember, I told you I've always wanted to go to San

Francisco. I think it would probably be worth the trip just to see that Lillie Coit put her bare legs through a window and try to lure me inside!"

The stab of jealousy was also good for me, I told myself, while clenching my teeth. "Stop it," I finally burst into laughter, poking him sharply in the ribs.

We both began to laugh, and I thought how wonderful it would be to have the company of a man who was always seeing the humorous side of things, never taking himself too seriously and not viewing life as a battlefield, as the straight-laced Martins had always done.

No wonder Uncle Joshua had thrived on the freedom he discovered upon finally breaking the chains of convention. No wonder I had struggled with those same traces. But all that was changing now; I intended to have the kind of freedom I needed and, I felt, deserved.

"You'll probably grow bored soon enough," I said, slipping my hand into the crook of his arm as we began to stroll the deck.

"I imagine it will take a while. When you mention boredom, are you referring to the newspaper?"

"Among other things."

"Life in the city?"

I shrugged. "And the people you're with."

"Present company excluded, of course!" He looked at me with humor in his eyes. "I don't know. I was never bored with Bering; he was a wonderful companion."

"Bering!" I stopped walking and looked at him, distressed. "What did you do with Bering? Poor dog!"

"Happy dog! I gave him to Jamie, and the last time I saw him, the two of them were in a mad chase up the flats in hot pursuit of a rubber ball."

I laughed again as joy bubbled through me like a fountain; I could hardly contain all I felt. As our eyes met, the magic between us was stronger than ever. How long would it take for it to wear off, I wondered? It would be an interesting challenge to try and keep it going . . . for a very long time.

The ship's whistle cut sharply through shouted goodbyes and the excited voices of boarding passengers. The gangplank was drawn, the last passenger hurriedly directed to the deck.

"Abigail!"

I did not have to turn around to know that Edith Vanderhoof was bearing down upon me. This time, however, I felt suddenly overly generous with patience and kindness.

"There you are!" she cried. "And look at you in that black suit and hat, with those blonde curls gleaming in the sunlight! Aren't you just the picture!" She broke off, staring wide-eyed at Scott. For once she seemed to have lost her voice.

She was dressed in a brown cloak and tiny matching hat. Her busy hands were enveloped in a brown fur muff, which I noticed immediately.

"I see you're taking back a memento of Alaska," I said, pointing to it.

"Yes," she cooed, her eyes never leaving Scott. "Mary gave it to me for a going-away present. Wasn't that nice of her?" Slowly, her eyes dragged back to me, and a pleased smile lit her small face. "And you seem to be taking home a memento as well!" she teased.

Feeling slightly embarrassed, I turned to Scott. "Miss Vanderhoof, I'd like to introduce my friend Scott Morgan."

"Oh, how do you do!" she gushed, her eyes raking over him again. "It's such a pleasure to meet you!"

"Scott is from Portland. If you remember, I asked Mary if she knew Scott, since Mary comes from Portland as well."

Beneath the ostrich plume drooping from her hat, Edna's narrow brow furrowed in confusion.

"You remember," I continued, feeling mischievous, "he is the young man who chops wood. Mary mentioned his line of work."

I glanced quickly at Scott, knowing that he, unlike other men I had known, would not take offense, would even enjoy the humor.

"Oh." Her voice faded, her smile withered.

"It's a pleasure to meet you, Miss Vanderhoof," Scott took over. "I hope that you have enjoyed your stay in Juneau." He spoke in his most cultured voice, drowning her with charm. I lifted a gloved hand to my mouth to conceal the smile.

"I . . . why, thank you!" As she looked him over again, she seemed to decide that he was a suitable companion after all. She fixed her dark eyes upon me again and gave me a smug little smile. "Well, your trip to Juneau seems to have paid off," she said, laughing nervously.

"Yes, I would say it has paid off rather handsomely, wouldn't you?" I looked at Scott, whose eyes were dancing. I knew it was taking great effort on his part not to burst into laughter.

Edna leaned over, rudely whispering, "And to think, *I* was the one looking for a rich husband!"

"Perhaps you didn't look in the right place," I whispered back, smiling at her.

"No, perhaps not," she mumbled, her eyes sweeping over Scott again.

The situation was getting entirely out of hand, but having suffered through so much stress the past days, I felt I had earned a good laugh or two.

I cupped my hand to my mouth and whispered in her ear. "Next time, look for a man who chops wood for a living. They are, by far, the most romantic!"

She jerked her head back and looked at me, trying to decide if this was all a joke.

"It's true," I said seriously.

A faint smile wavered on her lips as her glance flew back to Scott.

"Nice meeting you, sir."

"The pleasure was entirely mine," he said, dazzling her with another smile.

She gave a shrill laugh and disappeared into the crowd.

He turned back to me, his eyes scrutinizing me a bit differently.

"I'm going to have to stay on my toes with you," he said, lifting his brow. "I'm constantly seeing something different in your nature."

"It isn't too late to change your mind," I said, as the last call to board was delivered amidst shouts of *bon voyage!*

"I'm not about to change my mind," he said, suddenly reaching down to press a quick kiss to my lips.

Someone in the background gasped at such an open display of affection. I imagined it was probably Tom.

"Well," I said, taking his arm and drawing him away from the crowd, to a private corner where we could speak freely. "It's entirely possible that I will require a diversion from the newspaper from time to time. Another adventure, perhaps."

He threw back his head and laughed, a wonderful, rich sound that was caught up on the wind to drift across the channel. "You're a girl after my own heart," he said.

"Yes, that may be true," I replied honestly, staring up into his green eyes.

"Well," he said, as his eyes moved slowly over my face, "if everything else fails in our pursuit for adventure, we can always set out for the Yukon."

"True. Or . . ." I opened my purse and reached deep in the lining, touching the small bulk of the folded square of tablet paper. The map.

"Or we could come back here after spring break-up and look for the one-eyed Indian."

He nodded. "It would make an interesting story. . . ."